The Promised End:

From Mid-Life to Old Age and After-

Selected Stories

Ron Singer

The Promised End:

From Mid-Life to Old Age and After-

Selected Stories

Ron Singer

THE PROMISED END: FROM MID-LIFE TO OLD AGE AND
AFTER
Copyright©2019 Ron Singer
All Rights Reserved
Published by Unsolicited Press
Printed in the United States of America.
First Edition.

Attention schools and businesses: for discounted copies on large orders, please contact the publisher directly.

For information contact:
Unsolicited Press
Portland, Oregon
www.unsolicitedpress.com
orders@unsolicitedpress.com
619-354-8005

Cover Design: Kathryn Gerhardt

Cover Image: Elizabeth Yamin: "Crosscurrents," 2-11-15, 22" x 30", mixed media on paper, copyright by Elizabeth Yamin, 2015.

Author Photo: Elizabeth Yamin: Ron Singer at St. Saviour's in Chora, Istanbul, May 2013. Copyright, Elizabeth Yamin, 2013.

Editor: Saidah Wilson

ISBN:978-1-950730-31-5

CONTENTS

Part One: Mid-Life   7

Garbage   9

The Silent Treatment   24

A Dream of Trains   37

Glen's Vintage Tin   51

The Technicolor Meal   64

Part Two: Old Age   69

W^4 ™ (Whole Wide World of Wrestling)   70

In Ethiopia, Once   80

A Reading at the Library   96

Spots   109

The Curing of the Blind (c. 2015 C.E.)   120

A Game of Lies   125

The Card Players   137

A Nose for A Jacket   146

Their Countries of Origin   161

When the Barber Died   180

On Elizabeth Bishop's "One Art"   188

Running the Diagonal   194

The Key   208

Part Three: And After--   245

Total Body Crumble   246

The Old Avatar   257

Part One: Mid-Life

Nel mezzo del cammin di nostra vita
mi ritrovai per una selva oscura,
ché la diritta via era smarrita.
   --Dante, *Commedia*, 1-3

(Midway in the journey of our life
I came to myself in a dark wood,
for the straight way was lost.
   --Hollander, transl.)

Garbage

When I put out the garbage, I expect it to go away. On Wednesday nights, as soon as the cab gets to my neighborhood, I lean forward and peer through the window. If I see unpicked-up garbage, my heart goes pitter-patter till the driver turns the last corner and I find out whether they've picked up on my block yet. On the rare Saturdays when I sleep in, I actually like being woken up by the clattering cans and the truck crunching the garbage. As soon as the men move on to the next house, I turn over and go back to sleep with a feeling of personal accomplishment.

Right now, I'm up in Maine at my summer place. Been here two weeks, one to go. The kids are in camp, their mother's off in Europe someplace, and the day before yesterday, I got myself into what you might call "a little situation." Relating to this matter of garbage disposal.

Friday night, I had zilch in the way of sleep. The fucking crows were cawing all fucking night, and the asshole dogs in the next cottage interrupted every one of my dreams with their goddamned yipping. As soon as it was light I gave up, crawled out of bed and wandered up the hill to the road, only to find that the guy who usually hauls my garbage had left it there with a little note for me: "Sorry, too much!" This brief communication was rolled like a fat joint and stuck through the knot of one of the five large clear-plastic bags I'd dragged up from the shed the night before. Rolled inside the note were the two bucks I'd left --the going rate.

I almost had a fucking heart attack. I ran back down to the cottage and, without even washing my face or making coffee, I got dressed and grabbed the keys to my old blue pick-up. I ran to the garage, gunned the engine a few seconds, and backed her up the hill to the garbage, which was already covered with sunlight, moisture and flies. Cursing, I wadded the note and money and flung them in the bushes. Then, still cursing --and resisting an urge to retrieve the two bucks-- I started hefting the bags unto the truck bed. It was a lot of fun. After heaving the first three bags, I had to clamber up and move them back to make room for the last ones. This close contact, you might say, rubbed my face in my own garbage, for as I worked I relived the seafood party I'd thrown on Wednesday night. Three entire bags came from that bash: salad, corncobs (two dozen), shells (clam, mussel, lobster) and wine bottles (ten). Ah, yes, the wine: Pinot Chardonnay, domestic. The pretty labels reminded me not only of all the times over the years when I've been bilked by the local Yankee wine merchant, but of the uncommon hangover I'd enjoyed all day Thursday. French prices for a California hangover. The heaviest of these three dinner bags contained the bottles, plus the remains of several lobsters, whose festive color and castanet-like claws seemed to mock me with personal malice.

When I was done, I climbed back into the cab and sat with my hands trembling on the wheel, all dressed up and no place to go. The town dump was out --you need a sticker for which summer residents (like me) are ineligible. That was why I paid the guy with the truck.

When I got tired of sitting there, I drove up onto the highway and into town, where I inched through the usual Saturday shopping aggravation --the hot-rodders who stop every ten feet to schmooze with their friends and the law-abiding oldsters who take the preposterous speed limit -- twenty-five-- literally. Then I headed up the coast with a vague notion that, since it was less developed there, they might not have as strict dumping ordinances --or enforcement.

Halfway to the next town, I impulsively hung a right down a steep hill into what looked like a construction site for new condos along the shore. Since the place was already an eyesore, and since no one was around, I braked and backed down a dirt slope into what seemed destined to become a carport. It was only after I'd edged back into the shadows of this half-built structure that I noticed a piece of construction equipment right behind me, looming over my truck. In fact, it was so close that if I had backed up a few more inches I would have smacked right into it. The only part of the thing I could see in the mirror was a huge metal jaw, the shovel of a bulldozer or crane. The machine had been left with its buckteeth chomping into the ground, and for some reason --nerves, who knows what? -- that bothered me. It reminded me of a portcullis that had barely missed slamming shut on my ass. At any rate, I got out of there before the women started dropping rocks or hot oil.

I headed east again, up the coast to a sad-assed place with nauseating air pollution from a fish-rendering plant --and lots of vacant lots. Now the folks in a town like this aren't going to care much about five teensy bags of garbage, are they? On the outskirts I got into a line of very slow traffic going up a very steep hill --so steep I began to feel the garbage slipping back toward the windshield of a little green sports car on my tail. When the driver, a blond kid, noticed what was happening, he began beeping like crazy, and his girlfriend stood up and pointed frantically at the moving garbage. I gave them the finger, hung a screeching left, and headed up an even steeper hill I had never been on before. This hill, it turned out, climbed and climbed, up into a poor neighborhood with cheap little shingle houses overlooking the whole town and a good bit of the coastline, a neighborhood that had obviously been built before the sharks arrived and started selling off the view by the inch. Somehow, on the way up, my garbage had stabilized. When I hesitated at a stop sign because I had no reason to turn either way or to go straight ahead, the fun began.

I had been there no more than ten or fifteen seconds when I was approached by a sort of generic teen-ager, who came running from the back of one of the little houses. She was pale, skinny and leggy --stork-like -- and definitely a minor. She wore tight little white shorts, a pink tank top, white high heels, lots of perfume and eye makeup, and a gold chain identifying her as a "Cheryl." If I was a wise guy, I might say this girl was trouble with a small t(ee).

Cheryl asked if I was lost, and when I'd briefly explained the situation, with a straight face she politely offered to show me to "a good place." Before I could answer, the bimbo ran around the front of the truck, swung the passenger door open, and hopped in. After a very short silence, I became excited by her tawdry youth, and she, I guess, by finding herself inside an older stranger's pick-up (!) truck.

When the brazen little thing reached across and gave my red beard a playful tug, reflex caused me to tweak one of her little birdies. After that, there was no going back, it all became automatic and unstoppable. Before I could even think about throwing this jailbait back in the water, we had stopped downtown for a six-pack and parked in some bushes behind the firehouse, where we killed the package and she sat on my lap backwards for a while. Then I tossed the empties (and the rubber) into the bushes and we took off again.

Laughing, feeling refreshed, but a little nervous, and wondering how best to ditch Cheryl, I drove around and schemed, while she smoked and enjoyed the view. Finally, I made a tentative offer to drop her back at the stop sign. Big mistake. Obviously hurt, she called me a bastard, then wouldn't look at me or say another word. My feeble excuses sounded stupid, even to me. Since I didn't know her very well, I decided I'd better be careful, so I changed my tune and started gabbling about places to go and things to do. Something also warned me not to offer this kid any money. She still didn't say anything, but the gloom seemed to lift, at least partially. By the time we were back at the stop sign, the cunning little voice in my brain had told me that, sometimes, the safest thing to do in a risky situation is to take more risks. Since no one was around, I explained my change of heart to Cheryl's young body with my hangman's hands. That worked, it made her perk right up. She said she had some things to do for her mother, who was at work, and told me to be back at six sharp. A last smack on the lips, a bright smile, and she wriggled off toward her little house. I revved the engine, turned right, and careened back down toward the ocean.

That day a fresh wind was blowing from the west, and as I sailed along I realized I hadn't been smelling any fish pollution, but when I reached the bottom of the hill and made some more turns, I noticed that my garbage had really started to reek. Of course I knew I should hurry up and get rid of the stuff, but I'd already made other plans. How much fun it would be to wait until dark, then sneak into the dump with Cheryl! A nice secluded place with lots of scary things to make the bopper hop right back up on my lap again.

All afternoon I wandered around killing time, looping back and forth on some newly built roads that formed a network of clover leafs. Around two, I stopped on the old coastal bypass at one of those little white restaurants that call themselves diners, where I had some weak coffee and hot chili with bread and butter. As I was paying, I mentioned to the waitress that I hadn't smelled the fish, and she said times were bad and they weren't running any Saturday shifts. I bought gas near the diner and drove on, listening to a ball game on the radio. Around four, I pulled over again, this time for a nap at a scenic turn-off.

At six sharp I was back at the stop sign, with two more six-packs and a big bag full of hoagies, chips and stuff, on the seat next to me. Once again, the streets were empty, and I could smell supper from some of the houses --mixed with my garbage. After about thirty seconds, Cheryl came running up. She poked her head through the passenger-side window and, spotting all the goodies, flashed a big mercenary smile. Beside the little white purse she'd had with her earlier, she was now carrying something long in two grocery bags, one upended. She was grasping the middle of the bags tightly together so they wouldn't come apart, and when she handed them to me through the window I pulled them apart and found a gun --a rifle-- plus a bunch of loose shells and a big red flashlight.

It was her brother's twenty-two, Cheryl explained innocently, hopping in and shoving the groceries toward me. I laughed and said it was better the gun was in my hands than in his. She was working on a major-league wad of gum and wearing the same pink tank-top, but she had changed from the shorts to a denim mini-skirt which made her legs look even storkier.

"Let's go to the dump," she said. "Later. When it's dark. We'll use your garbage as bait to shoot rats. Whew, that stuff reeks! I mean, if you like. It's fun! All the kids go. But there's a big dance at school tonight, so the dump won't get crowded till way after midnight."

I didn't ask her why she wasn't going to the dance, I just assumed she had broken up with someone and I had caught her on the rebound, which was fine with me. I told her I'd had the same idea --going to the dump-- and she laughed. She pointed to her name on the chain, and I told her mine was Richie. (It's Bob.)

There was time to kill, but we couldn't return to the firehouse because a bean supper was in progress. In fact, her mom was there, and she made a little pleasantry about my maybe wanting to drive by to say "Hi." Then, she reached into her gun bag, fished out two clean, empty Coke cans, and poured two beers into them. This was in case we ran into any sharp-eyed cops on the road. A short stocky guy in a flannel shirt, with a neatly trimmed beard, driving his kid or his niece someplace, each of them enjoying a Coke. A pleasant picture. Since the dance wasn't due to start for a couple of hours, we took off for the high school.

Everyone in these parts has supper at the same time. In fact, once when I was driving through a tiny place called Arnold's Corner at supper time, I had a vision of all the residents eating a synchronized meal --lifting forks and spoons at the same time, all taking a sip of their beverage, and so on. Anyway, as Cheryl and I zigzagged through the back streets of town, we saw almost no one. Here and there an old man or woman was putting the unsold stuff from the yard sale back in the garage --fifty pairs of Bermuda shorts, two-hundred plastic plates and grandma's culotte. A few kids in vehicles like mine roared past, but that was about it. We saw a neon sign in front of a car wash that said, "IF MORE HUSBANDS WERE SELF-STARTERS, THEIR WIVES WOULDN'T BE CRANKS." Maine humor.

She had been right about the high school --it seemed deserted-- but when we had parked behind the building and were just starting to eat, a bunch of kids in a new red low-rider called "Bounty Hunter" came blasting toward us. Cheryl had had me park so we could see anyone coming from a long way off, and now she ducked down, sandwich and fake Coke and all, and giggled when I lost half my sandwich and sloshed beer on my pants, trying to get us moving. By the time "Bounty Hunter" was abreast, I had gotten things under control enough to reply to their friendly wave with a "Howdy" that made her choke.

Since she couldn't think of anyplace better, we headed out to the coastal highway and wound up at the scenic turn-off where I'd taken the nap. There were several vehicles parked there now, but most of the occupants looked like tourists or summer residents come to have a picnic and watch the free sunset. A couple of the cars and trucks did seem like they might belong to locals, but Cheryl peeped up from behind the door and said none of the folks looked familiar. Anyway, my truck has local registration, and there were those fake Cokes, which we took turns flashing while the other one tried not to laugh.

We stayed there more than an hour, chatting, listening to the radio, finishing the food and three more beers apiece, and fooling around so much (below window level) that I gave the sunset a loud cheer, which provoked polite amusement in the next vehicle. It would be a moonless night, and before taking off for the dump we checked the flashlight. The gun and the bag with the bullets were under the seat. When I asked, Cheryl claimed to have the registration in her purse.

To get to the dump, we drove back to the stop sign, hung a left away from the coast, then followed a gravel road three miles through some woods. I drove slowly, and by the time we got there the sun had long since gone down behind the surrounding trees. Inside, a dirt track skirted the woods, and we followed it around to where it ducked into a little hollow partly hidden by a still-smoking pile of mostly burned trash. (I was surprised anyone still burned the stuff. What an ecologically incorrect town!) I slammed on the brakes, and we flung the remains of our dinner through the window and went at it like crazy.

In the next two hours, we finished the beer, talked a lot, and climbed over each other a couple of more times. When we wanted to see what we were doing, we would turn on the inside light. At one point Cheryl suggested I stop using my truck to haul around garbage and put an old mattress back there, instead, like a lot of her friends had. I didn't ask her what their parents thought the mattresses were for, or what my friends would think mine was for.

The light was on now as she quickly and smoothly loaded the gun, showing me she was not too drunk to do so. This was lucky since it happened that, even sober, I had never so much as held a gun, except for those electric ones or whatever they are, in amusement parks.

"We'll use your garbage for bait," she said, jumping down easily with the rifle in one hand. I opened my door, stepped into space, and barely managed to hold on to the flashlight and land on my feet. I could hear her snorting with laughter in the dark, and I shone the light toward the front of the truck and saw her lurch toward me, doubled up, the gun still in her hand. When I put the light on her, she raised the empty hand in front of her eyes. Then, I flicked off the light and she reacted immediately by firing a shot. I jumped back, this time falling, but holding the light above my head to keep it from hitting the ground. When she finally stopped laughing, she reassured me from the dark that she was just making sure everything was "in working order," because, as she explained, she had once met a bear there.

"Now for the trash," she said, and I heard her stumble around to the back. I crept along my side of the truck and, arriving at the same time, we bumped heads. Holding on to the gun and light, we managed some heavy smooching, until she pushed me back, saying, "Let's take care of business first! There'll be time for plenty more of that later."

So Cheryl held the light while I lowered the tailgate and clambered up, barking both shins, but not minding. Then, one by one, I rolled the bags off the truck while she counted: One. Two. Three. Four.

"Wait!" she said, when I had my hand on the fifth, and again she laughed for a long time. When she could finally speak, she suggested we save this one to scatter on the lawn of the High School Principal, who went to all the dances in order to prove he was one of the boys --which he definitely wasn't.

"Just save the last bag for me," she sang wittily. I thought saving the last bag for him was an excellent idea.

Next, we used the flashlight to watch each other pee in the woods. It turned out she had forgotten her purse, with the Kleenex, so I left her there squatting in the dark while, tripping, laughing and waving the flashlight, I finally found the truck. I made her shout by starting up the motor, then turned it off and staggered back with the Kleenex.

By now we were so squiffed we felt no squeamishness toward my garbage. On the contrary, it might have been jewelry or fine lace, which we took turns sorting, while the other one held the light. Ostensibly to select the things the rats would like best, we picked over two or three of the bags, really hamming it up. The show started when Cheryl put the spotlight on me, and I did a little dance with half a grapefruit on my head. Then I did a sort of Carmen Miranda number with lobster claws for castanets. After I had played the corncob harmonica (lame), the lobster motif took hold. For her main act, Cheryl used a tail as a big red nose, holding it on with one hand and her white sunglasses, which she had been wearing ever since we got to the dump. Imitating a woman her mother worked with at the five-and-ten, she jumped around, chattering and wagging the nose. For my own finale I held up a big carcass as if it were an electric guitar and pretended to be Elvis singing a song I made up on the spot to the tune of "Blue Suede Shoes." It was called "Rockin' Lobster." The part I remember went like this:

Well, you can suck my claws and crack my tail,
Squeeze me till I spout like a whale,
Rockin' Lobster. Rockin' Lobster ...

You had to have been there.

When Amateur Night was over, we set the pile of selected appetizers out in a little clearing. Then we hid behind the truck and, taking turns, fired off about two-dozen shots apiece. There were lots of rats --at first-- and we --she-- may have hit one or two, but none fatally. By then the night had grown cold, so we got back in the cab, turned on the motor and heat, hugged and said nice things.

By the time we were back at the stop sign, it was after eleven. The lights in Cheryl's house were on, so we made it quick. She had told her mother she was going to the drive-in and the dance, and now she would just say she'd come home early because the kids were getting into some heavy drinking. Her friends would cover for her. When she had gotten her things together --the gun would go right into the back shed to be cleaned in the morning-- I offered to pick her up again the next night at nine. No, her aunt and uncle were coming to supper, so she'd have to stay in. Sunday would have been out, anyway, because her family was religious. As she jumped down, she coyly whispered, "Maybe Monday."

I drove home fast and wild with the tailgate clanging. Only fool's luck kept me from being pulled over. I was pretty sure I got home uneventfully, the only exception being when I zoomed around the curve in front of my friend Alice's house, hit the bump and banged my head on the roof of the cab. This was just out of town, where the main road turns toward my road, and just before the speed limit changes from twenty-five to thirty-five. I was doing about forty when I hit the bump. For some reason I noticed that Alice's place was dark, and her carport, empty.

The next day --yesterday-- I got up around noon, feeling the same way I had felt Thursday after the wine. I was scheduled for brunch with a young lawyer and his family in town and, having canceled the previous Sunday for a similar reason, this time I had to go. So, loaded with coffee and aspirin, freshly showered and all dolled up in new white painter's pants and a sky -blue tee shirt, I decided to take the Ferrari. You understand what was going on, don't you? Everything clean? Neat? Expensive? Besides, when I peered through the garage window at the truck, it seemed to have a "hit-and-run" look.

As I approached Alice's place, something jarred against my mental picture. As usual, the spindly little trees stood there in a row baking in the sun. And Alice's nice flagstone and olive-green-shingle house gleamed prosperously in the same sun. And the new blacktop drive...

I braked, forgot to put the clutch in, burped to a stop right in the mouth of the driveway, and jumped out. There were the contents of the fifth bag, spread all over the glistening asphalt. Either the bag had split open as it bumped off the truck or a raccoon had gotten into it later --but what did that matter? There were bugs, too.

I looked at my watch and started sweating. By local standards, it was a hot and humid day. There would be rings on my tee shirt and I might smell a bit, but there was no choice, I already knew what I had to do. It was like the moment when you bounce off a horse and have all the landing options figured by the time you start downward.

Fact: Alice's car hadn't been there last night, and she hadn't come and gone since. I knew because she couldn't have gotten past the garbage without leaving tracks. Fact: on Saturday nights, she often stays over with her old mom on the other side of town, in which case she would take her to church, drive her home, then come back here for lunch and the ball game, which began in --twenty-five minutes.

Those facts left me with three apparent choices, plus one real one. Choice: go home, change, grab a new bag, a shovel, etc., call the lawyer with a simple, plausible story, hurry back here and get to work. But I couldn't think of a simple, plausible story, and even if I could I might be late, still stooping in the driveway when Alice pulled up. Choice: leave the garbage for now, with a note saying I'd be back later to explain and clean it up. (It occurred to me to leave a buck or two.) But Alice and I happened to be on terms which made both this choice and the first one unacceptable. For, as luck would have it, she and I had gotten a bit familiar at my lobster dinner Wednesday night, and as she had been a little less drunk and a little less carried away by the moment, there had been the matter of a slap in the face. That had been our most recent communication and, as Alice had more than once previously noted what she called "a mean, vindictive streak" in me, my guess was that she would have the mess all cleaned up by the time I got back, after which there would be a staggering debt to be repaid --on her terms.

So, as I said, had there really ever been a choice? Just as I got back into the Ferrari, an old couple out for their pre-lunch constitutional paused to look askance at me and my garbage.

Leaning through the window, I smiled and said conspiratorially, "Damned kids!" and the old folks walked on, apparently satisfied. I quickly backed up the Ferrari. Sighing as if I had arrived late at a funeral, I turned off the motor. Then I opened the trunk, got down on my hands and knees, tossed in the first carapace, and something happened.

Call it a sea change. For was I mistaken, or was that Cheryl's nose in the trunk? And had I never before looked closely at a cooked lobster shell in bright sunlight? You know, once at an antiques fair I saw a whole oceanful of lobster-colored Fiesta ware, set out on a gigantic red table. Into the trunk went a sea green wine bottle and some pieces of pastel yellow and light-green melon rind. Then, with a second bottle poised in mid-air, I began to laugh. As Yogi Berra said, "It was *Deja vu all* over again." What was I going to do with the stuff in the trunk of the Ferrari?

It was like falling off the horse again. Of course, I could have just cleaned it out into another bag and left it with a buck the next Saturday. Dull! Perhaps it should have gone back to the construction site, or to the Principal's lawn. No, those, too, were ideas whose time had passed.

Of course, I already had the answer --and, with it, the courage to get the driveway spill completely cleaned up before Alice arrived, and the courage to get through the brunch reeking of sweat and garbage and with a headache four of the lawyer's extra-strength Excedrin couldn't touch.

And so that long Sunday passed. And then the night, through which I slept wonderfully well. And Monday morning and afternoon, which I have profitably spent on overdue errands and household chores. And now --soon-- not more than two hours from now, comes my reward. Yes, tonight the little lady and I will once again be hauling my garbage to the dump. This time, however, it travels first-class, and, although there is only that one bag, I take comfort in the fact that, what with my filthy white painter's pants and sky-blue tee shirt, I have already made considerable inroads on a new bag.

Ron Singer

The Silent Treatment

Three years had passed, and once again it was time to take the cure. I am someone whose exuberance frequently prompts him —me—to "lope into other people's emotional pastures." I heard this metaphor used a few months ago at a funeral for a suicide, to describe the manic phase in bi-polar disorder. My exuberance often peaks with a rash of ruined dinner parties, where I finish my wife's sentences and motor mouth about my latest triumphs (trivial) and setbacks (hilarious). Since I am a teacher, these sociopathic breaks tend to cluster around the long vacations, Christmas, Easter, and, especially, summer, when I lack access to my official victims. When my bad behavior becomes impossible to ignore, because others stop ignoring it, I take the cure: I subject myself, that is, to the silent treatment.

In undergoing this treatment, you might say, I am a kind of reverse Ancient Mariner, who (if you remember, from your own school days) would periodically feel compelled to take a break from his eremitic existence in order to seek out someone upon whom to unload his tale of sin and non-redemption. You might also say that the A.M.'s interlocutor/victim, the wedding guest, was an unwilling, unpaid, couch-less shrink. The transference --or was it counter-transference? -- was complex. I mean, all those dead men on the deck of a becalmed ship? And why, you might ask, did he not simply return to his first shrink, the "holy hermit" who had "shrived" him when he finally struck (Eng)land after his fatal journey? Or had the holy hermit died in the interim? (And I teach this poem!)

The efficacy of any treatment modality depends, of course, upon finding the ideal environment in which to undergo it. (Ah, psychobabble!) For example, I've heard that some people in talk

(!) therapy binge on sleep and comfort food. For the silent treatment, I have found the perfect environment to be the vast Navajo reservation in western New Mexico and eastern Arizona. I have a friend there, who lives near a Navajo-run community college ("near," by western standards --about a hundred miles away). The campus is just west of the Chuska Mountains, which straddle the two states. Thrice now, this friend, who knows an administrator at the college, has generously arranged for me to rent a room in their guest dorm.

A quiet, considerate man, my friend avoids visiting me at the college, and I, in turn, politely refuse his polite invitations to visit his wife and him. Both of us, presumably, are afraid that a visit might trigger a relapse into motor mouthing. While I am at the college, for form's sake, I do make a single brief phone call, during which I thank him and we ask about each other's work and family, relying heavily on the phrase, "Oh, about the same." This is in contrast to our several annual email exchanges, effusive, on my part, and politely lengthy, on his.

The dorm at the Navajo college is austere, but not silent, or even quiet, because some of the maids, secretaries and maintenance men congregate in the living room for much of the day, watching soaps, cartoons, and quiz and reality shows. For them, this cool, dark, windless room in the middle of an eight-sided building modeled after the traditional Navajo dwelling, the *hogan* (hoe-*gahn*), is a perfect sanctuary from the blinding, blistering, windblown environment outside. By watching their shows with the volume on the big TV turned all the way up, they, too, may be taking a silent treatment, of sorts. For me, of course, it is the environs of the noisy dorm that constitute the perfect setting.

A month ago, toward the end of July, I took the cure for the third, and probably the last, time. Once again I followed the drill I had established on my first visit, eight years before. Parts of each day were spent over mostly silent meals (of which more later), and parts reading, and keeping a circumstantial journal on my laptop. I did this reading and writing in the dead of night in my room and in the quiet library, where my company consisted primarily of local children playing video games with the sound off and without talking —after all, it is a library. However, the heart of my waking hours each day (I slept well, and, I assume, quietly) consisted of two self-imposed, consciously therapeutic activities.

The first was a long drive through the empty landscape in my small white rented car. After either breakfast or lunch, I would log about 100 miles on various two-lane highways (the sole paved roads), where my only company would be occasional other vehicles, either whizzing past me or whizzing past on the other side. (There was also the roadkill that these vehicles generated, but roadkill can hardly be called "company.")

I did not play the radio, and once every half hour or so, I would pull onto a shoulder. Turning the motor off, I would either wander over to a red sandstone mesa and stand looking at it for a few minutes, close up, or lean against the side of the car, peering at a vista in the middle or far distance. It would be just the wind, me, and an occasional crow out there. When it seemed time, I would get back in the car, start up, and head for the next mesa or vista. My routes were uncharted.

One such vista, which I came across on the second day of last month's sojourn, was particularly spectacular. In the middle of this dry, mostly flat country stands what looks like the remnant of a massive formation. This is a very high, thin slice of black rock, perpendicular to the road, and running westward, from a few hundred feet off the road all the way to the vanishing point, or, as I fantasized, to infinity. A very nice, professorial *biligana* (non-Navajo) woman with whom I subsequently ate lunch in the college cafeteria told me that this formation is known as a curtain rock, and that it actually winds about thirty miles down to the Navajo landmark called, for an obvious reason, Ship Rock. The curtain rock may have been formed when a magma-less volcano blew, spewing a pipe of air upward that lifted the sheet of rock. But my informant did not have any idea when (or even whether) this had really happened.

The second session of my day, the more important one, took place at dusk. Of course, dawn might have been better, since fewer people are around, and since dawn is a holy time for the *Di'neh*, which is what the Navajo call themselves. (It means "human beings," which makes you wonder where that leaves the rest of us.) But this being a quasi-vacation, I was too lazy to get up early, so dusk it was, right after dinner.

On the very first day of my first visit eight years ago, I had found the perfect place, the front steps of the college's administration building, a hideous modern excrescence with amber mirror glass, blasphemously shaped like a humongous *hogan*. Thereafter, every day of all three visits, at around eight o'clock, I would sit silently on these steps, a long flight made of cement. They look out across a parking lot to the soft, wooded, medium-high Chuska Mountains. Sitting there, I would watch the shadows take over the world. More to the point, as I watched, it was with the distinct consciousness that I was clearing my head of the myriad words that always buzz around inside. Each evening, little by little, the crowded page would turn to a white sheet. By the end of each of the first two cures, the words would be there when I needed them, but *they* would wait for *me*.

Almost no one interrupted these nightly vigils. Every single Navajo that came up from the parking lot would see me, avert their eyes, then detour to the walkway on either the left or right, which leads around the building to the back door. They did this, presumably, so as not to cross my line of vision to the mountains, or even, perhaps, so as not to cross my field of thought.

The only person who ever stepped inside my space did so on the very first evening of this, my most recent visit. The intruder was a beach-bleached-and-baked *biligana*, who affected a quasi-Navajo style: silver bracelet, turquoise ponytail holder, etc. Coming from the lot, he did a double take, then loped up the steps two at a time with outstretched hand. He named himself (very un-Navajo) and said he was from California.

There was not even an initial, token show of deference. After a quick, "Hey, how ya' doin'?" he pointed out that, since the sunset was on the other side of the building, he wondered what I was doing there, or, as his tone suggested, what the hell I was doing there.

"I'm here for the quiet," I explained. "I'm here to dry out."

"Dig," he said. "Booze?" And he made the glugging gesture.

"Nope," I said, making the yakkety-yak gesture. "Talk." Understandably, he looked puzzled.

"It's like this," I explained. "I talk too much. It builds up, builds up, until, every so often, my motor just won't seem to quit. You know those little flaps of metal they used to have in carburetors, the 'butterfly'? Well, mine gets stuck on 'open.' This really gets on everyone's nerves, mine included. So … "I gestured to the space around us and, affecting a youthful argot, added, "Chillin', man. Just chillin'."

"Dig!" he replied. "Oh, wow, that's why you're here? You came all the way out here, like, just to be quiet! Wow! Like …

far out! Hey, we have something like that at school. I mean, I go to this really cool private school, like, we call it 'Quaker High,' but its real name is 'San Demiento Friends,' and, like, twice a week for almost 20 minutes, we sit there in absolute silence. A hundred and fifty of us, all in this big room, all saying *nada*. You ask a lot of the kids: "Borrrr-ing!" "Embarrassing!" Their parents all like to eat in, like, restaurants that play foreground music.

"Not me, though," he assured me. "I kind of dig the silence. See, I spend a lot of time in my own head, anyhow." He glanced at his big watch. "Wow! Got to split, man, hit the library, mega-reading to do for my N.S. class. Nice talking to you."

"'N.S.'?"

"Navajo Studies. Really cool. Hey, have a good evening."

"Good evening to you, friend. If..." But he was gone.

Why had this young man, who was about two years older than my own son, stopped to talk to me? He was being nice. He probably thought that, despite my stated intention, I was lonely, starved for conversation.

As well he might have, since, as I had immediately realized on my first visit, Navajos —the men, especially-- are very silent people. Out there, you don't jump into someone's space or step on the backs of their sentences. Any but the slowest, most careful entry, with clear signs of invitation, into a conversation, constitutes loping into someone else's emotional field.

That whole week, it did not rain, and I read in the local paper that this was part of a long, harmful drought. As for me, the days passed, the cure kicked in, and the emptiness became more and more enjoyable. By the third or fourth evening, as I sat there on the cement steps, I would mostly think of nothing.

But later, in the middle of the night in my room in the now-silent dorm, writing in the journal with the only light the glow from my monitor, I would consider many things. Navajo silence is a fullness. Here in the windy, scruffy, under-populated semi-desert, silence is fructifying.

For a contrasting style of silence, consider this anecdote:

Back in the early days of our marriage, years before our son was born, my wife and I took a vacation trip to Honolulu. One evening, we were waiting on a movie line right in front of two local girls who were having what might be called a conversation.

Girl One: You go MacDonald's?
(A pause of, perhaps, five seconds.)
Girl Two: Yah.
(Pause.)
One: Who'd you go that place with?
(Pause.)
Two: You know, some guys.
Pause.
One: Greg?
(Pause.)
Two: Yah.
(Pause.)
One: Jerry?
Two: Uh huh.

And so forth.

On the fifth day, sensing that my cure was complete and wanting perhaps to try out my new less-social skills, I made a move to break the silence. I had spent four days quieting down. I had eaten three meals a day alone, except for a few people who joined me, the professor who told me about the rock formation, and one or two other *biliganas,* academic types. The Californian did not seem to eat there, at least not when I did.

By the time of the geology lecture, by the way, I felt the need for only a few appropriate questions and comments. "Are there any other formations like that?" "It *does* look mysterious." "Mm, hmm." You get the idea.

On the fifth day, at breakfast, without making a conscious decision, I carried my tray from the end of the cafeteria line all the way across the room to a trio of *Di'neh* men who were the sole occupants of a table beneath a window. Without speaking, I made a small gesture toward a vacancy a few seats from theirs and sat down. One of the three was on the same side as I was, facing the other two, whose backs were to the window. They were all youngish, maybe in their late 20's or early 30's, and all were dressed cowboy style, except for the headgear, caps, which they kept on while they ate.

As I sat down, one of the men across from me broke the non-eye-contact rule long enough for the quickest of nods. Then, they went on eating —a little faster, it seemed to me-- and left without a word or even another nod. I may have been wrong, but I guessed that rather than fleeing my unwelcome presence, they were simply being courteous, providing me with unbroken space.

That evening, they were at the same table. Again, I joined them, this time without the preliminary gesture.

"Y'ah'teh," the man on my side said, not looking up from his food." ("Hello.")

"Y'ah'teh," I replied. The two others nodded; I nodded back.

The next, and sixth, day, which was my last full one before leaving, we were seated at lunch again, when the floodgates broke. One of the men asked why I was there.

"For the quiet," I said.

They accepted this explanation without comment, and a few further bits of neutral information were exchanged.

Then, without preamble, the facing man who had nodded the first time made a sort of speech. A straight-arrow type, he explained that he was an army vet and had come here on the G.I. bill, to try to "get me some college." He told me his name, "Larry," not his Navajo name, the spirit of which, as I knew, can be worn out by too much use. I told them my name. More nods, no handshakes.

While the rest of us kept eating, Larry talked. He had just returned from towing a friend's car, which had hit a big rock in a construction zone on the main east-west highway, tearing a hole in the gas tank and flattening the muffler. Could they get the money for towing to a distant garage (there were none closer) and for the repairs, major money, from the incompetent construction company?

I knew he did not expect an answer or, for that matter, anything more than a neutral nod, which would be taken as a proper show of sympathy. I nodded.

Then, the man on my left really broke things open, spontaneously offering a long, autobiographical monologue interrupted only by several silences into which I did not intrude. His friends sometimes smiled, but they did not say anything, either.

First, he introduced himself, more formally than the first speaker, offering both first and last, non-Navajo names. I'll call him "T.R." Un-Navajo-like he proffered a handshake, which proved to be soft. A very interesting person, a little grim, alive and full of experience, although, as with many, even most, *Din'eh*, I caught a whiff of despair. The gist of his speech was as follows:

For five years, T.R. had traveled the country with his uncle, from Pensacola to Walla Walla, working as a silversmith. He spoke good English, and like many other older students, he explained, he was at the college, which he found to be a uniquely congenial learning environment, to bite the long-delayed educational bullet. T.R. ended by saying he had grown up near Gallup (a big town just east of the Reservation), and understood Navajo pretty well, but couldn't really speak it, and that people over by Tuba (Tuba City, to the west) were "even more Navajo" than those in the town where the college was located. (I am unsure why I do not name this town, but for some reason I am still —almost three weeks later-- reluctant to do so.)

T.R.'s monologue continued long after we had all finished eating. As he spoke, we played with the remnants of our food. Finally, he stopped. No one said anything. The four of us just got up and carried our trays over to the bussing station by the door.

"See you around," we allowed, on both sides. I did not mention that I was leaving.

That last night in my cell, I replayed this my first real "conversation" in five days. It was very stimulating, but very sad and un-Navajo. I felt a bit like an A.A. member who had stood by watching helplessly while a couple of fellow members binged. T.R. especially, I thought, was a motor mouth like me, talking just to keep from crying.

The next day, I was home, and as it had seemed to Lemuel Gulliver, "home" seemed anything but. The noise made my teeth rattle. Back in Psychotic City, everyone seemed to be talking at the same time. Cell phones, telephones, chat rooms, non-stop nattering all day and night, in bars, cafes, parks, coffee shops, on corners, buses, subways, everywhere. Of course, I did realize that, until recently, I had, myself, been a prominent member of the chattering classes, but this did not make me enjoy the state of things any better.

Somehow, though, after a few initial days of panic in the midst of all the noise, I was able to step back, drawing on my reserves of quiet from the week on the Reservation. I was calm again. My family noticed, approvingly, at first. But after a few more days, as my silences became prolonged, they began to worry.

"Like, Dad," said my son, fourteen, his pale brow furrowing, "you never say anything, anymore. I don't think you've said more than two words the whole time you've been back. What'd they do to you out there? It wasn't like this the other times. You were... mellow, then. But this is ridiculous."

He looked as if he were about to cry. I shrugged and tried to smile.

"He's right, dear," my wife chimed in. "What are you doing, practicing for the grave?"

"Mm," I said.

She was right. It was as if something had flipped my switch to the "permanently off" position. Interesting. And it was also interesting that I thought about this phenomenon as if it were happening to someone else.

After another mostly silent week, I began to be infected by their alarm, to worry about their worry. As they would voice this worry, which my wife called "concern," I would nod in sincere agreement.

Then, she started making noises about my seeing a "real shrink, or else." The idea of trying to talk to a complacent, paid stranger repelled me. Instead, I reasoned (or stalled), why not wait for the school year to begin, when my switch would surely flip back on, the minute I stepped back into the classroom? But what if it didn't? I pictured myself standing there in front of a group of freshly summered faces, some puzzled, some laughing.

"Say something, Mr. ----," a concerned student would prompt. "This isn't like you. Speak."

With that imagined scenario, and the realization that actual school was less than three weeks off, things came to a head. One afternoon, I locked myself in my study and fell into a sort of trance in front of my computer. Without quite knowing what I was doing and with no sense of time passing, I went online, and after I had surfed hither and yon, something snapped.

The best way I can describe this "something" is to mix some figures of speech. Suddenly, the floodgates sprang open, and once again the words flowed, like shit through a goose. I was like a man with a distressed bladder who, after an agonizing car trip, finally makes it to a rest room, and stands flooding the porcelain.

Not to be solemn, but I can also call what happened a revelation of sorts. I thought I had found the —an-- answer. Triumphantly I *loped* into the living room, where my wife and son were both busy, she at her computer; he, reading. As usual, it gladdened my heart to see my two dear ones thus "gainfully employed."

"I've got it, I've got the answer!" I blurted. They both looked up, wearing their by-now familiar worry faces.

"Listen," I said superfluously, "I think I have an idea. I just googled a tourist site in West Africa. You know, they talk a lot there, and I bet it's the kind of talk that's really infectious. So I started checking airfares and hotels." I waved a piece of paper at them, with figures on it. "I've already decided: Lagos, Nigeria, where I learned that they have ten or fifteen million people and only part-time traffic lights. It's a problem with the power grid. Can you believe that! Lagos, the heart of noise! I mean, the car horns alone! I can get my shots and passport and everything else taken care of this week, then fly out Monday morning, they still have seats. Twelve hours later, I'll be there. Bingo! Lagos."

When I came up for air, the ludicrousness of my African travel notion descended with a thud. I looked around, dazed. What had happened? Although the room was pleasantly cool, I was sweating as if I had reached the apex of a fever.

"So. What do you think?" I asked, but the question was rhetorical. As usual, my loved ones did not disappoint.

"You're not really going to do this, are you, dad?" my son asked, also rhetorically. "You're joking, right?" He was wearing his loopy grin. "That's really funny."

My wife was smiling, too. "You'll be all right now, dear," she said, looking at me over her half-glasses. "I don't think you need to start packing yet."

A Dream of Trains

"Hello?"

Other than two or three from my parents, this was my first call since I'd gotten home. My voice was loud but modulated.

"Bob? Is that you? Listen, this is Charlie. Charles Frescobaldi? How you doing, Bob?" It was the neighborhood contractor who had inspired the dropped ceilings for my subway designs. We had been sidewalk acquaintances. "So, I ran into Eleanor the other day, she told me you're ... that you were released." Charlie's dialect is nervous, educated Brooklynese. I pictured his big round head and imagined him running a hand through the thick wavy black hair. I heard faint sounds of ice tinkling, then swallowing, and imagined he had moved the telephone away from his mouth. "How do you feel?"

"Better, thanks. How are ..."

"Good, good. Listen, I happen to have a nice job for you. Can you, er, work yet?"

Well, I thought, I sure can --at least I hope so. But why did you call *me*, Mr. Fresco? Because you knew I'd be cheap? No, that was ungracious.

"Sure."

OPERANT THERAPEUTIC MODALITY. Monday, February 20, 2006

"Artsy fartsy!" I screamed. I jerked my head toward the drawings. Obviously, the flavor of the month was Therapy through the Arts. In addition to the usual mimeographed notices of fire regulations and so-called activities, the walls of the otherwise tasteful corridor were papered with saints, phallic projectiles, severed heads, and giant parentals menacing diminutive offspring. Across the top of this display was a strip of oak tag with a caption in large black curlicues:

Mason Clinic Proudly Celebrates The Creativity Of Our Clients

DR. JARVIS MASON'S CASE NOTES (1). Tuesday, January 17, 2006

It's just the same old story… la la.

Profile: Robert Green ("Bob"), Caucasian male, age 38.

Diagnosis: clinical depression.

Predisposition: 3 early checkouts in family, 2 on maternal branch; patient has suffered from chronic D. at least since onset of adolescence.

Pre-trauma symptoms: low self-esteem masked by rigid routine; absolute "reliability"; workaholism; occasional puffs of escaped rage.

Triggering episode: After 11 years [1994-2005] of awful bed lock, wife, Eleanor Herrick, leaves him ("*bo*-ring") for another (!) woman [Friday, August 5, 2005]. She keeps apartment (hers, he moved in when they hooked up). He loses job, moves to worse neighborhood, immediately traumatized, and over subsequent 7-mo. period [August 2005-January 2006] sinks steadily.

Crisis and aftermath: Hits bottom, sticks head in oven [January 14, 2006]. Parents, expected later that afternoon, turn up early (on a hunch), save him. Grade-A health insurance through wife (tax lawyer, large white shoe firm, separation not yet formalized). And, yesterday, here he is.

Current state: fetal, locked in private room, 24-hour supervision @ 10-minute intervals.

Medication: SSRI's [selective serotonin reuptake inhibitors], normal dosage, for now. If no luck, we'll switch him over to MOWIES [monoamine oxidase inhibitors].

Prognosis: Way too soon to say.

IMAGINING THE C.C. RIDER. Saturday, April 8, 2006

It's my idea, all mine. It used to be the Loomis ice cream parlor; now it will be the C.C. Rider dance club. (Pity the neighbors.)

Although I had been inside the parlor only two or three times, none recently, of course, I remembered it well. Pink marble counters, pale green fixtures, etched glass windows, black and white tile floors. And, most important, the vibrations, caused by the subway, which ran right below the building. Especially when you were standing at the cash register, if a train passed you could feel these vibrations running up your legs into your bowels.

Vibrations to Vibes. The C.C. Rider. Old fashioned, ultimate chic, conversation piece. I would transform the lovely ice cream parlor with its high tin ceilings into the kind of subway car they had around 1950, fifteen years before I was born. I leaned stiff-armed against the kitchen table. Eyes wide open, I imagined …

… metal fans, dark green, slowly spinning overhead. Maps, posters. Straw seats with little rectangular handles on top, also dark green. Loud laughter/ conversation, pulsing techno/

bodies. Tinkling of glass. Old wooden cash register. Tokens, anyone?

DR. MASON'S CASE NOTES (2). Wednesday, February 15, 2006.

I like Bob Green. For starters, the man can wield the English tongue. In today's session, he used some interesting imagery. In his own words:

"A couple of months ago, I think it was, I was trudging up a snowy hill from the subway after a long day of futilely searching for a job, when a huge Doberman, leashed luckily, jumped right at me. His snout turned into Mick Jagger's face, screaming into a mic. And his asshole master, some drugged out punk with brain piercings, thought it was really funny."

Prognosis: This is a very talented, creative guy although his D. is deep. If the family pitches in, if we can put him back together with ongoing SST's plus talk-talk –i.e. the usual combo—plus the modality flavor of the month, which is tailor-made for Mr. G--and, if, after all that, he can get a job and keep it … yes, a lot of ifs. But this guy just might make it.

A DREAM OF TRAINS (1). Thursday, February 24, 2006

Understand that in my former incarnation I was an architectural draughtsman with a large downtown firm. My parents, presumably with Mason's approval, brought to the clinic all my instruments (except the compasses), plus the special paper I had requested. Understand, too, that presumably in keeping with its therapeutic purpose, this putative art course is called "Visual Fantasies."

I think I'll tell this in narrative form.

TWO PLANS FOR THE RELIEF OF SUBWAY CROWDING

With trembling hands and in silence, I hang the drawings from the stainless-steel clothespins in front of the whiteboard. The class consists of myself, the young instructor (female), and two other "clients," Frederick M, a tall fat man with sandy hair and a permanent expression of fury on his florid face, and Dorothy S, a thin middle-aged woman whose gray face is a circus of tics and whose fingers incessantly tap out the same tunes which, over the years, I myself have played. We two men wear patterned sport shirts, the instructor a dark-green shirt, very becoming, if I may be so bold. The instructor and I wear blue jeans and Frederick, brown corduroy trousers. Dorothy wears a plain well-cut navy blue woolen dress. During one of the morning assemblies, Mason reminded/explained to the community (the unlocked members) that a few months back he had, "for morale's sake, determined to outlaw bathrobes and slippers in public spaces, except, of course, for the physically incapacitated."

As the always pleasant instructor coos encouragement and my two fellow students stare into space, I announce the title, then begin my lecture. At first my voice is violently tremulous and much too loud, but as I proceed the trembling subsides to a tremor and I am able to modulate the volume.

"The concept behind these fine perspective pictorials by the [*sic*] eminent architect Robert G. [no surnames here] is simple. In every subway car, there will be two levels. I note at the outset that the cars themselves will not need to be an inch higher than at present, since all modifications are to be made to their interiors. It should also be acknowledged that these modifications have been inspired by the work of Robert G's friend, the noted neighborhood contractor, Charles F., whose work with the dropped ceiling, albeit controversial, has revolutionized the re-design of historic residential townhouses." At this point, Frederick barks a loud cough and his red face grows even redder. Dorothy, almost imperceptibly, frowns. I try to ignore these reactions.

"Note that our plan is to lower the first ceilings to six feet, leaving two-feet-four-inches above. Ladders, either permanent ones extending vertically at either end of every car, or removable ones slanting up from the station platforms through the large custom windows, will provide access to the upper level." I pause to drain half the water from the large Styrofoam cup that is practically an appendage for most of us, since a well-known side effect of many of our medications is thirst.

"You will also note," I resume, aiming my pointer at the first drawing, "that PLAN A calls for people who are six feet or taller to ride lying down on the upper level." By now, Dorothy has begun to peek shyly at me, and Frederick, to pace the room. For obvious reasons, moving around is permitted during classes.

I drone on. "PLAN B, on the other hand, adds to the design of PLAN A intermittent vertical compartments wide enough to contain a single person, exact number to be calculated by demographic survey, and reaching from the floor of the car through to the ceiling of the upper level. Passengers six feet and taller will be directed to these compartments. The upper level will now be reserved for those passengers who elect to lie down and are willing to purchase a special gold transit pass for that priv ..."

At that point, Frederick startles us all by interrupting, in his usual booming voice:"... privilege, the theory being that many harried commuters already look as though they would gladly pay a surcharge for a seat, so how much more willing would they be to pay to lie down? Conceivable, but admittedly problematic, are two additional dimensions."

I cannot help noticing how well he has caught my tone. The instructor watches uneasily for signs of impending violence, but since class participation is encouraged (and often hard to come by), she allows the interrupter to continue. Dorothy is still studying either her feet or the floor.

"The first addition," thunders the intruder, "will be to subcontract the upper levels to the subway prostitution firm, *Darlene's Rush Hour Services for Gentlemen*, of which I happen myself to be founder and C.E.O. You may recall," he digresses from his own digression, "that it was one of our gals who wrote the best-selling memoir, *Tightly Packed Pants*. The second ancillary dimension will be the employment of jobless youth to awaken passengers in time for their stops, recompense to take the form of gratuities."

"Those sure are problematic dimensions," Dorothy finally mutters, licking her chapped lips.

My best course is to humor him. "Thank you, Frederick," I say before he can continue. "That presentation displayed the crisp succinctness we have all come to expect from you." He nods brusquely, smashes a fist into a palm, then sets off around the room again.

"It will be apparent," I drone on, "that PLAN A is the more egalitarian, although I will be the first to admit that even it is open to allegations of height-ism, which, as we all know, in this city is often tantamount to racism. Nevertheless, I feel certain that the more fundamental issue for the city council will prove to be space utilization versus revenue return. Let me close with a caveat: I plead with the authorities not to regard the plan —whichever version is ultimately selected—as a panacea for the city's future fiscal ills. Such a misuse, such a misjudgment, would lead inevitably to gross overcrowding of the new facilities, making a mockery of the initial rationale for redesign. Ladies and gentlemen, I thank you."

Frederick, without interrupting his circumambulation, smashes his hands together twice; Dorothy, expressionless, rapidly and silently taps her fingers together several times. The instructor smiles (widely) and nods (vigorously).

"Very good, Bob," she says. And since this has been my first-class presentation and I have been at the clinic for barely a month, she adds, "Welcome aboard."

The next morning when I came down for breakfast, my drawings were up there with the rest in the corridor. They had even been allocated their own small bulletin board just to the right of the others, where the light was excellent. And I must admit to a surge of pride as I read the caption, which I could guess the art teacher had prepared:

MASON CLINIC CLIENTS ARE NOT ONLY TALENTED. THEY CARE ABOUT THEIR CITY!!!!!

DR. JARVIS MASON CASE NOTES (3). Tuesday, April 4, 2006

BG discharged! He's still on the SSRI's and I'll be seeing him as an outpatient, twice weekly, at first. Says he's been offered a job and, beat this, it actually has something to do with trains! (He waxed mysterious when I asked for more details). I think I may have a bright idea that will benefit us both.

CREATING THE CC RIDER. Saturday, April 15-Friday, June 2, 2006

When Charlie Frescobaldi saw what a skillful, prompt, willing worker I (still) was, I became his right-hand man for the whole project. The boys (cocaine snorters, pill poppers from Manhattan with obscure financial backing) quickly came to know and love us both. From start to finish, Frescobaldi showed great finesse. Within the first few days, contracts had been signed, advances rendered, and we had been authorized to send the bills to their accountant, a box number. Within another week, Charlie had finagled several thousand extra for me, for "expanded services."

I did perform expanded services; these were the busiest seven weeks of my life. As I told Mason during one of our-now weekly evening meetings, "There are times when I even long for the quiet times at the old firm, the days when there was even time to mark time. At times."

"Understandable," he chuckled, "but insincere, of course. You love this job, Bob, it's obvious. Which is wonderful. Don't forget to invite me to the opening."

This lighthearted allusion to the old problems, the cool way I now dealt with Eleanor (we legally separated in early May), the work —everything went so well. During another session, I fatuously said to Mason that a busy, successful life is the best bulwark against mental illness: one lives a crazy life in order not to be crazy. Nodding sagely, he took a hit from his pipe.

Blueprints, whiteprints, drafting film, tracking cloth, they disappeared so fast it was as if they had been stolen. Floor plans, section drawings, mechanicals, wiring diagrams, outlets, fixtures, switches, doors, windows, security systems, energy systems. Permits, subcontractors, short cuts, palms to grease, sloppy workers to be brought up to the mark: Charlie was particularly effective in these human areas, even scary. And it all had to look like a goddamned old subway!

Problems, of course, were legion. For instance, when a workman's flying hammer shattered one of the five-by-eight sections of mirror behind the original Loomis counter, matching the old glass cost us two thousand and many, many phone calls. Also, one of the investors, a twitcher named Joey Marx, announced that he had fallen in love with the chandeliers, and ordered us to keep them. But they clashed with the new décor and would have been shredded instantly by the overhead fans. Compromise: after a few hissie-fits and several wasted hours of aggro, he had them installed in the dining room of his own (undoubtedly tasteless) new condo.

When the parquet floors came in fifty percent above estimate, there was another huge palaver, this one even including a few threats and epithets cribbed from the Godfather movies. Of course, there were consolations, too. "Bob deserves another three grand," Charlie opined at an opportune moment a few weeks ago. Bob got it.

Somehow, an inch at a time, we crept forward. Concepts became blueprints, which were scrutinized, modified, approved. Demolition (the flying hammer), then renovation. Sounds simple? Ha!

One detail chosen from ten thousand: would the straw seats Charlie spotted in a junk shop do? Well, no, they would rip people's pants to shreds. Could you lacquer them with currently available products and still have them look forty years old? Of course you could, for a price. But it turned out there were only eight, and we needed six more, two long, four short. Here and there, rushing all over the city a la Keystone Cops, and with great agony because the damn seats all had to match, Charlie and I eventually hunted them down. I then designed the new booths, incorporating the eight short seats. It was a grand moment when we stood there and watched them being bolted into place.

Bear with me, I find these details consummately interesting. Each booth consisted of two of the transverse seats and a dark maple table. The notion of covering the tables with graffiti was dismissed as anachronistic: 1950, not 1973. Along each wall, the men set in place a booth, then twelve feet of the long seats, another booth. The bottoms of the little bare light bulbs above the tables were frosted, which sacrificed authenticity to comfort and ambiance. On the walls were replicas of the old poster ads and maps, the latter more schematic but less accurate than the ones we prefer in our new Age of Information. The ads, finned automotive monstrosities, demurely smiling Miss Subway candidates with soft pre-gym- workout bodies, were easy enough to find, but they cost a bundle. As the smiling shop owner said, "Sorry, gentlemen, these are a very hot item."

We built the huge bar across the back wall, designed as a large open-fronted conductor's booth, complete with control panels (computerized bill and inventory records) and even a little window (purely decorative) behind. The hefty entry fee would be collected in front, of course, inside, at two "token booths." As the bouncers funneled in the customers, they would move through turnstiles, chosen both for the feel and to slow the traffic just enough to prevent mob scenes at the booths. Beyond the booths, on both sides, cattycorner to the big dance floor, were twin DJ stations with all the appurtenances thereunto. The juice that these stations sucked was the main obstacle to our initial hopes of making the place green. (These days, green buildings can count not only on tax breaks, but on big write-ups in feel-good nature publications.) The design of the front of the room also gave us a major security bonus. The managers, one in each attractive, difficult to burglarize token booth, could keep an eye on both the DJ's and the dancers. The bouncers, who could be summoned by buzzer, were seconds away.

We open this Friday, June 2, 2006.

MASON CASE NOTES (4). June 5, 2006

What a blast! Besides, for me, Christmas may come in summer this year. Feature Article: "A Dream of Trains: The Pathology Is the Cure, Stupid." By Jarvis Mason, Ph.D., Fellow Royal Society for the Quashing of Depression (RSFQD), etc. etc. To appear in *Journal of Alternative Modalities (JAM)* (editor: the wife's cousin, Robin Bates!) Yes, Friday night I went to the opening of the club Bob just finished designing: absolutely brilliant! All that train business while he was hospitalized is completely explained: sub(way)limation, you might say.

I can see it already: a narrative first-person by Bob, cleaned up and footnoted by me --the case history, in effect. Therapy through the Arts, Mason Clinic modality of the month triumphant: the imagery (symbolism?) of depression: tunnel as night, phallic projectile smashing through the darkness, ambivalence thereunto, the whole nine Freudian yards. What's in it for Bob? More catharsis, maybe even a few commissions. For me? Heh heh, this will be so big it will: a) bloat my already gargantuan reputation, and b) bring in some (sorely needed) new clients! Maybe I should leave that "Stupid" off the title. Unclear: with it, rude; without, clichéd?

A DREAM OF TRAINS (2). Wednesday, March 1, 2006

Since patients at the clinic took two "classes," I also enrolled in Creative (i.e. Cathartic) Writing. Here, from the early days, is an example of my literary *oeuvre*.

NIGHT.G---- stands alone on a dark platform. From the black tunnel shines a single light, a beacon. An equipment train rumbles into the station, a string of flatbed cars cluttered with miscellaneous machinery and equipment. There are large generators that look like cement mixers, piles of wire and cable, pipes, drums, and so forth. Oddly, the train clatters silently. G--- is aware that the train is clattering, yet the dream is silent. Slowly, without stopping, the cars pass, and he scrutinizes each with pleasure. It all has the air of a display. He reads the caption: THE CIRCUS IS COME TO TOWN. Like clowns, two or three men sprawl impassively among the equipment, their faces covered with greasepaint, their limbs akimbo. They do not wave, and neither does G--- , who has perceived in the beacon a command to bear witness at a ceremonial procession. The last of the cars disappears into the tunnel.

THE CALL (2). Monday, June 5, 2006.

My new love (hooray, no sexual dysfunction whatsoever from the SSRI's!), Kay (gorgeous, met her at opening, women's clothing designer, business client of, yes, Eleanor's) is in Rome. She promised to call this afternoon. The sun streams through the little window above the sink onto a corner of the beautiful teak table. Should I call her? No. Wait. There, it's ringing. *One.* Here we go. Make them wait ten rings, but no longer, or the machine will pick up. My beautiful new lemon-colored kitchen, designed exactly according to [*Two*] the specifications I left on the table when, shall we say, I almost checked out. [*Three*] Clear the throat, lick the lips. Kay? No, still too early there, let's see, about six. I bet it's old Frederick, calling to cut me in [*Four*] on Darlene's Rush Hour Services. I stretch my hand toward the warm light. That hip lawyer (also from the opening)? [*Five*] Did he say a beach house? Some other client, through w.o.m. So soon? [*Six*] Thank you, Eleanor, thank you, mom and dad. The boys again, they want dance clubs in [*Seven*] fifty provincial cities, all subway car replicas. The old table, where I left the kitchen plans right before investigating the interior of the oven. [*Eight*] Jarvis Mason calling with his "Great Offer" (teasingly announced at the opening). [*Nine*] *Thank* you, Eleanor, thank you, mom and dad. Who knows, someone from *Ho and Ho (House and Hotel)* or *ZANY (Zone Out New York)?* [*Ten*] Were there reporters present, then, lurking in dark corners?

Whatever. Now.

"Robert Green speaking."

Glen's Vintage Tin

...no longer exists --at least, not under that name. The big rolling field littered with old cars is still there, and so is the Quonset hut backdrop, but not the black and white sign that was large enough to be read from the road. The expert sign-painter (Glen) had stenciled huge, bold, clean letters onto the side of the shell of an old red truck that sat twenty or thirty feet up in the air atop a stout white pole:

GLEN'S VINTAGE TIN

The pole is still there, but there is no more truck and, so, no more sign.

"How many passing motorists do you suppose pointed at that sign before it came down?"

"Lots. Glen was in business for more than forty years."

"What happened to him?"

Pearly sighed, made a sound like a car running down a road, and used his own thick right index finger to chart its progress. "Last October, he sold the business --his house, too -- kit and caboodle. Bought an Airstream and took to the open road." He made the noise and the finger movement again. "He's living in a trailer park in Florida now."

Over my shoulder, I could see the metallic red, white and blue tape around Pearly and Bobbie's garden. As the wind moved the tape, it glinted in the sun. Three weeks earlier, Pearly had told me that his friend and my landlord, Harvey Houghton, a wildlife biologist, had told him that the tape would keep the deer out.

"Does it?"

"Yep. Not the turkeys, though."

"What can you do about those?"

"Not much." Then, he winked and made a thumb-and-forefinger shooting gesture. "Good eating."

"Yep," said Bobbie, wagging her big head.

"But can you shoot them now? Aren't they out of season?"

"Oh, you can, you can. No one's going to mind."

"No one's going to say anything," Bobbie agreed.

I looked across the highway to the "for sale" sign on the big white farmhouse. It had belonged to Bobbie and Pearl until they sold it to the present owners ten years ago. Bobbie had told me more than once what good neighbors these people were, and Pearl had nodded vigorously when, each time, she would add the hope that the new owners would be as good.

Bobbie and Pearl --Schofield-- in their sixties or early seventies, now lived in a spiffy double trailer with a big garden, a big garage, and a big mowed field, all set back from the tarred road. The three of us sat on big Adirondack chairs under an old tree (big) halfway between road and trailer. It was about 4:40, and I knew I should leave soon so Bobbie could go in to make supper for her mother, an Alzheimer's' sufferer who likes to eat no later than 5:30.

"Harvey's maple tree lost a branch in that storm the other night," I said. "The one right next to the house. Old age, I guess."

Pearl stared at me with feigned alarm, then leaned over and clasped my shoulder in his strong hand. "My Gosh, Dave!" he said. "Do you think that'll happen to us?"

I'm fifty-one. Bobbie and I --and Pearl, too-- laughed hard.

"Why'd Glen leave?"

"Same as a lot of the other old folks around here: couldn't take the winters anymore," Pearl explained.

"Did Mrs. Glen go with him?"

"Well," he said, "there is no 'Mrs. Glen.' At least not for the last thirty-five years."

Bobbie grinned. "Nancy. She ran off with an all-female band."

"What kind of band?" I quipped. "Heavy metal?"

Bobbie gave me a "those men!" look, and Pearly, bemused, glanced back over his right shoulder. I looked that way, too, just in time to see their black-and-white cat duck into the tall weeds beside the garage.

I know a bit about Maine and Florida. A lot of Mainers relocate to Florida, mostly in or near the Panhandle, to fish and play golf with each other. Those with money keep two places and become snowbirds; those without --like Glen, presumably-- just move.

"By now, I bet he's realized he can't take the Florida summers, either," I said. "You ever been down there in August?" There was nothing anyone could say to that.

Soon I stretched, made noises about getting home, and accepted three huge zucchinis, which Bobbie went and got from the trailer while Pearl and I strolled back to my car. They said their "come agains," I said my "come up for a beer and a sunset." Then, I started back through town toward the long hill that led back to all that empty space and time.

Space: Harvey's ramshackle old farmhouse is situated in the middle of a state park on a large cleared field surrounded by woods. During the 30's, when the federal government bought out all the local hardscrabble farmers, including Pearly's dad, Harvey's late father had been the only owner not to sell. The cause of this apparent exception was that Harvey's dad had been not a farmer, but a writer, a Depression-era refugee from New York, and his was the only place not buried under a mountain of debt. The Feds had subsequently given the land over to the state, stipulating that it be set aside for public use. The Houghton farmhouse backs onto a spectacular view of five or six spectacular mountains, and Harvey only rents it to me because he needs to pay the taxes. My motives are that it is cheap and wonderful. My only regret is that I have to kill several dozen mice during those summers when they decide to come inside. My wife and I have been coming here for six years now.

Time: Jean, my wife, was in Vermont visiting the kids (two) at camp and would not be back for two more days. Meanwhile, my responsibilities consisted of heating up the food she had left and driving down to the lake in the late afternoon to swim for about twenty minutes, then to read on the grass until the mosquitoes and black flies closed in. It was early August already, but the hot, humid weather had given the biting insects an extra lease on life. After Jean got back, we would still have more than three weeks here. (You guessed it: we're teachers.) There would still be empty time, but we'd spend it together. You may have inferred why the kids, nine and eleven, opted for the full eight weeks of camp. The pattern began four years ago, after the first summer of whining and the second planning a complicated schedule of visits for them to other people --with children-- some of whom returned the visits, which Jean and I agreed was very unfair of them.

As I headed up the hill, just after I passed the turn where tar gives way to dirt, I had an odd premonition: the house had been robbed or vandalized. I bumped along the washboard a little faster than usual, but, when I turned from the driveway onto the field, I could see that my premonition had been wrong. At the top of the field on its little rise sat the old farmhouse, looking shabby, as usual, but unmolested. Above it, and the mountains, clouds raced about their business across the dark blue sky. Maine, the way weather should be --and still is, sometimes.

Another year passed, and we were back in Harvey 's house. I managed to climb out of the deck chair, which was under the tree with the lost limb, and to get inside in time to catch the phone. (Actually, I made it by the seventh ring, which probably meant I had four or five to spare.) I had been reading a book about central Asia, and did not mind being interrupted, even though I was in the midst of yet another gory massacre.

It was Pearly, calling for the first time ever. Until then, we had been on a drop-in, and invited-to-drop-in, basis. I had sat under his tree twice so far this summer.

"Dave? Pearl Schofield."

"Pearly!"

After we had checked each other's well-being, he got right to the point.

"When's the good wife due back?"

"Tuesday." She was visiting the kids again.

"Well, Bobbie's afraid you might starve, so how about coming down here for supper tonight?"

"Sounds very good. What do I wear?"

He laughed. "Come as you are. But wash your hands."

We briefly negotiated the other terms: six o'clock, and I would be permitted to bring a bottle of wine I already had -- white, since Bobbie was roasting a chicken-- plus a cottage cheese-container full of raspberries Jean had picked and left for me with the admonition, "You don't have to bake, or anything, Dave, but don't let them go to waste." Part of that was sarcastic: I don't bake. But I had only eaten about an inch of raspberries since she had left, so there were still plenty to bring.

The terms set, I was ready to sign off, but first Pearl said, "Oh, and there'll be a surprise guest, too."

The anomaly of the invitation had made us both a bit awkward, and I wondered if the "surprise guest" was a way to deal with this awkwardness. I surmised that it would just be Harvey, who lived forty minutes away in a biggish town for this part of the world, Farmington.

Farmington was right, Harvey wasn't. It was Glen. Back.

When I arrived at six on the dot, Glen was already there. Like Pearl, Bobbie and me, he looked scrubbed and brushed for the occasion. He was a long grizzled fellow with a little mustache and dark, cracked, leathery skin. He wore brown hush puppies, jeans and a faded blue work shirt. Pearl introduced us, we shook hands, and I said I had heard a lot about him, which prompted an "Uh oh!"

We sat right down at the big Formica table in the dinette. I had only been inside the trailer once, and that had been to use the "facilities," which were on the left end behind the door next to the washer, drier and freezer. Now I was surprised by how roomy the trailer seemed.

We ate a delicious meal, most of it local -- from their garden (green beans and salad) and well (water), the village bakery (bread and cookies), nearby farms, which sold in the village once a week (potatoes), Harvey's berry bushes (the raspberries), and the nearest supermarket, in Farmington (coffee, ice cream, milk and the chicken). Actually, the chicken had probably been an out-of-towner, since all the local chicken industry-workers have switched to processing credit-card transactions at MBNA, a converted shoe factory on the highway east of Farmington. (The "M" does not stand for "Maine." It used to stand for "Maryland," but no longer stands for anything.) There was also my wine, from Chile, also via the supermarket

"Where's your mom, Bobbie?" I asked, as we tucked in. I had only seen the old woman once, when she had been outside when I arrived one afternoon, and I had gotten a nod for my "Hello."

"She's in Holton with my sister for the week." Bobbie tried not to look indecently happy.

"So you couldn't take the Florida heat, eh, Glen?" was my opening gambit.

"Nope," he said, his mouth full. He chewed, swallowed, then added, with a wink at Pearly, "plus I already missed the Maine winter."

"There wasn't much of it to miss," Bobbie said.

"Were you back in time for the blizzard, though, Glen?" Pearly asked. There had been four inches of snow May 14th.

"Yep. I got out my old snowshoes and tramped around in the woods."

That was about how the conversation went. Glen and I took to each other. I found him easy to talk to, and, if I read him right, beneath his polite inquisitiveness, there was that mild condescension tinged with jealousy so common among rural

Americans toward people foolish --and rich-- enough to live in cities. Most of what I told him about myself, and my family, proceeded from Pearl's or Bobbie's initiatives.

"He's a school teacher," was one.

"What age do you teach?" Glen asked. When I told him --college-- that led to another joke. "Well, you're lucky it's not high school. He doesn't have to deal with the likes of us, eh, Pearly?"

"Oh, I wouldn't say that, Glen. We were the two best students in our whole graduating class, Number One and Number Two. Which of us was first again now, Glen? I can never remember."

"You. Of course, there were only eight graduates that year."

"And, a year later, they shut the school down and began busing the students to the new one," Bobbie said. "That's where I went."

"We broke the mold," Pearly added.

And more of the same.

The most interesting parts of the conversation concerned Glen's livelihood --or livelihoods. Starting in high school, he had been a seasonal blueberry worker and had also shown an aptitude for tinkering with car and boat engines. After school, he had gradually worked his way toward "Glen's Vintage Tin," which fixed up and sold used cars, including some old ones: the Model "A" is the "vintage tin" of choice in this area. For forty years, he had also bought, sold and swapped used car parts. I realized from all these facts that Glen had been a competent, trustworthy businessman. He had one other vocation.

"Art," Pearly proclaimed, after Bobbie had failed to draw it out of Glen, himself, with, "Come on, Glen, tell him what else you did."

"Rode snowmobiles? Got drunk? --Once or twice. Played bingo? I don't know what you mean, Bobbie." But, of course, he did know.

We had reached the coffee-and-dessert stage. The best way to describe the way Pearly pronounced "art" is to say it was somewhere between "at" and "aht." It turned out Glen had made just about all the most beautiful signs in the area between Farmington and our village, including his own sign, of course, plus other kindred masterworks, such as the big map of the area's lakes, roads and mountains. This, he had hand-painted on a piece of plywood, which he had then framed, lacquered and fixed to the side of the village general store. Every car or pick-up truck that has arrived at the store for the past twenty years has nosed to between either one or two, or twenty or thirty, feet (depending on which parking space they take) of Glen's map. Of course, it is the lake, mountains, and quiet, unassuming, friendly competence of the inhabitants that make people like me --and the inhabitants, themselves-- love the village. But Glen's map is certainly at the top of the list of the minor wonders of this part of the world.

Another topic of conversation was Glen's health. I don't know if "topic" is accurate, though, since it crossed the table only once before it was dropped. Pearl and Bobbie had already been in contact with Glen, and they would not go deeply into this subject in front of a relative stranger, but Glen's appetite lagged far enough behind the rest of ours' that I sensed something was wrong with him even before Bobbie asked her question:

"Have you seen the man in Skowhegan yet, Glen?"

"No use," was all he said. "I told you, the Florida quacks were sure."

"I see," Pearly said. Bobbie's mouth was moving as she played with her dessertspoon. I just sat there, trying not to make eye contact with anyone or to avoid it too obviously. Through my mind flashed what might have been said if Glen had already left.

"I guess he wanted to see one more Maine winter, after all," I might have said.

And would Bobbie have added: "At least he doesn't have to worry about losing a limb"? No, I doubt she would have said that.

In actuality, two or three quick jokes --nice, neutral ones-- took us back to happier ground. By then, it was getting toward seven-thirty, which meant it would be dark sometime between ten and thirty minutes from now, depending on your elevation and whether or not you were in the woods or the mountain shadows.

"Well," Glenn said, looking at his watch, "better get on the road soon," and with a few age and eyesight jokes, an exchange of "pleased to have met you's," a compliment for the cook, and some hugs and handshakes, he was gone. I should say that his own piece of vintage tin --at least, that night-- was a red sixty-six Dodge Dart. It was, as they say, a real cream puff.

Bobbie, Pearl and I stood in the driveway together, and it was good to be outside. I must say that ninety minutes in the trailer, big and comfortable as it was, was enough for me to think I understood why they spent so much time under the tree waving to their numerous passing friends and acquaintances.

"It sounds like he's ... not a well man," I said, after Glen had pulled out of the driveway.

'He's got that fast-acting kind of lung cancer," Bobbie said.

"From smoking?" Glen had not smoked or smelled like a smoker that evening, but he had the look.

"Well, no," Pearly explained. "He always was a smoker, but the 'quacks,' as he calls them, told him the kind he has doesn't come from smoking. More likely, it was from the way they used to burn off the blueberry fields every other year, back then, and dust them with fertilizer from big trucks. No one wore proper masks or anything."

"I see," was all I could say.

It quickly became clear that this was not a good time to be outside because, as Pearly put it, as soon as they got us on their radar screens, the mosquitoes and black flies would do to us what we had done to the chicken and ice cream. So I made some noises about heading up the hill, myself, and began my valedictory "Thank you's."

Pearl interrupted. "Let me tell you one last 'Glen' story before you go, Dave. It will give you a better measure of the man."

"Sounds good," I said lamely.

"Well, you know this story, Bobbie, don't you --Harvey and the stock car? -- so I hope you'll forgive me. Or, maybe, you want to go back inside."

Bobbie smiled. "Yes, I know the story well," she said, but she made no move, and, as her husband told the anecdote, I could tell that she still enjoyed it.

"Well, Dave, by now you must realize there's a bit of a wild side to Harvey."

"I've noticed." Harvey had been through three or four wives, and his unreliability and generosity as a landlord also suggested a certain looseness of character.

"Well, when he was in high school, he used to drive stock cars. Once, when he had just bought a new one, he took it over to Farmington to 'GVT,' as everyone called it. By then, Glen had had his home and business there for, oh, maybe, ten years. Bobbie?"

"Yes, I'd say it was about ten. Maybe eleven."

"Anyway, Glen painted this beautiful flame design on the car --the car was black--and big red numerals. I happened to be there when Harvey pulled in with his carrier to collect the car. He was suitably impressed by Glen's work, of course, all 'oohs' and 'ahs.' Then, he asked what he owed him.

"Glen pretended to think for about three seconds, scratching his chin and all. Then, he said, 'Let's see. *Nothing!*' Harvey was puzzled, of course, but Glen explained: 'Do you think I take money for helping people commit suicide?' "

I burst out laughing, and, although the story obviously had a very long beard, Pearl and Bobbie chuckled right along with me. After that, we finally said our good nights, and I thanked them and headed back up the hill. This time, instead of a false premonition about burglars and vandals, I remembered something that had happened in the city the previous winter. It was nothing momentous, so I was surprised to remember it now.

I had been riding on a subway express train, and, as we slowed down to pass a local station, I saw several people in motion on the platform. The train's roar made it seem as if they were acting in silence, but, in my mind's ear, for some reason, I heard them. One woman was clicking toward the exit on high heels, another was chewing gum with a loud smacking sound, and a young musician-beggar was singing and playing the guitar.

That was what I saw and heard again that night, as I drove up the hill through the woods toward the house.

Ron Singer

The Technicolor Meal

Mr. Peavis was a fussy eater. Everything had to be just so, or he simply *could* not eat. Furthermore, his fussiness was of an unusual type: each meal of the week had to be a different color. On Wednesday nights, for instance, he had his red supper, which might consist of tomato soup, red meat, cabbage (red), watermelon, and red wine. What is more, the table service had to be the same color as the food: red plastic cutlery, plates and cups; red paper napkins and tablecloth. Ketchup was the condiment on Wednesday night —no mustard or mayonnaise.

The regimen was hard on Mrs. Peavis. For one thing, red meals tended to cause heartburn; green ones, gas. Much of the time, the only way she could herself manage to eat "normal" meals was by using food coloring. On Wednesday night, this meant red dye number two. Red dye number two on rolls, on potatoes, on string beans, in coffee, on layer cake. Fortunately, for all his color fussiness, Mr. Peavis was also imperceptive about color. It did not take an artist's eye to see that the dyed cake was a brownish purple.

Besides the carcinogenic possibility, which she knew about and feared, Mrs. Peavis could not be said to enjoy these dyed meals. The eating experience had become confused for her. After seven or eight years of marriage, she had lost even the ability to enjoy an occasional restaurant meal with a friend. She had long since ceased complaining: anything for domestic tranquility. She was a thin, hard-bitten woman, in contrast with her short, plump, bald, florid husband. Once, by the way, Mrs. Peavis had suggested to Mr. Peavis that she color his food along with hers so that he, too, could enjoy normal variety (and so that she would only have to make one meal!). He had flown into a rage. He did not believe in food coloring. What could be more unnatural?

Saturday night was the technicolor meal *chez* Peavis, the one to which guests could be invited. Since the rule for this meal was "one, only, of a color," the guests were less likely to suspect that anything was amiss than they would have been at a monochromatic meal. Even Peavis was sensible enough to grasp this.

The guests this week were old friends, the Trilbys. Mr. Peavis rubbed his hands together proudly and greedily as his wife put the final touches on the cake, a chocolate layer with white icing. The meat was red, the wine pink, the vegetable yellow. The appetizer was a carrot mousse, molded to the shape of Mr. Peavis's favorite animal, the Bengal tiger —without stripes, however, to avoid color duplication problems.

"Wonderful, honey, wonderful," Mr. Peavis beamed, reaching up to pat his wife's shoulder. She smiled and started to say something, but just then the bell rang. Mr. P. bustled to the door.

"Bill, Phyllis," he said, shaking hands with the tall, stout Mr. Trilby and patting Mrs. Trilby on the shoulder. "Let me take your c... "

He noticed the brown paper bag in Mrs. Trilby's hand.

"Here, Wally," she said.

"Oh, thanks, thanks," he muttered, snatching the bag.

And that should have been the end of it, for in a moment he would have spirited the gift away, to be produced again at the appropriate meal or, if necessary, even thrown out. But Mrs. Trilby was too fast for him.

"It's ice cream, Wally. Dinah said she was making a chocolate cake with white icing, and we thought vanilla ice cream would hit the spot."

With the announcement of the flavor, Mr. Peavis's last, slim hope melted into the air. The rule for the technicolor meal might have gone unbroken had the ice cream been any of a number of fruit flavors. Even raspberry might have been winked at —called a purple— in such an emergency.

He fished desperately for an excuse not to serve the ice cream: too many sweets (everyone knew he loved sweets), his wife's dislike of ice cream (she had eaten it often with the Trilbys), the harmfulness of artificial flavoring (this brand used natural flavors exclusively). He was stuck. Come to think of it, why hadn't this happened before? All those dinner guests, and never a contribution to a meal? Finally, he fell back on his first idea: to forget about the ice cream. So, without saying anything to his wife, he put it in the freezer, and only then did he remember to take his guests' coats. He also recovered his tongue.

"I won't offer you drinks because we're having wine with dinner."

The meal might have been pleasant, but Mr. Peavis was fairly dripping with anxiety over the ice cream. Now the dishes had been cleared, the cake and green herb tea (both couples were anti-caffeine) set out. He started to cut the cake, hoping his guests would be too polite or full to mention the ice cream.

"Big or small, Phyllis?" he asked by way of camouflage.

In the event, the betrayal came from an unexpected quarter. For, with a horrifying scrape, his wife pushed back her chair and uttered the dreadful words:

"Oh, we forgot the ice cream, Wally. I'll get it."

And, before he could recover, she was on her way to the kitchen.

"Delicious slab, Wally," Mr. Trilby remarked conversationally, leaning back and stretching. Beads of sweat appeared on Mr. Peavis's visible parts, and he clasped his hands tightly. He said nothing.

In a moment, his wife was back, carrying the ice cream in its original container, a blood-red little tub. She stood behind Mr. Peavis's chair. All eyes were on him.

"Big or small, Wal?"

Now the room began to spin, and he placed his trembling hands over his eyes and emitted a small cry not unlike a meow. Then, he ducked, because he saw a giant roast beef hurtling through the air right at him. It looked like a bottom round, or maybe a rump roast, and it must have weighed a good six hundred pounds. Closer and closer it came, hissing, its juices dripping, until at the very last moment it veered, and shot out of his field of vision.

Then, one on each side, coming from the walls, there materialized two huge pieces of toast: eight-foot square slices of lightly- browned Wonder bread, the normally appetizing odor of which was magnified ten-thousand fold until it might have been the collective reek of history's atrocities. Closer and closer the big slices came, slowly, ever so slowly. Mr. Peavis was not aware that he had begun to shriek.

All the while, his wife stood behind his chair, the ice cream and scoop in her hands, a peaceful little smile on her lips. The Trilbys watched with detachment. Two minutes later, the room in shambles, Phyllis Trilby walked out to the foyer with measured tread and picked up the telephone.

Ron Singer

Part Two: Old Age

"With submission, sir, we both are getting old."
--Melville, "Bartleby, the Scrivener: A Tale of Wall Street"

Ron Singer

W⁴ ™ (Whole Wide World of Wrestling)

When the level of mayhem could no longer satisfy, the governing body of W⁴ ratcheted it up. Among the featured newcomers were Cannibal and Pygmy. Cannibal was a spandexed giant imported from an unnamed Pacific island, who wore an elaborate mask modeled after Hannibal Lecter's (Anthony Hopkins'), in *The Silence of the Lambs*. In mid-match, Cannibal would extricate himself from the mask, and, like Lecter, proceed to rend his screaming antagonist, or, if you believed the skeptics among us, to rend the high end tear-away latex body suit the victim wore over his —or her!-- actual flesh.

The second featured newcomer was Pygmy. Ostensibly from an unmapped region in Africa, Central Asia, or South America, Pygmy was a headhunter. Entering the ring without the requisite equipment, the small, quick athlete would dart away from his slower opponent, nevertheless enduring a modicum of punishment. At some point in the match, he would be thrown through the ropes down onto the apron. Only then would his female associate poke her smiling face from under the ring and slip Pygmy the tools of his trade: knife, scalpel, a diminutive hatchet, and the garotte, with its polished wooden handles. The tiny, but nubile, associate would proceed to distract the referee by means of a game of peekaboo, running helter-skelter beneath the ring and darting into and out of it, so that, whichever way he turned, she would be behind him. Meanwhile, Pygmy would perform the apparently lethal decapitation.

Again, of course, our skeptics purported to deconstruct the ruse. According to them, the actual head of the hapless and apparently headless victim was stitched inside a body suit, from which vantage he would look out through the nipples as Pygmy struck off his second, papier-mache' head. But regardless of our belief systems, we granted the headhunter our uncritical affection, for, like most of us, a ninety-pound professional wrestler would always be the underdog. As for Cannibal, suffice it to say that he only did what we dreamed of doing.

Whichever of the two new stars was featured in a given match, making virtual mincemeat of yet another young Adonis or old fatty, and flooding the ring with either human blood or red paint, a plethora of bells, whistles, sirens, lights, and rattling thunder (or sheet metal) would provide cover for any slip-ups. When the head was off, or the flesh eaten, all would go dark, and an awed hush would descend, broken only by the scrabbling feet of the custodians (presumably), who rushed into the ring (presumably) to clean and clear it. Some minutes later, the lights would come back up, and it was as if nothing had happened. There sat the spanking white canvas ring with its gleaming brass stanchions, padded turnbuckles, and so on. And there stood the stoic referee in his polished shoes and immaculate striped shirt and black pants, arms folded across his chest as he awaited the arrival of the next contestants.

It was, of course, only a matter of time, hype, and the accumulation of suitably impressive resumes before we would get to enjoy the inevitable clash of the giant, Cannibal, and the pygmy, Pygmy. What was especially thrilling about this prospect was that W^4 officials began dropping broad hints to the effect that audience participation might be permitted. We held our collective breath.

Six weeks ago, I received a notice in the mail that reminded me of my draft notices during the Vietnam War. (I was deferred twice, the first time for a fish allergy; the second, in order to attend graduate school.) Several other documents were enclosed. I opened the notice with proverbially trembling hands.

W⁴ ™ (Whole Wide World of Wrestling)

(their address and fax number)

________ (date filled in)

Dear ____________ (my name filled in),
Congratulations. You have been selected to participate in the featured bout, CANNIBAL_V. PYGMY. Please plan to arrive at ______ (time filled in) on ______ (date filled in) at __________ (name of arena filled in).

INSTRUCTIONS:

I. Signatures and Fee

For each of the enclosed forms (see below), in the spaces provided, append your **SIGNATURE** and the **DATE**. Then, using the pre-addressed envelope, return the first and second copies of all four forms (see below), along with a check for ______ (amount filled in), to cover the costs of one-time health insurance for this event. **(Note that the U.S. Postal Service will not deliver mail that does not have sufficient postage.)** Retain the third copy of the forms for your own records. A copy of the insurance policy will be forwarded to you at least one week before the date of your scheduled appearance.

2. Enclosures

1. Agreement to participate in match (APM).

2. Medical liability waiver (MLW).

3. Participant's fee/financial remuneration waiver (PF/FRW).

4. Interview Agreement form (IAF).

3. Medical

In addition to the signed, returned MLW, please instruct your primary care physician to forward to us, either by fax or regular mail, a short statement on letterhead to the effect that (s)he knows of no medical condition which might make it hazardous for you to participate as a spectator-performer in a **W⁴** ™ **(Whole Wide World of Wrestling)** event. This letter must be received by _____ (date filled in).

4. **If you are accepted for participation**:

--Please appear at ________ (address of side door) of ______ (name of arena) at the time indicated on your letter of invitation (above.) Your name will be included on the list of those authorized to receive a (**one**) complimentary ticket. In order to claim your ticket, you will be asked to produce an official photo I.D. (such as a passport or driver's license.)

--Please wear non-marking athletic shoes and loose-fitting trousers and a long-sleeved shirt, both made of durable materials. You should **not** wear a "costume" of any kind, and you should wear either no head gear, or a baseball cap without a logo or with a logo that in no way replicates or competes with that of the **W⁴™ (Whole Wide World of Wrestling).**

Important: Prior to the day of the event, please commit to memory the following details incident to participation:

--You will be seated ringside to the west of the apron between two representatives of the N.Y. State Sports Medicine Department (NYSSMD), who will both be wearing conspicuous name tags.

--When the match reaches the 8:07 mark (there will be a large digital clock on the wall directly opposite your seat) ... **[in the interests of suspense, I will skip this next part –for now]** ... Thereafter, no matter what happens, **DO NOT RETURN TO THE RING.** At the conclusion of the match, assuming you have signed and returned the enclosed Interview Agreement Form (IAF), you may be asked by one of the television announcers to say a few words, as follows:

"Announcer: So ______ (my first name inserted), What did it feel like to actually participate in a **Whole Wide World of Wrestling** event? Was it a dream come true?

You (smiling): Yes. Awesome!

Announcer: Glad you enjoyed it, ______ (my name repeated). Back to you, ______ (name of other announcer inserted)."

Please do not forget to commit the contents of this impromptu interview to memory.

We look forward to receipt of the necessary documentation pursuant to your participation. Again, congratulations. And remember, "Many are chosen, but few are body-slammed." (joke)

Yours in the spirit,

——————— (signature)
President, CEO, W⁴ ™ (Whole Wide World of Wrestling)

A week before the event, I rescued a notice in my spam box to the effect that, all paperwork having been completed, they looked forward to my participation. Attached was a copy of a policy for single-day health insurance coverage. In the notice, there was also what I assumed to be a joke about Cannibal and Pygmy paying me a "personal visit" in the event that I failed to show up. What were they thinking! I memorized the instructions immediately.

Any description of this very special evening must prove anticlimactic. Passing through the metal detector at the main entrance to the arena, I confess to a degree of stage fright. But when I encountered the heady sights, sounds and smells of the frenetic crowd, I was once again myself. (My only regret is that regulations no longer permit these arenas to be smoke-filled.) As I took my seat, the two physicians nodded simultaneously and cordially in my direction.

The under-card passed in a slow-motion dream until, at last, the main event arrived. By the time the contestants and their gaudy entourages had completed their grand, Caesarian (i.e. Roman triumphal) entrances, and the referee had managed to forestall mayhem until the bell could ring, I was already on high alert. As the grapplers closed, I focused half my attention on the big clock on the opposite wall, and half on the riveting proceedings unfolding within the squared circle.

For the first 8:04, back and forth swung the pendulum of arranged combat. There was only one civilian intervention. At 4:02, a fat, bald man wearing a blue track suit and glistening white tennis shoes was supposedly knocked unconscious with a rubber folding chair by Pygmy's heavily made-up assistant (who seemed less short, in person). This man's job was to stop the chair from descending on a dazed Cannibal's head, when he missed a drop kick and plunged down onto the apron. I felt a slight twinge of envy at my colleague's rather baroque role, until he nearly ruined it with a tasteless, hammy finale. Regaining consciousness after only a few seconds, he rubbed his pate vigorously, then began to dance around the assistant, as if he were daring her to bonk him again. A discreet word from one of the omnipresent physicians made him behave himself. He returned to his seat wearing an expression that could equally have been chastisement or lingering mock-befuddlement from the blow.

At last: 8:04! Wonderful! Barely in time, at the precise moment the facial savaging seemed about to commence, I got to carry out my scripted instructions: "... you should stand, roll up into the ring, and, without exerting undue force or otherwise behaving in a manner that might inflict injury, gently push Cannibal away from you and off the top of Pygmy. After that, without hesitating, roll back out of the ring (trying not to fall), and re-take your seat." In the event, I got to push a crazed Cannibal off a recumbent and ostensibly unconscious Pygmy. Although my role was crucial to the match, I do not wish to overstate it: I entered, I performed, I exited.

The remaining 7:53 played out with no further spectator intervention. But, as the final bell sounded (and sounded and sounded), it began to look as if nothing could keep the bout from ending with at least one fatality. Then, suddenly, the crowd was hushed, as down the aisle hurried a most unexpected trio. Costumed so as to suggest the three main western monotheistic faiths, and holding up the skirts of their robes, they rushed and rolled into the ring and, in pantomime, cajoled the grapplers into uncoupling and giving each other the kiss of peace. The Match was over; the crowd (we) roared.

But that, of course, was not quite the end. Escorted by the two physicians, I proceeded to the television table. There I received (unscripted) a kiss on the cheek from Pygmy's nubile assistant, and, as a further surprise, at the conclusion of the scripted interview (see above), a certificate of appreciation from W^4, signed not only by the CEO, but by both of the now glistening combatants. During my interview, the pair stood alongside me, part of the TV tableau, beaming at everyone in sight, arms wrapped in awkward comradeship around each other's shoulders (one being more than a foot taller than the other). The three clerics waited patiently to one side, all the while bowing and smiling silently. As for the bald man, given his histrionics, I was unsurprised that he was not even interviewed. Since the match had been (predictably) a draw, the big crowd appeared to exit the arena pleased, but not completely sated. Not that I dream of being invited to participate in a second match....

It is time to tear away my own mask. As you may or may not have guessed, I am a former academic, an erstwhile Associate Professor of Comparative Linguistics (my specialty: Middle-

French Phonology) who, laid off and pension-less during these difficult times, must now be content to sustain my wife and myself by grilling eponymous burgers at "The King." In the autobiographical spirit, too, let me explain the context of my moment in the wrestling sun. It was, you see, my sixty-fifth birthday. My present was the expense money entailed by the W⁴ ™ appearance.

The birthday party, which took place the next evening, was also wonderful. My youngest grandchildren had constructed a hat for me in the shape of the paper crown distinctive to my employer's mascot, but home-made and, hence, much nicer. I was also given two T-shirts, stenciled by my two talented teen-age grandchildren. To moderate applause, I modeled these shirts, in turn, at the party, then put them away so as not to soil them. And what had been stenciled on the shirts? I blush to think of it. Since my name is George, one is a picture of me as Curious George. As my wife explained: "You're a playful intellectual, dear, and a curious fellow." On the other shirt is a somewhat idealized image of me, sporting blond ringlets: Gorgeous George. Do you remember him?

In the middle of the party, right after dinner, came what I may call the main event. My wife had arranged for separate telegrams to arrive from the wrestlers. From Cannibal: "Happy B-day, George, Baby. No hard feelings!" And from Pygmy: "Georgie, Mister. You saving my bacon! Much thenk." After that, I sat back and happily surveyed the table. The cake — chocolate with pink, green, white, red, and yellow icing—was topped with (what else?) a picture of me pushing Cannibal off Pygmy (vanilla ring, chocolate stanchions, etc.).

Then, just when my happiness was at its apogee, a small voice at one ear whispered, "But it's all *fake*, George." (Did the voice refer to the sport or to the ingredients of the cake, such as, presumably, Red Dye Number Two?)

"Never mind Killjoy over there," riposted the voice at my other ear. "Happy birthday, George, you only live once." Yes, true, very true. And, since it *is* true, I vowed never to forget either this wonderful birthday party or the magnificent gifts attendant thereunto. With that happy thought, I made the first cut.

In Ethiopia, Once

"How did the rest of your week go, George?" The question was asked by Edna, a South African journalist whom I had interviewed on Monday. It was now Sunday.

"Well, on the one hand..." I gestured, "I did three more interviews. But on the other..." a second gesture, "I was almost eaten by a lion." Everyone laughed, and I explained. The anecdote featured a malfunctioning car window in a game park on the outskirts of the city (Nairobi). The hot-and-foul breathed lion had cased the car and its occupants, then walked off.

"Must have been a vegetarian," said Devi, Bill's waggish roommate.

Bill was the mild-mannered son of my dentist (father) and eye doctor (mother). Reared in an affluent New Jersey 'burb "minutes from the city," he was a little Clark-Kentish. Devi, an Indian-American from the same place, was tall, thin, and wired. Old friends, they both now worked for a U.N. group monitoring the distribution of food and other aid at refugee camps across East Africa and the Horn (Ethiopia, Eritrea, Djibouti, and Somalia). Or, as Devi quipped, "We make sure no more than 90% is stolen." This job required frequent trips to places where it was too dangerous for them to live. Since Edna was the Reuters rep for the Horn, operating, like the roommates, out of Nairobi, she, too, traveled a lot. Edna was Bill's significant other.

The four of us were relaxing at the pool in Bill and Devi's apartment complex in Westlands, an upscale suburb of Nairobi. We were enjoying *apres*-squash drinks. Bill was in his early thirties, and Devi and Edna looked about the same, which made them all a bit more than half my age (60).

"What happened with that guy I introduced you to?" Edna asked, referring to the Managing Editor of *African Zeitgeist*, an important news weekly. If it is not obvious by now, I had come to this part of the world to write an article about local journalists.

"Well, not to make too fine a point of it, it was a fiasco."

"Oops," said Edna. "Sorry. What went wrong?" So I told them a second story, this one much more elaborate than the lion story.

I had telephoned and made a date for a working lunch with the editor, a Kenyan Asian, but after that everything went wrong. First, some pickpockets on the bus I took from my guesthouse had a go (unsuccessful) at my wallet. Flustered and hot, I then had trouble finding the restaurant, a steak place in the Downtown Business District that the editor had suggested. Since I hadn't quite caught the name, which turned out to be "Prime Eats," I wandered around for a while, until the penny dropped. Luckily, or maybe not, I still managed to arrive early, but only because the editor was late, which I excused because I knew he was a busy man.

After he had bustled in and spotted me in the dining room, we shook hands, and he moved us to the bar. While I ate and anticipated the interview, he ignored me, watching cricket on the big TV, gobbling down some food, guzzling a beer, and chain-smoking. Perhaps, his frantic behavior stemmed from the fact that the match, some kind of cup final, involved his original homeland, India.

As soon as it ended, looking at his watch, he suggested — then, insisted- that, since I was the one who had initiated the interview, I should pick up the check. Outraged, but reluctant to create "a scene," I acceded as gracefully as possible. Given that Nairobi restaurants can be expensive, the check luckily turned out to be manageable.

As we were nodding our very cool farewells out on the sidewalk, he seemed to notice how angry I was. At any rate, he turned on the charm. "But, please, George, you must come to my home this Sunday for lunch. We can do the interview right after we eat. *Inshallah*, I'll call you that morning and pick you up in my car." But he never did call.

"I thought the plan sounded good," I concluded, "especially the *inshallah* part. Isn't that some kind of oath?"

"Well, no, George," Devi explained, "not exactly." Bill and Edna looked amused. "Let me preface this by saying that I am, myself, of partly Muslim extraction. Okay? '*Inshallah*,' or 'God willing,' is what we Muslims sometimes say instead of really doing anything. E.G. '*Inshallah*, I shall not have any more children,' says the pregnant mother of twenty. "

"Oh."

"What a jerk!" Bill said. Edna just shook her head, and we changed the subject.

So that was how I came to be poolside that Sunday afternoon. Rather than call the rude editor again, I had opted for some r & r.

While I had been telling my story, a genial young African Kenyan waiter served us a second round of beer and soft drinks. There were four other parties at poolside that afternoon, two white, one Asian, and one African. (By chance, although racial mixing is common among better-off Kenyans, ours was the only racially mixed group.) The Africans were a family of five, all fat. In Kenya, there is a piquant saying for what happens when your ethnic group comes to power: "It's our turn to eat." While the mom supervised the children, the father swam laps in the small pool, which he had to himself, splashing water onto the apron with his vigorous strokes.

Although only Devi and I had played squash, we had all been into the pool. After Bill signed for the drinks, we sat at our table in the broiling sun, the four of us politely trying to edge our chairs under the too-small umbrella. In an *ersatz* way, it was like the scramble for Africa.

For a while, we chatted about this and that. For the benefit of Devi, who had not heard it before, I summarized my intended article, mentioning that, before coming to Nairobi, I had spent ten days each in Dar es Salaam and Addis Ababa. Then, Devi and I reprised our fairly even squash match, which he had won. He was good; I was —am—too old for the game. Bill had watched from a small gallery above the court, so the account was for the sole benefit of Edna, who had arrived afterwards. It turned out that, like many South Africans, she was, herself, a squash player, and she and Devi conducted a mild pissing contest about what might happen if they were to play, an eventuality they had previously broached.

"Who do you think would win, George?" joked Edna, who was wearing a black one-piece bathing suit, and was the fittest-looking member of our party.

"It depends who's better," I non-answered.

"The wisdom of Solomon," Devi said.

After that, he and Bill told me more about their work. Since many visitors to this part of the world pass through Nairobi, and since they had obviously given the spiel before, they sprinkled in a few well-rehearsed, harrowing details about violence and deprivation. Mostly, however, they stuck to facts and generalizations, their tone bureaucratically dispassionate.

This was obviously the kind of conversation that, sooner or later, falls into the doldrums, and, after ten or fifteen minutes, it did. The reader may be surprised by how I got it moving again, so let me blame Edna.

"Had you ever been to this part of the world before, George?" she asked.

A lucky gambit, for I had, indeed, been to East Africa, visiting several countries over six weeks in the early 1970's. This was a parent-sponsored, post-college trip, all by myself, since it was meant to be (and was) an adventure.

So I answered that, yes, I had been there, and offered a few details: the bar in Mombasa where I narrowly avoided a fight with a British commando on r & r from Yemen, the dusty streets and open-air food shops of Addis, and so on. My sparse travelogue seemed to arouse Edna's journalistic instincts.

"Come on, George," she said, "those are the kinds of stories everyone tells. Give us something a little more ... interesting."

This posed an "interesting" problem, which I quickly considered. Much of what had been most interesting about the trip was, for various reasons, unrepeatable, at least in a poolside conversation on a Sunday afternoon in Nairobi in early 2011. How about my newly acquired Tanzanian drinking buddy, a college student who went on about how he was the only person in sub-Saharan Africa who did not believe in *juju* (magic), and whose mother replied to the letter I sent him six months later, informing me that, the week after I had left, her son had contracted a mysterious fever and died?

Or how about my encounter with the gorgeous fifteen-year old whom I met at a dance club in Kisumu, on Lake Victoria, and had sex with five or six times (careful here, time and age distort this kind of thing) during a single, delightful night, all without benefit, or even mention, of contraception? Nor did the girl ask for money or anything else. Of course, I took the initiative, as I was perhaps expected to do, buying her breakfast the next morning and handing her a substantial, but not ridiculous, sum, which she accepted without protest. But those are the kinds of stories I don't think you can tell these days. Whatever else you may think of it, the one I did tell was politically correct.

"Okay," I said bluntly, "I'll tell you a story about Ethiopia. There are two parts. I'll start with the first one. But I have to warn you, this isn't going to be what you would call 'cute,' like the lion story. So. Shall I?" Looking interested, they all nodded, so I bulled ahead, practically uninterrupted.

"Now that I think of it, this is more of an image than a story. It comes from a very long, slow, hot train ride through the Ethiopian desert from Addis to Dire Dawa —do you know where that is?" They all did. "Anyway, sitting directly opposite me was a woman with a tiny child. Although she was wearing what I remember as elegant clothing, an embroidered shawl, and so on ..." (Bill complimented my memory) "... both she and the child were emaciated and drenched in sweat. In fact, they looked as if they might be starving. The child —a baby, I think, although I had no idea how old it was-- seemed barely alive.

"During the ten- or twelve-hour trip, the woman made no effort to nurse the baby or to give it any other food. She just stared into space. Come to think of it, I guess you could say this was another example of '*inshallah.*' The detail I remember most vividly was that big flies kept swarming over the child's face, which the woman made no effort to brush away. I'm not sure why that sticks in my mind.

"Of course, there are also many things I *don't* remember, but still wonder about. Had I brought any food along for the journey and, if so, did I take it out and offer to share it? In the long hours during which we sat across from each other, did the woman and I make eye contact? Who were our fellow-passengers, and what were they doing?

"The only other thought that does stick in my mind was that this mother and child were traveling toward their deaths. Did she get off the train when I did, at Dire Dawa? Because I met death there, myself. Or does that sound too melodramatic?"

On that note, I finally wound down. As you can imagine, this anecdote, or whatever it was, was something of a conversation-stopper. Everyone had been listening raptly, but, when I finished, there was a sort of stunned silence. Then, Bill recited some facts about hunger, poverty and illness. Devi said nothing. Edna mentioned the pathetic beggars she always encountered in Addis and other cities of the Horn: the blind, the orphaned, the limbless, the starving, those who were aged and destitute, and those whose limbs were twisted by polio or other crippling maladies. These comments, with their "nothing has changed" theme, were followed by another silence, which Edna once again broke.

"Well, George," she said, shielding her eyes from the sun, "that was jolly! But you said there were two stories. Is Part Two more … cheerful? Has to be, eh? Want to tell us that one now?" She shined a high-wattage smile on me, and, sheepishly, the roommates also smiled.

"Well, no," I said, embarrassed, but managing a tiny smile of my own. "Actually, the sequel is just as bad. Suppose I save it for another time. But, if you like," I added," I can recite the ten plagues against Egypt."

"Just the first two or three, George," suggested Devi. "Skip the frogs, please."

This little … whatever… did the trick, barely, moving the conversation back onto the expected tracks of, first, some hectic banter; then, a few further thoughtful and sober, but not too gloomy, reflections on Africa's enduring problems; and, finally, out onto the broad and tranquil plain of ordinary chatter. By now, the afternoon, still very hot, was turning into evening, so the talk turned to dinner plans, in which I was included.

When we left the pool, Edna hurried home to catch up on some e-mailing. The roommates and I went up to their flat, where we showered and dressed. At seven, I said goodbye to Devi, who intended to go dancing later on "with some ladies." Bill and I were dropped at the restaurant by a genial young taxi driver whom they had on call. We were joined almost immediately by Edna, who came in her own car. When she generously offered to drive us both home after the meal, Bill gave the driver the rest of the night off.

It was a very posh Indian place (no smoking), recommended by some friends of Devi's, and new to Edna, Bill, and, of course, me. When we had been seated and were studying the huge menus, an Indian family of four, ostentatiously rich, bustled in and was shown to a nearby table. As the Kenyan-African waiter began pulling out chairs, the father, a small man wearing a light blue safari suit and gold-rimmed glasses, stopped him in his tracks.

"Just a moment!" he barked. "This table is unsatisfactory. Have the manager come over here immediately! I specifically reserved a corner table next to the verandah. Didn't he tell you that, you fool?"

The waiter muttered something and sprinted off, presumably to find the manager, who was nowhere in sight. Many of the other diners, including Edna, looked very embarrassed. To my great surprise, mild-mannered Bill went ballistic.

"I fucking hate it," he spluttered, *sotto voce*, "when rich people throw their weight around like that. Some of these fucking bastards are really uncivilized." As he spoke, Bill's red hands gripped the edge of the red tablecloth, and, for an exciting moment, I wondered if he might be about to spring to his feet, change into his Superman costume, charge the martinet, and escalate the verbal attack, maybe even punch him in the nose.

Luckily for everyone, I suppose, there was no phone booth. Anyway, before it could come to that, the flustered (Indian) manager glided up, as if on roller skates. Apologizing profusely, he escorted the half-placated complainant away, presumably to a more suitable table. The wife had assumed an imperious air of her own, and, apparently used to their father's tantrums, the children obediently trailed after. The occupants of the other tables overcame their embarrassment and resumed what they had been doing before the altercation, or whatever it was. The offending server was nowhere in sight. The entire episode had lasted no more than two or three minutes.

"I'm really sorry, folks," said Bill, still angry, "but I fucking *hate* that kind of behavior."

"So do I," said Edna, matter-of-factly.

"Ditto," said I, and we returned to our menus.

Soon, we ordered. The hors d'oeuvres were promptly served, and we began to eat. Everything was excellent. I like Indian food, and this was at least as good as any I had eaten in New York, or anywhere else.

"How about that sequel now, George?" Edna suggested, when the waiter had replaced the small dishes with huge ones and was refilling our beer glasses. "The Dire Dawa story?"

"You sure?" I asked. They both nodded. If I need to explain myself, the proximate cause of Part Two of my Ethiopian adventure must have been Bill's muffled outburst. Of course, my poolside account of the train ride had prepared the way. Anyway, Edna was (again) the instigator.

Part Two was told in stages over the next hour, during which we finished the meal, dishes were cleared, and negotiations conducted over the check. For a while, this interrupted narrative worked well. Most of the story must have been fairly amusing, since my audience's interest never seemed to flag. I'll tell the bulk of it without their comments, which were few, anyway.

"Sometime very late, our train pulled into Dire Dawa, which was the terminus. When we had wearily disembarked, and the other passengers had gone their way, I realized I had a problem.

"As part of my itinerary of adventure, I had been traveling from town to town without bothering to make hotel reservations. I would just turn up, walk around, and pick a place. Decent rooms always seemed available; prices, manageable. I traveled light, with only a few changes of clothing and a camera, but no camping gear. Of course, in the pre-ATM era, my most important possession was my book of travelers' checks. Midway through the trip, I still had almost $1,000 worth. The checks were deep inside a zipped pocket in my cargo pants, nestled against my thigh. I also had some cash, of course, in another zipped pocket.

"By now, I think it must have been ten or eleven, and the "town" looked like a long dusty street lined by small, darkened buildings, none of which was obviously a hotel. Luckily, there was a moon, although I can't remember how full. After standing there indecisively for a few moments, I decided to follow my nose.

"Five minutes later, I reached a two-story building made of mud bricks, I think, with a sign above the door, in Amharic, and a faint light glowing through a window. I banged on the door, feet scuttled, and it was opened by a tall, thin young man wrapped in a white cotton shawl and carrying a small oil lamp.

"'Hotel?' I asked.

"'Yes,' he nodded.

"'Room?' I asked.

"'Yes,' he nodded.

"He beckoned, and I followed him through some winding corridors past several closed doors. Stopping at one, he turned the knob and gestured me in.

"'This one?" he asked, in English, shining the light into the room. 'Two *birr*.' (As I recall, this was then the equivalent of about twelve cents, U.S.)

"It was an empty, windowless room, about fifty or sixty square feet, with a dirt floor and a hole in one corner. The room was redolent of the uses previous occupants had made of the hole.

"'Better room?' I asked.

"He beckoned again, and we wound through the corridor to another door, which he also opened. Inside was the same room, but with a rolled-up raffia mat standing in a corner.

"'Four *birr*,' he said.

"'No, thanks,' I said. 'Any more rooms?'

"'No, same,' he said.

"With the optimism –rashness—of youth, I reasoned that, if there was one hotel in town, there must be other, better ones down the road. He shrugged and showed me back to the front door, closing it softly behind me.

"Adrift once again in the desert night, out on the long road, I proceeded, meeting no one. For a while, there were no more lights or signs, either, and I began to consider turning back. But I fell into one of those "just a little farther" moods and trudged on. After a while, the road dipped, and I crossed a sandy patch about twenty feet wide, which I assumed was a dry riverbed. Up on the other side, after five more minutes, I came to another sign and another dim light. Again, I knocked, and, again, a man with a lamp came out. I can't remember much about this man. Maybe, he was older than the first one.

"'Room?' I asked.

"'Yes,' he said, and we repeated the routine from the first hotel. The only differences were that this one had no rooms with mats, and the rooms may have smelled even worse.

"'No, thanks,' I said, without asking the price.

"By then, even my sense of adventure was wearing thin. It had been a very, very long day. So, I trudged back down the road and re-crossed the dry riverbed. By now, clouds seemed to be rolling in, and the moon was playing peek-a-boo with them. I woke up the first guy and took the deluxe, paying in advance.

"When he unraveled the mat, the equivalent of turning down the covers in a five-star accommodation, it looked as if it had never been used. When I lay down on it, at the far corner from the hole, it seemed no softer than I imagined the dirt floor would have been. But it felt clean and crinkled reassuringly. Exhausted as I was, I managed a fair night's sleep, wrapped against the desert night in my one jacket and all my spare pants and sweaters."

I paused. By now, Edna, Bill and I had finished stuffing ourselves and had declined dessert. As we waited for the check to be divided onto our three credit cards, I sensed that I had led us into a –another—conversational *cul de sac*. It lay just ahead, a surprising reversal of what, so far, could have been one of those amusing anecdotes which, I have read, are favored by "old Africa hands."

"Want to guess what happened?" I asked. "This is the bad part."

"Can't imagine. Let's have it," said Edna.

"Sock it to us, George," said Bill.

"To make this quick, what happened was that, sometime during the night, it rained. Very early the next morning, when I was packed and ready to leave, I looked for the attendant, to say goodbye. Making my way to the entrance, I saw him standing in the now-open doorway.

"Outside, a hullabaloo was in progress. People were shouting and running back and forth along the road. Traffic, consisting mostly of big trucks, was lined up as far as I could see, but in only one direction, away from the train station.

"'What happened?' I asked the hotel man.

"'Go and see,' he said, pointing ahead. 'Big rains in north.'

"Threading my way through the crowds, I approached the riverbed. It was now a torrent. A bunch of men with a heavy rope were tugging at a big truck that had intrepidly tried to cross and made it just far enough to drop its front end into the rushing water. For a minute or two, I stood and watched, shaking my head.

"Of course, if I had chosen the other hotel, I would have been marooned. For how long, I had no idea, but since the daily train left at eight a.m., I would presumably have missed it. Why would that have mattered? After all, I had no fixed itinerary. Somehow, though, the thought of being stranded across the river in Dire Dawa, cut off from the train station, distressed me.

"Later, having eaten some local food at the station, I rode back to Addis, seated across from people who left no impression. As the train chugged along, I felt that I had somehow survived one of those adventures I had come to Africa to experience."

"Well," said Edna, "and so you had."

"What's the bad part?" asked Bill.

"Heh, heh," I laughed mirthlessly. "Sure you want to know? I was told by a fellow passenger that, during the night, a large number of people –hundreds, maybe thousands-- had drowned. It seems that many of the homeless took shelter in the warm sand of the riverbeds, down where the wind did not reach."

"And when it rained," Edna said, "they drowned in the flash floods. As they must have known they might, at any time. That still happens, you know."

Bill capped the story. "The lives of the poor are a lottery."

We briefly fell silent, then, each with our own thoughts. While we waited a few more minutes for the credit cards to reappear, my dinner partners drew upon their own experiences to amplify what they had just heard.

Edna recalled an anecdote about the separatist, ethnic-Somali, Ogaden region in Ethiopia. After a visit from a Dutch reporter, those residents who had been brave or rash enough to speak with him had been brutally beaten by Ethiopian soldiers.

Bill told about how, a few months earlier, a Somali warlord's very lucrative gun-running operation to both sides in that conflict was uncovered by a U.N. colleague who worked on arms control. Twice, the warlord's thugs barely missed gunning the man down on a Nairobi street. He was now back home on leave in the U.K. Bill tapped a forefinger against his temple.

The check settled; we left the restaurant. The night was cool and clear, full of stars. In her puddle-jumper, Edna drove Bill to his apartment complex. Then, since the next day was a workday and she was not staying over with him, she drove me home to my guesthouse, which was on a quiet side street not far from her apartment building. When we reached the compound, I got out to ring the bell. The guard quickly appeared and opened the gate. I leaned into the car and shook Edna's hand.

"Thanks," I said, "for the ride, for everything. I'm really grate…"

She cut me off. "You're welcome, George, it was a pleasure meeting you. And the story you told us… those people in the train? the flood? … well, that's how it is, isn't it? I shan't soon forget that story. Best of luck with your article." She seemed about to say more but did not.

A bit awkwardly, we shook hands a second time. Then, she backed away from the gate, turned, and bumped off down the dark street toward the main road. I walked quickly into the compound, and the gate clanked shut behind me.

Ron Singer

A Reading at the Library

Prelude: Art Farms.

Before I swore off them, I sojourned at four art farms, one of them, three times. I came to hate these places. Almost every "fellow" at the communal dinner table acted as if he or she were entitled to a blow-by-blow account of your day's labors. You might think writers and other artists would be more imaginative in their table talk, but, no, they apparently saved their imagination for the privacy of their studios. Not to overstate the point, but they seemed like social cretins. Of course, many visual artists and musicians are dyslexic.

"So how did it go today, John?" asked a stocky, bald, smiling young painter who came to the table every night wearing his palette on his sleeve —and on the rest of his clothes. Since I had been at this particular farm for a week, the painter must already have asked his question four or five times.

"Not too bad." ("I winged a few birds with my slingshot, indulged in several hours of sexual fantasy, and took a long nap," John (I) would (not) add.)

"But what *are* you working on?" demanded a heavily made-up, bird-like woman, a fellow writer who resembled Joyce Carol Oates. "Come on, John, give us the goods!" The woman had butted in while I was mumbling my reply to the painter. She looked like she might be a plot thief.

"Thanks for asking. Well, today, I wrote 800 words and deleted 799 of them." But she did not even hear this little joke, because she had already turned toward a music critic, who was ticking off on his fingers, the ten best Beethoven piano performances of the last hundred years.

At the Library

A Cloud No Bigger than a Man's Hand:

By now it was 11:30, which felt like a good time for a break. Having eaten a large breakfast at the café, I thought I would just loiter by the riverside. So, packing my things, I exited the library. One of the two unpainted benches facing the river was already occupied. They were about two feet apart, parallel to each other, both in dappled sunlight. A cool breeze was blowing.

"May I?" I pointed to the bench on the left.

"Please," the occupant of the other one replied in a resonant baritone, making a "be my guest" gesture. I sat down. Using a brown paper bag for a placemat, he was eating what looked like a fish-salad sandwich on what looked like whole-grain bread. Beside him sat a large plastic water bottle.

"Beautiful day," I said.

He swallowed, then took a swig from the bottle. "Hope you don't mind…" He gestured to the sandwich.

"No, no, please."

"Well, as we locals are fond of saying, this sure is an example of 'weather like it used to be.'"

"Isn't that the state tourism motto?"

He smiled. "You're not from around here, are you? Actually, the motto is 'Worth a Visit, Worth a Lifetime.' "

This led into a round of show-and-tell, starting with introductions. Although his manner was dry, it was cordial.

"Charlie Scovill." (He spelled the surname.)

"John Roberts. Like the judge."

Reaching across the gap between the benches, we shook on that. As we continued talking, Charlie finished his sandwich, wiped his mouth on an unbleached paper napkin, drank some more water and, closing the bottle tightly, put it in the bag.

"What do you do, Mr. Scovill?"

"'Charlie,' please. You mean, besides reading magazines in the library? I'm a retired newspaper man."

"Huh! I had you pegged as a CEO, or something."

"Well, my last job was Editor-in-Chief of the local paper. Four or five years ago, when I reached the mandatory retirement age, seventy-two --which, by the way, I had decreed, myself-- I became Editor Emeritus. You might say I was 'hoist with my own petard.'"

"*Hamlet.* What does 'Editor Emeritus' mean?"

"It means that, when I get too exercised about the way the paper is being run, I go see the publisher and let off some steam."

"How often does that happen?"

"Oh, about once every ten minutes —seriously, I limit myself to one visit every five or six weeks."

"That must take forbearance."

He laughed. "What about you, John? I thought I saw you working on a manuscript in there." He gestured over his shoulder toward the library. "You mind if I ask…?"

"Not at all. A thriller about cyber-murder."

"Hmm! Up-to-date."

Since, as is already clear, I *did* mind talking about my work, I changed the subject. "You a family man, Charlie?"

"Widower, with grown children. You?"

"Amicably divorced, no children."

It occurred to me that one reason we had already become so chatty might have been that we were both lonely. Of course, we were both also connected with "the writing game," albeit in different ways.

"How long have you been a writer?"

"Well, it was always on the back burner. For thirty years, until I retired in 2007, I earned my bread as a clerk in a New York State government office."

"Hmm. Which one?"

"Motor Vehicles. By the time I retired, I was a Unit Manager."

"Quite a success story!" Was he being sarcastic? "So, then..." He stalled for a moment, fiddling with the paper bag. "Oh, yes, speaking of writers, did you happen to come across that big room in the basement?"

"The Community Room?"

"Yep. Well, you may have missed the notice on the board to the left of to the door. A bi-weekly writers' group convenes there."

"Is that so?"

"Sort of an open-mike set-up. If you're interested, there's one Thursday, at 2:30. You don't have to commit, sign up or anything, you can just show up."

"Hmm. Does everyone have to read?"

"No, there are usually about ten of us, three or four readers, including a couple of regulars. The rest just listen, and there's usually some Q & A. Last summer, a Boston lady read from a historical novel that I thought was exceptional --very suspenseful. I'm waiting for it to come out."

"What was the subject?"

"It was based on her life as a hidden child in the French countryside during the Nazi occupation. I know that doesn't sound very original, but the details were exquisite. Actually, she read twice. She must have been encouraged by our fulsome praise the first time."

At this point, the conversation flagged. I made some noncommittal noises about Thursday, and we shook hands and went back inside together.

Amanda Stallworth Reads. "Comments, Anyone?"

Squaring up the pages in front of her, Stallworth cleared her throat. She said she was working on an untitled novel about the Spanish Armada of 1588. You remember, the grand plan to overthrow the monstrous Protestant queen? The fleet of Spanish sailing ships that God dashed against the rocky Irish coast? She told us that, thus far, she had completed a draft of the first third of the book. Either from modesty or because she did not have one, she did not mention a publisher.

The chapter she read was from the point of view of one of the boys manning the huge Spanish cannon that were supposed to blow the English to oblivion. She described the hour when the wind was unexpectedly starting to shift. The gunner boy was fully aware of the disastrous implications of the shift.

Stallworth read for eight minutes. I enjoyed her crisp, no-nonsense prose. Since her listeners/readers were presumably familiar with the broad outlines of the story, she had to deal with the problem of how to keep us engaged between dramatic incidents, which she tried to do by means of characterization and *obiter dicta*. In this regard, her vessel drew some water. The *obiter dicta* weren't bad: tidbits about currents, winds, navigation, and naval warfare in 1588 that sounded like they went well beyond Google. The characters were the problem.

I could tell this even from the single chapter she read. Her people were wooden and too obviously chosen. When she mentioned King Philip back on his knees at the Escorial, this reader, for one, was hoping she would depart from the historical record to visit him with a fatal lightning bolt. As for Elizabeth, although Stallworth would presumably allow the Queen a few bits of codpiece tearing, I knew she would keep cutting back to the big battle before anything really sadistic or salacious could happen.

As I listened (having committed to read, after all), I was very interested in what the ensuing discussion would be like. I had already gained confidence in my own powers. My novel would seem funny and nasty, I anticipated, and the technical bits, I hoped, would measure up to the Stallworthian standard.

When the chapter ended, Ms. Brooks, the Head Librarian and our moderator, opened the floor for discussion. Three hands were raised: the lumberman-poet, Gene Eaton; Alicia Bernstein (non-fiction); and Charlie Scovill. (Ms. Brooks had introduced everyone.) I was glad to see these hands, because I did not like the idea of commenting right before it was my turn to read. I would keep my powder dry.

Bernstein praised the historical details, provoking a murmur of assent around the table. Eaton generously alleged that he could smell the brine and gunpowder. Although his hand had not been raised, at this point, Mike Billings, a burly lobsterman (who was "only a reader") chimed in.

"Yes, sirree," he said, in a ringing tenor. "When things start airing up out there in the chapter, you feel like you're stuck on the ship, yourself. Hey, I don't envy those fellas!"

After everyone finished laughing, it was Charlie's turn. "Well, Ms. Stallworth," he said, folding his hands and looking down at them as he spoke. "That was nicely done, very professional. You've handled the central problem well: how to interest people in a story they already know. You've done quite a good job with that." Since, by this point, even I was waiting for the other shoe to fall, I glanced at Stallworth, who looked as if she had battened down the emotional hatches: her face was closed and expressionless.

The shoe fell. "Just one suggestion, if I may. The characters in a serious novel, which yours is --although one could quibble, and call it genre fiction—have to be a bit more... developed than yours are." It was as if he had been reading my mind. "It's okay for the ones we already know from history to be predictable, a bit on the flat side. But, in a large cast like the one you've assembled, some of the characters that take turns occupying center stage should be more rounded, less predictable. The gunner boy, for instance: it shouldn't be too hard to individualize him, to make him more than a poor, scared kid in an impossible situation. You could give him a backstory that ..." Charlie drew breath and looked up. "But I'd better stop right there, before I hog all the time. Anyway, I'm sure you get the idea. You're the writer, and, I think, a good enough one to deal with this problem without my help."

"Well," said Ms. Brooks, blowing out some air, "if I may say so, that was vintage Charlie Scovill. Are you okay with that, Ms. Stallworth? Everyone? Are we ready to move on? Mr. Roberts, please." Stallworth tried not to look shattered.

Selected Works, Past & Present.

Novel #1 (completed 2003, unpublished): *Teach Her a Lesson*: In the milieu of New York's East Village, a corrupt police detective murders a prostitute and tries to pin the blame on a former English teacher who became homeless when he suffered a nervous breakdown. The murderer leaves many false clues, all of which are details from *Macbeth*. For instance, he slices open the corpse and cuts off her head. *Macbeth*-ophiles (of which I am one) will recall that, early in the play, the protagonist dispatches the traitorous Thane of Cawdor by "unseaming" him "from the nave unto the chops," and impaling "his head upon our battlements." Since the demented ex-teacher roams the neighborhood alternately muttering and shouting snatches from Shakespeare … you get the idea. Probably out of some perverseness of my own, I won't reveal any more about this novel, except to say that there is, indeed, a Macduff figure, a nemesis who settles the murderous cop's hash.

Novel #2 (WIP, begun Winter, 2011-12): An On-Line Offing. WIP is a thriller. The protagonist uses the Internet to try to murder a hated cousin who repeatedly humiliated him in childhood. His "inspiration" is the recent case of a college student who caused his gay roommate's suicide by posting on Facebook a hidden home video of the roommate's encounter with another man. In my novel, the protagonist mounts his campaign against the cousin (who faintly resembles my ex-brother-in-law) by videotaping a motel tryst with his secretary. He posts a copy of the video on Facebook (or, as he jokes, "Dickbook"). Since the killer can't assume that a video showing a fat, bald middle-aged man bonking a thin, plain woman in a generic motel will go viral, he also sends copies to the cousin's wife, children, and ailing parents. The idea is to induce a fatal coronary in the cousin, who has already had two un-fatal ones.

My Turn to Read:

"Um," I said, "since this is my first appearance, perhaps the other readers should have precedence, in case we run out of time. Suppose I defer and read last, if there's any time left?" Did I detect a flickering grin from Charlie?

"No, please," said Ms. Brooks, glancing at her watch. "That's very generous of you, Mr. ---John—but we're right on schedule. So ..." She gestured, inviting me to begin.

Girding my loins, I picked up the pages I had set aside while Stallworth was reading. Although it took me a few sentences to get the tremor out of my voice, I thought it went well. I had chosen excerpts from two chapters. The first was sort of technical, the part where the protagonist hatches his scheme and begins to figure out how best to record and disseminate his cousin's indiscretion. The second describes a few of the childhood humiliations. People laughed at my jokes and seemed absorbed by the narrative and cyber-details. When I finished, I was relieved to see that only two hands were raised.

Billings, the lobsterman said, "Well, that was very good. I can't wait for the —excuse me, everyone—for that bastard to get his come-uppance!" It was unclear which bastard he meant, but no one asked. Alicia Bernstein complimented me on the "mix," as she called it, of technical detail and absorbing narrative. Since she had not yet read from her own work, it crossed my mind that she might be recruiting me to her corner. Charlie sat looking down at his folded hands. Was there a hint of another little smile?

The Scovill Verdict:

After the last readings, by Bernstein and Eaton (the lumberman), Ms. Brooks thanked and dismissed us. Charlie held the door of the conference room open for me.

"John," he said, with a little bow, "have you got a few minutes? I'd like to chat about your book."

"Sure," I said. "Thanks." I was being counterphobic. "Shall we go outside?"

He agreed, and we walked upstairs together. As we crossed the lobby, I noticed that Ms. Brooks was back at her post already, speaking on the phone. She did not look up. Charlie and I silently exited the library and headed for the riverside, where there was a moment's hesitation while we decided whether to share a bench or each to take his own. We settled on the latter, with him on the right again. We each leaned an arm across the back of our bench, so we were more or less facing one another. I put my folder down on my bench.

"Shoot," I said, opting for directness. "What did you think?"

"Well." He cleared his throat and cracked two knuckles on his right hand. "First, let me say that you're a live wire, John, a very entertaining writer. But I'm afraid your book has a problem."

"Oh?" I tried to sound unfazed.

"Yes." He frowned. "Actually, there are two, related problems." He cleared his throat. "May I be blunt?" He looked me in the eye.

"You certainly may not," I did not say. "Suppose I kick your ass, instead, or punch you in your ugly face?" Actually, I raised my right hand a few inches off the top of my bench, in a "be my guest" gesture.

"Good," he said. "I hope these comments will be useful." He frowned again. "The problem is, well, I'm afraid you don't quite know what you're doing. The related problem —the underlying one—is that you don't really have a book here." His expression was pained.

"Oh?" My voice sounded tremulous.

"Actually, you have two books —sort of --the thriller with the tech stuff and the thinly disguised memoir. I don't mean to impugn your credentials, but how much do you really know about the Internet? Even a codger like me, too old to be much of an authority, can tell you're faking the tech stuff. The malice towards the cousin is plausible enough --that was the part I enjoyed most-- but the tech stuff... I mean, what it really evokes is an image of you anxiously surfing the web for tidbits to use in your book. Take that video of the gay roommate. It was on YouTube, not Facebook. Not good. As for ..." I could feel my face growing hot. Luckily, we were in shade.

"...the memoir?" I interrupted. This may sound as if I was putting a big "kick me" sign on my backside, but what I really wanted was to get this hazing over with.

"Yes, the humiliation rings true enough, but there's a big problem here, too. Again, to be blunt, that sort of stuff has been written to death. You skirt the problem by turning a real-life situation into the backstory for a thriller, or something like that. But you wind up falling between the stools of genre fiction and literary memoir. I hate to say it, John, but that's a beginner's problem. Not only do you fail to ..."

At this point, I tuned Charlie out. He nattered on for a while, but I was no longer listening. I was trying *not* to listen. My mind darted in twenty directions: Hemingway's dictum, to write only about what you know (my thirty-year day job issuing learners' permits?); what the other writers had just read -- clinging to the shreds of *schadenfreude*, I focused on Gene Eaton, the mediocre poet. My mind raced on: I was back in bed with my ex-; back in my childhood, when my grandfather had saved me from being snatched by a passing pedophile; playing Store in my grandparents' grape arbor with my little cousins; how much money there was in my checking and money-market accounts; and, finally, why Charlie Scovill was such a sour old fuck.

The reader is free to find the common thread in these desperate flights of thought. Maybe, the thread was actually a point, to which I kept returning like a moth to flame. I think I had already sensed that Charlie's devastating criticism of my WIP (RIP) was equally true of my *Macbeth* novel. In both, from a grain of reality, I had sown vast fields of mendacious, strained prose. In both, ill-matching parts were jammed together like jagged halves of a broken egg.

When Charlie muttered some nonsense about "no hard feelings," the torture session was finally over. He stood up and extended his hand. In a fog, I stood up, too, grabbed my folder in my left hand, and shook his cool hand with my clammy right one. Muttering something about lingering at the riverside, he said goodbye and sat back down. I fled the scene, hurrying past the library entrance, back toward the parking lot.

"Thank God *that's* over!" remarked either my good or bad angel. "But it was all true," said the other one. "You're finished."

"Why," you may ask, "did Mr. Scovill choose to demolish Mr. Roberts, a relative stranger who had never caused him the slightest bit of harm?" Well, *you* may ask that reasonable question. I was beyond reason.

Postlude: Back at the Cottage.

By the time I pulled out of the parking lot, it was four thirty-seven. I was not sure how to spend what was left of the afternoon (or the day, or, possibly, my life). I thought of going to the café for a late-afternoon snack, but, as always, I was chary of fleeing to food. So I drove —slowly and cautiously-- back to the cottage.

As soon as I was inside, I tapped the computer and was greeted by my faithful screensaver, a garish Marsden Hartley sunset in several of nature's least natural colors. Dropping the folder on the table, for about two minutes I stood staring at the screen. Then, without even checking my email or changing my clothes, I walked slowly down to the dock. After reassuring myself that I had no intention of jumping into the deep pond, I spent the rest of the afternoon drifting around in my rowboat. Even when the mosquitoes started to bite, I did not want to go back inside. But, eventually, I did.

Spots

A Thursday, and Professor Dortmund was on his way to the Public Library to check three footnotes before sending his latest monograph off to the publisher. Trundling down the steps to the subway station, Dortmund imagined the pleased smile the woman would wear as she tore open the envelope, removed the rubber band from the protective cardboard sheets, and cast her first glance over the thick sheath of white pages, each with its twenty-seven perfect rows of black type.

It was as if this thought had generated momentum in the universe, for no sooner had Dortmund set foot on the platform than he spied the bright headlamps of the train coming through the tunnel. A few seconds later, he was speeding comfortably along in an air-conditioned car of silver metal and blue and pink plastic. Had this immaculate car even been used before? The pink floor was made of a glittering hard-rubber substance that reminded the professor of dish-detergent commercials.

With a seat, and the adjacent ones on either side, all to himself, Dortmund occupied his time looking across the car and out the window at the dirty sunlit cityscape. He also studied the other passengers, inwardly sighing with relief as he noted that the sparse midmorning collection of riders comprised exclusively people of an appearance every bit as law-abiding as his own. He noted further that there happened not to be a single so-called "person of color" in the car, but he was careful to classify this observation as chance observation, rather than an expression of racial chauvinism.

Twelve minutes later, the train pulled into a hub station, and a third of Dortmund's fellow passengers disembarked. Their places were taken by a larger number of newcomers, mostly Black, and the professor observed with pleasure that the group included neither rowdy young people nor anyone overtly intoxicated. His self-image of evenhandedness was enhanced by the fact that he was as pleased with this group of good citizens as he had been with the previous group.

When a large, muscular "ethnic" youth ("What am I, then," he chuckled, "an 'ethnic elder' "?) boarded at the last moment and took the one remaining place, to the professor's left, Dortmund really did not much mind. For one thing, the young man was deferential to his neighbor's prior claim: he sat compactly so as not to make contact. Even better, the newcomer immediately opened a paperback book, attesting not only to his literacy, but possibly even to an intellectual strain. What was more, now that the train had gone underground, the book would afford the professor a new diversion.

But what was this? With breathless glances, the professor found himself reading a narrative in which a young woman seemed to be disrobing in front of a male friend, meanwhile recounting a strange ordeal at the hands of kidnappers. In his own, more refined way, Dortmund was as absorbed in the story as was his seatmate, who read doubled over, his open mouth creeping closer and closer to the text, threatening literally to devour it.

"On her belly," the two passengers read,

... in a straight line running from the navel to the very edge of the pubis, were three large red dots. "They look like ... blood," Dick gasped, unable to tear his eyes from the slightly protruding rosy lips of her vagina. His fingers trembled. "They are," Maria said faintly. "They said it was a warning, that, unless we immediately broke off our effort to penetrate their network, they would catch me again and rip open three separate parts of my body." She shuddered. "I'd better go wash the spots off."

Dick watched the rich globes of her behind callipygiate toward the bathroom. When she had closed the door and he could hear the water running, he looked down at her panties, which lay crumpled on the floor where she had dropped them. With a mixture of disgust and fascination, he noted the spots of dried blood on them, obviously smears where the fabric had pressed against her body. As he heard the tub begin to fill, unable to control his mounting ardor, Dick bent to retrieve the flimsy garment with one hand, even as the other tremblingly unzipped his already burgeoning fly.

Like Dick, the professor had become very excited, indeed. "Well, well, this 'Dick' must be quite a contortionist," he joked to himself, trying to calm down. When his seat mate, by now bent almost double, quickly closed the book, the professor could not but inwardly applaud the decision, although he did feel a pang of disappointment not unlike that of a child who has had a delicious morsel of candy snatched by a bigger child.

The book was not reopened, at least not before the professor's stop had arrived, and, by the time he was disembarking, he could honestly say it was better this way. As he climbed the stairs into the hot August sunshine, Dortmund was once again ready for the task of checking the three footnotes to his monograph, which staked out a small corner in the large field of cetacean musicology.

Never content to devote all his energies to a single mundane task, Dortmund was planning the most efficient itinerary for checking the three notes even as his feet carried him to the correct subway exit. Coming up from the ground, he noted in the corner of his eye a poor man paying angry, mute courtship to a prosperous-looking woman, dancing around in front of her as she tried to avert her eyes.

And, with that, the day went wrong. Since the closer he came to the start of a task, the greater would wax the professor's enthusiasm, what was his chagrin when, reaching the library door, he did not find it in its normal, ajar position. With an implosive sensation in the vicinity of his heart, he read the funereal print of the notice on the closed door:

SUMMER HOURS: THURSDAY, CLOSED.

"Damn it to hell!" he transliterated. For the next few seconds, he just stood there, muttering further imprecations, as if the force of his will might change the words. Being a practical man, however, he managed to accept the setback, decided to treat himself to a new book, and concocted a few other errands he might run in this neighborhood. First, however, he must telephone his wife to announce his changed plans.

"Thus does adversity become the stepmother, at least, of invention." He chuckled at his own wit.

True it is, too, that a man makes his own luck, for, upon entering the phone kiosk, Dortmund saw neatly folded between phone box and plexiglass wall, a fresh copy of that day's paper. He chuckled again: more than 20% of his subway fares and incipient phone call had thus been effortlessly recouped. Not to mention the anticipated pleasure of reading a free paper on the way home.

An hour later, the professor was back in the train. Between his legs rested a shopping bag containing several small parcels, and across his lap was the spread-open newspaper. His only anxiety now was that he would reach his stop before he had time to complete his favorite sections: local news, including crime; sports; and classified advertisements, which he often found particularly humorous or poignant.

In the event, this fear was justified, for Dortmund never finished a single section of the paper. He had, alas, been exhausted by several days and nights slaving over his monograph, by the library disappointment, and, perhaps most of all, by the ridiculous, but prodigious, exercise of self-control that had been required while reading over the young man's shoulder. Before the empty train could creep past the first two stations, the professor had nodded off.

Not that he went without a struggle. Thrice did his leonine head droop and the top of his torso tack left toward an old woman. And thrice did he recover, blinking and shaking himself awake. But the fourth time that Dortmund began to nod, he knew he must sleep and so, with a sigh, he quartered the paper, put it into the shopping bag, and turned his body so that his head would most likely plop against the subway map, fortunately not too filthy, behind the empty seat to his right.

It began as a dream of trains. Night, and Dortmund stood alone on a dark platform. From the black tunnel there shone a single light, a beacon, and an equipment train rumbled into the station. This train consisted of a string of flatbed cars, each cluttered with machinery and other equipment of varied sizes and shapes. There were large generators that looked like cement mixers, piles of wire and cable, pipes, drums, and many other objects and materials.

The odd thing was that the train clattered silently: he knew it was clattering, but the dream was silent. Slowly, without stopping, the cars rolled past the professor, who scrutinized each with pleasure. It had the air of a display, and Dortmund's sleeping mind read the caption: THE CIRCUS IS COME TO TOWN. Like clowns, two or three men sat impassively among the equipment, their faces painted with grease, their limbs lolling in different directions dictated by comfort. They did not wave, and neither did Dortmund, who had perceived in the beacon a command to bear witness at a solemn procession. Finally, the last of the cars slid off into the tunnel.

Then, somewhere, a dog barked or, more likely, the sleeping professor heard a sound like barking. In this next part of his dream, he was back on the street, briskly gliding along two blocks from the library, trying to get there before it closed. His task was to look up the lyrics to a song he would use for an epigraph to his monograph, which he now carried in a big brown portfolio. But he could not think of the name of the song. The melody, he thought he had, but suddenly it was another one, and another and another, and all of them seemed appropriate.

Then (still on the sidewalk), he stumbled, and he noticed that his slippery shoelace was once again undone. This trouble had all come of stopping to shine his shoes the week before. Already late for a lecture, he had unwisely neglected to remove the laces. Since that error, the shoelaces had come undone at least ten times. The left one, especially, would not stay tied, and the left was the culprit now, just when he was in such a hurry. Executing a tricky maneuver, he managed to keep his portfolio leaning against his left thigh while he knelt on the right knee to tie the accursed shoe.

But what was this! Dortmund heard panting and felt something warm and wet against his cheek. Raising his eyes, he found himself nose to nose with a brown and white cocker spaniel. The dog's big loose pink tongue flopped uncomfortably close to the face of the professor, who felt hot breath blowing into his eyes. He stared fiercely into the dog's own muddy eyes, feeling foolish, but full of offended dignity, which precluded his backing off.

Once again, the dream turned. Dortmund was back in the subway, this time in the midst of a rush-hour crowd. Now he was in a hot old airless train, caught in a press, his body welded front-to-front with that of a short young woman wearing a perfume smelling of primroses, edelweiss, or some other flower remembered from childhood. All he could see of this aromatic female was her golden hair, which hung well below her shoulders to the vanishing point, but her large, exciting breasts were digging into his navel, creating a natural, but highly embarrassing, temporary physical change in the beleaguered professor.

And what now? All at once a business card materialized in the air before his eyes:

DARLENE'S RUSH-HOUR SERVICES FOR GENTLEMEN PAY WHAT YOU PLEASE

Rush-hour prostitution! What was the world coming to? And, bizarrely, he visualized a book that he knew to have been (co) authored by this same Darlene, prominently displayed in the store in which he had just actually purchased his own volume:

TIGHTLY PACKED PANTS: MEMOIRS OF A SUBWAY GEISHA

But, even as he read the title, he realized with fearful joy that an expert hand was unzipping his fly.

"'Down, hysterico passio, down, I say,' "Dortmund quoted from Shakespeare's towering masterpiece, *King Lear*, as his head struggled to regain control of the underlings. With great effort, he managed to snuff out that naughty dream, but, alas, just as the train came up into the daylight, yet another swam right into the previous one's place.

Now he was in an establishment called the House of Aquarius, one of those big furniture stores in the slums, where one can acquire, at least temporarily, expensive pieces of furniture for a small down payment and several signatures on a complex document. As Dortmund scanned the piles of plush velveteen, the sets of chrome and glass, the mattresses and cushions still in their plastic wrappers, he sensed something anomalous. It was not the single salesman on duty, a thin middle-aged fellow with pencil mustache and eager-to-please eyebrows. Nor was it the furniture, the usual sad, garish jumble. Then he understood: it was the clientele. Every customer was known to the professor, at least by sight.

There was the big fellow he had seen the other day in front of the licensed betting parlor, a rascal with pug nose, square jaw and beefy arms, presently engaged in scrutinizing the price tag on a dinette set. There was the barber, from Dortmund's own corner, converted in the dream to a mob type who, Panama hat pulled low, was peeling bills from a huge wad and counting them with a thumb he kept licking. The barber was purchasing a living room set with an African motif: synthetic zebra-skin chairs and couch, red and black paintings of topless African maidens and long warriors in the sunset. Then, with a gasp, the sleeping Dortmund spotted Darlene, herself, arrayed in black slit skirt and red fishnet stockings. She was testing couches, perching on each for a moment before jumping to the next.

"Ah, eee, no, it's him!" exclaimed the professor at the sight of another familiar customer. For it was his seatmate with the book. But the young man had deteriorated since that morning. His hair was stringy and filthy with grease, his eyes red and furious, his brown pants shiny and frayed. Instead of the heavy mustard-colored work boots he had been wearing, he now sported down-at-the-heels black high-top sneakers with broken laces. And from the youth's back pocket protruded what the professor knew could be absolutely nothing other than a shiv.

As Dortmund watched in alarm, this young person, who was most certainly a mugger, began gingerly to sit down on a gigantic waterbed. Given the clientele, the professor hoped that management had possessed the foresight to stock only the most puncture-resistant plastic. By now, the young man was seated, and, as he leaned slowly backward, he seemed to be debating whether to take his sneakers off before fully reclining.

"Wait, wait!" cried the professor, rushing forward.

Too late! The mugger had made up his mind. With a big, happy smile, he swiveled around and dropped his legs onto the bed. Instantly, there was a loud pop, and Dortmund threw up his arms as the room began to fill with water.

At that moment, he awoke with a start, acutely aware that he had reached the precipice of an acute embarrassment. As he ground his teeth and tensed his muscles, willing every nerve to remain perfectly still, Dortmund's eyes flashed to the three passengers opposite him. These were (and the catalogue was essential to the professor's efforts at self-control) a gray-suited business type lost in a (presumably normal) book; a thin old woman who blushed and averted her eyes; and a tall, fat, red-faced man with tiny eyes, pig snout, and a small pile of curly brown hair that resembled a potholder.

"It … must … not … happen," the professor vowed with iron determination. And, after a few moments of perhaps the greatest exertions of his life, he knew that he had prevailed. "It" had not happened. Sighing deeply, he pulled out his handkerchief and mopped his face. He had won. The train stopped. Dortmund saw that it had reached the station before his own. He smiled coldly, glad that his will, his brain, or whatever it was that governed his life, had once again prevailed.

A few minutes later, he unlocked the door to his apartment.

"I'm home, dear," he called from the foyer, less heartily than usual, to his wife, who sat in the kitchen reading a magazine and eating a big peach.

"Good, good, you sound tired, Norbert," she mumbled, absorbed in magazine and peach.

"I am. A little," he admitted, trudging down the hall.

Relieved to be home at last, when he reached the end of the hall, he wearily lowered the shopping bag to the floor and entered the bathroom. Flicking on the light, he locked the door behind him and lowered both pants and underpants. After a thorough inspection, satisfied, he pulled everything up again. Next, he bent over the sink, opened the taps, and waiting for the water to warm, looked into the mirror. He was so startled by what he saw that he emitted a small cry.

For there, right there in the mirror, on his own face —on his chin, forehead and left cheek, to be exact—were three large smudges. And these smudges gave him an uncanny resemblance to a common, disgusting … bum. Undoubtedly, Professor Dortmund reassured himself, these marks had been caused by accidental contact with the newspaper print. But not only did this explanation lack any power to reassure him; it positively heightened his alarm.

"For who knows," he thought hysterically, "that paper may have previously been in the possession of some maniac who smeared it with deadly plague germs."

Snatching the soap from its nest beside the sink, Dortmund held it under the hot water tap for just a moment. Then, with vicious strokes, he began to rub the big green bar back and forth, up and down, all over his smudged face. The spots began to fade.

Ron Singer

The Curing of the Blind (c. 2015 C.E.)

Two months later, both eyes cured by retinal lens implants, a miracle of modern science (technology, anyway), as I lay in bed in the early morning with my arms wrapped around my sleeping wife's warm back, I remembered, still with animosity, a man I had encountered in the waiting room of the eye clinic.

The clinic was located in a converted mansion a few blocks east and south of Bethesda Fountain, in Central Park. A posh facility in a posh neighborhood, its waiting room looked like an old-fashioned parlor. On the light green walls hung four portraits of middle-aged men. At the time, I presumed the subjects were all doctors, although only one was wearing a white coat, with a stethoscope dangling from a side pocket. Like ancestors in the gallery of an aristocrat, these four could equally have been men of distinction, bumblers, or something even worse. Now that I think of it, they must have been trustees.

It was at Bethsaida that Jesus healed the blind, not Bethesda (where he healed the lame). Unlike those miracles, the ones at the clinic are performed not upon the virtuous, the sorely afflicted, or the needy, but on anyone with minor eye problems and major insurance. BTW, when Jesus cured the blind man, he did it in two stages —two procedures, if you like. After the first, the man said people looked like trees, so Jesus laid hands on him again. Oddly, in Gioachino Assereto's painting of this miracle (c.1640), Christ is touching the blind man's nose with an index finger: The Immaculate Nose Job.

When I came to the clinic to have my first eye fixed, among the half dozen people in the waiting room was the one I mentioned at the beginning of this story. While I waited impatiently for my name to be called, my wife had her head buried in a book, *Anna Karenina*, which she was reading for the umpteenth time. The culprit-to-be was frowning at his red smartphone —stock tables, I assumed. He wore an expensive-looking black suit that hung loosely on his shrunken frame, and he had big hands and elephant ears.

Full disclosure: I was already annoyed, because the receptionist had announced that the surgeon had been in a fender bender on his way to work and was running late. He was a wonderful doctor who had performed a complex eye-saving surgery on a friend of ours —I'm not sure of the details, but it was certainly not lens replacement.

Ironically, it was the doctor who precipitated the disturbance. Bustling into the waiting room, mask down on the chest of his pale blue scrubs, he treated the old man the same way he always treated me: a firm handshake, followed by heartfelt reassurances. "A complete success, Ned!" he beamed. "No complications. She's awake now, resting comfortably. You can go in, in ten minutes, and take her home in about an hour."

Already sounding obnoxious, the old man thanked him profusely, and he hurried back to the operating room. Then, "Ned" glued his smartphone to one of his big ears and began pressing buttons. Thanks to this second miracle of modern technology, I was forced to learn quite a bit about a total stranger. He spoke in a loud whisper, an apparent concession that only served to accentuate his sense of entitlement, as if he were sneering at the rights of lesser mortals. To be fair, the whispering may actually have been dictated by a vestigial sense of delicacy. After all, it was his wife's eyes, a fairly intimate topic, about which he was broadcasting. But I certainly did not think of that. What I did think of was those exploding cell phones terrorists sometimes use. Was *he* blind? Right in front of him on a coffee table was a placard: NO CELL PHONE USE.

"I guess some people can't read," I remarked conversationally, to a sensible-looking woman sitting on the other side of the offender from me. If the broadcaster heard this rebuke, he ignored it. The woman shrugged, looking embarrassed.

The situation reminded me of the time, five or six years ago, when, at my wife's suggestion, I had gone for a hearing test. "Your hearing is fine," the audiologist said, after reading the results. "Actually, for a man of sixty-one, it's remarkable."

"Then why..."

She smiled. "Spousal deafness."

"Hi, this is Edward Worth returning your call. I'm at the eye clinic with my wife..." (Message, apparently business.)

"Hi, this is Ned calling from the clinic. Just wanted to let you know Penny is doing *great*. Complete success. Love you." (Messages to two or three friends/relatives.)

In full sentences, peppered with small talk, that was also the gist of two more calls, these with live humans, and each lasting a few minutes, before he cut them off with, "Lots more people to call. Love you."

Then came the long one. With Penny's procedure as a prelim, Ned responded with relish to an apparent request for advice: "You'll have to figure that out for yourself, Steve ...how to make the most of... I agree ... promising venture ... bottom line... careful ... folks you're partnering with... terms in writing... up-front money..." etc. etc. The interlocutor must have been a young man, perhaps Ned's nephew or son-in-law.

The alarm sounded; my wife awakened.

"Been up long?" she yawned, stretching.

"About ten minutes. I didn't want to wake you."

"Thank you, dear." She yawned again. "You look so grim. What were you thinking about?"

I told her, trying to laugh off my seriousness.

"Huh!" she said, fully awake now. "You're still bothered by that guy? Yes, he was a jerk. But he was just happy his wife was okay."

"I suppose." We stood up, each on our own side of the wide bed. As I was about to head for the bathroom, and she to the kitchen, to start the coffee, I fired a parting salvo. "Well, *you* didn't act like that when *I* went under the knife."

"'Under the laser,' you mean. Of course, I didn't! I'm not a man."

I let it go at that.

Later that day, I took the subway up to the library. As I emerged onto the street, I saw someone a few feet in front of me who looked like Ned Worth, at least from the back: tall, bony, white-haired, wearing a fancy blue belted raincoat. He had his hand on the shoulder of an overweight, slouching, younger man, who appeared to be eating something. Since they were going my way, I hurried after them, wanting to see if they really were Ned and his relative, and if so, what they were saying.

Pulling alongside, I snuck a glance. Not them. And the younger man was a younger woman, a twenty-something with cropped hair, messily eating a bagel with cream cheese. Deciding to eavesdrop, anyway, I dropped back a few feet, then matched their pace.

"Listen, Bobbie," the man said (and, in the course of the two blocks I shadowed them, there were several more 'Listen, Bobbies')"... counting on you ... mistakes, dear... hell, your mother and I ... doozies ... goes with the territory...excuses ... 'bad bosses'... 'unfair' ... this time ... home run!"

The lecture went something like that. Bobbie's "response" was to blush (her neck grew crimson), to keep eating, and to utter a few quasi-affirmative noises. When they turned into a storefront realty office, I proceeded to the library, where I settled down in the stacks.

Opening a book (no glasses!), it dawned on me that my wife was right: I had overreacted. Since she works part-time in a posh antique shop, she "knows these people." And, maybe, the coincidental pep talk on the sidewalk made Ned Worth's phone calls seem less obnoxious. I'll even admit that folding his advice into the good news about his wife was just the sort of thing I might have done. But let's keep this in perspective: I'm not about to join the Entitled Old Bastards Fan Club!

A Game of Lies

The night after my first meeting with my cousin Martha, I had a double-dream. First, I was in bed with a group of strangers, all of them women. Nothing, however, was happening, sexual or otherwise. The scene shifted to a dark street, where a small man I assumed was a gypsy —or more correctly, a Roma or Sinti—was stalking me. On my way to Pannonia, I had stopped in Berlin where, in the sprawling park known as *Tiergarten*, I came upon a memorial to "gypsies" killed by the Nazis and their allies, including Pannonian Fascists. As in the first dream, nothing really happened on the dark street. Both dreams were silent.

Since my retirement six or seven years back, I had already traveled to Italy, France, and the British Isles. I will not use the real name of the central European country I was now visiting, not from coyness or from fear that I don't know enough to describe it accurately, but from delicacy. Since this country's problems are legion and I bear it no special grudge, I have borrowed the name of the Roman province, "Pannonia."

I woke from my double-dream thinking about my favorite stalking incident. It featured my father's younger brother, Aaron. A short man, Aaron had once mimicked the swaggering gait of a huge, shirtless "Negro," who was striding through Washington Square Park looking as if he would welcome a confrontation. As a boy of six or seven, I was shadowing my uncle, and, like many of the onlookers, laughing hysterically. But I also dreaded that, at any moment, the giant might whirl around and catch us in the act. This was during the 1950's, the heyday of American racist mythology.

Why did I come to Pannonia? Perhaps, the trip was an old man's way of acknowledging his own past, of reconnecting with a generation of despised, now mostly dead relatives. These were the same people Martha had abandoned, but for her own reasons. As a child, I had felt so different from my parents that I often entertained the commonplace notion that they were not my real parents. By the time I was in high school, I was terrified of being sucked into the quicksand of my family's lugubrious sensibilities. You might even say I was a coldhearted proto-snob. When I went off to college in 1961, I left the family behind —forever, I hoped.

Aaron and Martha were the exceptions. Aaron was hilarious, kind-hearted, and totally disreputable, but by the time I visited Pannonia, he was long since dead. I think I sought out Martha because she, too, had been nothing like the rest of the family. For one thing, she was not a blood relation. Also, like Aaron, she loved jokes —funny ones, not the "ho-ho" variety in which several family members specialized. She also enjoyed serious conversation, which even we older children got from her straight up, not ruined by condescension or fulsome praise. Martha embodied the adage that, to get respect, you must give respect.

Was Pannonia also a furlough from my present life, the centerpiece of which is frequent contact with my daughter, her husband, and their two children? Although I love these people dearly, I confess that I often find them wearing. Finally, I may have been trying to escape from my old man's semi-isolation and fears. Am I suffering from memory lock, or did Baudelaire or Rimbaud (or someone) write:

My immortal soul, redeem yourself,
in spite of the day alone and the night on fire?

Who am I, then? A sixty-eight-year-old widower and former high-school Social Studies teacher, in generally good health, and lucky enough to possess a modest amount of what is called "disposable income." That about sums me up.

My first day in Pannonia, the day before the meeting with Martha, I visited the Jewish cemetery, where I was stunned to come upon the gravestones of three people with the same surname as mine: "Shepherd." All three had died in 1945, presumably among the Jews who were deported, then slaughtered, at the war's eleventh hour. I have never felt a personal connection with the Holocaust. So far as I knew, although we had a few ne'er-do-well Pannonian relatives-by-marriage, there were no blood relatives. As for Holocaust victims in other European countries, if we had any of those, they were never mentioned. Like me, the people of my parents' generation may have preferred to burn their bridges. Irrationally, however, even though my surname is fairly common, I identified the corpses in the cemetery with the relatives I had forsaken.

"'Mind the gap!' You must have heard that announcement in the Berlin Metro, right, Cousin Jerome?"

"Yes, I did hear it, Martha, all the time, both in English and German. But please call me 'Jerry.' No one has called me 'Jerome' in over forty years."

I sipped my lemonade. The day was sunny and hot, about 28 degrees Celsius. Martha, who had ordered an Espresso, chuckled, and it struck me that she still chuckled the same way she used to, at the childish antics of the gaggle of children in her crowded kitchen. The gaggle had comprised her three, myself, and several other cousins. This was about sixty years ago, and she had changed so much, otherwise, that the old chuckle startled me.

In those days, Martha had been so fat that, when she chuckled (or did anything else), her chins shook and the plastic apron she wore over her housecoat rustled. She also had to keep pushing her black-rimmed glasses back up on her nose, because she sweated so much. Now she was a tall, bony, threadbare, but spry, old woman (about 85, I think). She still wore glasses, but the current ones had clear plastic frames. She also still had a big mole on her left cheek.

"Sorry. 'Jerry,' it is. Well, anyway," she explained, "I guess you could say that *I*'minded the gap.'"

I thought I understood this cryptic utterance. Martha had moved to Pannonia shortly after the Tonkin Gulf Resolution (1964). Already a leftist, she must have been further radicalized by this seminal lie. By now, most Americans assume their politicians are liars, and there is probably a rock group called "Mind the Gap."

By the time she left the U.S., Martha's children were all in their teens. By then, too, she and my cousin Ben, her sententious academic husband, must have been sick of each other. Ben was the kind of man who enjoyed pulling nickels from our ears, then giving them to us. I think Martha divorced him before she left, but maybe he divorced her, for desertion. Through the fragile, but still extant, family grapevine, I do know that Ben has long since remarried. But I have no idea to whom; nor do I care.

The rest of that first meeting with Martha was spent reminiscing. She listened with a tired smile to my account of another well-worn story about Aaron. In this one, also from the 1950's, he had chaperoned two of his nephews, Ben (already Martha's husband) and his younger brother, Willy, to a lecture in New Jersey. The plan was to find a place to eat supper first. But, when their bus dropped them near the site of the lecture, they discovered that there was only one option, a small, upscale place. They went in, anyway, and, while they were waiting to be seated, Aaron looked over the fancy menu.

Knowing him, at this point, he probably winked at his nephews. Then, turning his winning smile on the *Maître d*, without preamble he said, in his most posh accent, "Well, then, my good man, you do serve terrapin soup here, don't you?" As he knew, they did not. "Pity. In that case, I guess we'll just have to look elsewhere." And I imagine him shepherding his nephews back outside while the man stood there, open-mouthed.

Although she must have heard this story many times, Martha laughed. "That's right, Jerry," she said, "Aaron was a real wag." Neither of us mentioned that his wife had divorced him when he drew all their money from a joint savings account one day and lost it at the track.

As she had already told me, Martha was a freelance translator. After about an hour's conversation, she announced that she had to return to work. But first she invited me to a gathering of "a few friends" at one of their homes the next evening, specifying that drinks and dessert would be served (which implied that dinner would not). "You'll get to meet some specimens of the Pannonian intelligentsia, Cousin Jerry," she said. "My friends. A bunch of characters!"

I accepted the invitation readily, not only because I am always interested in meeting new people, but because I was curious about the kind of friends Martha would have. She gave me the address of her friend's place, and directions from my two-star hotel, which was in the hills just outside of town on one of the main tramlines. I had already ridden the tram, the screeching of which happily evoked the trolley cars of my Bronx childhood.

The next evening, the weather was still hot and humid. (When I got home a week later, I would read about severe rainstorms and flooding across central Europe, including Pannonia. There were pictures of people rowing down the streets in the cities and towns.) Arriving a few fashionable minutes late, I was handed a small plate of cookies and a glass of the local sweet wine. Martha brought me over to a group of five who were seated on a couch and straight chairs. Like her, three of them were wearing old-fashioned, well-worn clothes, but the other two were conspicuously chic. The woman wore garish make-up and a black-and-white art deco outfit, and the man sported a sort of modified toreador suit. One of the un-chic women was strikingly beautiful.

"This is my cousin Jerry from New York, everyone." They made room for me on the couch, and Martha introduced them, one by one. The women were both journalists. One of the men was a colleague of Martha's. The toreador was a playwright, and the last man was a poet and the night manager of a small hotel. Introductions completed, Martha left us for another group.

After some pleasantries, they asked me what I had done in Pannonia so far. I told them about the cemetery and about my visit to the excellent art museum that afternoon. I mentioned that a guard whom I had chatted up had told me that, even on the streets of her hometown, Sarajevo, smoking was now banned.

"The wave of the future," remarked the stylish woman, sounding disgusted. She took a long drag on her cigarette, which she smoked through a holder. "No one in the whole world will be permitted to smoke anymore. There will be a pandemic of suicides." Everyone laughed. About half the other people in the room were smoking, two or three, pipes; the rest, cigarettes.

"Were there any paintings you particularly admired, Mr. Shepherd?" asked the tall angular beauty, whom I had already mentally undressed.

"Well, there were so many ... it's hard to say. But I certainly won't forget Jan Steen's 'The Pregnant Bride.'" There were several knowing nods. This painting depicts an old man leading his obviously pregnant bride away from a party, while a wag makes the "cuckoo" sign behind his back.

"Have you visited our celebrated Cathedral yet, Jerry?" asked the toreador. I said that I had. "Did you happen to encounter the toothache statue?" Since I had not, he enlightened me.

Apparently, in the Apostles' Nave of the Cathedral, visitors come upon a statue of the Gothic Man of Sorrows, or "Toothache Lord." The soubriquet stems from a legend. A group of drunken fools were stumbling around the church one night when they came upon the statue and mocked it, claiming it looked as if our Lord were suffering from toothache. They even went so far as to tie a cloth around the statue's head. Immediately, every one of the drunks was stricken with severe toothache, from which they did not recover until they had abased themselves before the statue.

As the story was being told, my fellow-listeners wore knowing smiles, and when I laughed at the punch line, they all joined in. At this point, predictably, our talk turned to politics. The beauty referred to what was called "The Big Lie."

"The Big Lie is that Pannonia is now a democracy."

The others nodded knowingly, and the night manager explained. Speaking in heavily accented English, and looking over his shoulder from time to time, which I surmised was a vestige of the Soviet era, which had only ended in the early 1990's, he repeatedly apologized.

"I'm sorry, Mr. Jerry," he said, "I don't want to spoil your visit, but …" and "I don't want to interrupt the conversation, but …Sixty-six percent of our population voted for this right-wing government of ours. And every month, they are enacting terrible new laws, such as media censorship with severe penalties, including prison, for even the most trivial offenses. Their latest one, would you believe it, is straight from Franz Kafka. It imposes fines on people for being homeless!"

"That's ridiculous!" I said. "How are they supposed to pay?"

"Exactly," said the beauty.

I did not have to ask the hotel manager how the right-wing party had managed to wrest two-thirds of the vote from the incumbents. The general shabbiness and sense of deprivation in what I had seen of Pannonia confirmed what I had read before the trip: in six years, the previous party had ruined what had already been a weak economy.

As is often the case, politics, which fueled the conversation for a while, killed it. As our group dispersed, to my regret I noticed that the beauty appeared to be attached to the toreador. The party quickly wound down.

Martha and I agreed to meet again at our café, this time for lunch two days later, just before I was scheduled to decamp for Vienna. As she showed me out, since no one asked me for contact information, I just uttered a general goodbye to the room. It was only about ten-thirty, and the trams were still running, so I declined her offer to escort me back to my hotel, and easily found my own way. Back in the large, comfortable room, I read myself to sleep over the memoirs of a heroic policeman during Pannonia's abortive rising against the Russians during the 1970's. By the time he wrote the book, the man was working as a janitor in Toronto.

I spent most of the next day on two long boat rides along the Danube, disembarking from the first one at the celebrated Castle for an hour or two. When both ferryboat conductors glanced at my transportation pass and waved me aboard without asking for additional fares, I wondered if their largesse was a vestige of the Communist era. As the boat meandered through the city, stopping along both banks, the fresh river breezes were a welcome relief from the heat and humidity. My day ended with dinner at a small, quiet place Martha had recommended. The food was fair.

When we met again the next day, it felt as though the ice had been broken at the party, as if I had passed some sort of test. Ordering beer and sandwiches, which I insisted I would pay for, we settled down for what I hoped would be a long talk. The first few sips of beer quickly turned the café into a confessional.

I began by bluntly asking her, "Tell me again, Martha, exactly what made you come to Pannonia? Of course, I heard stories, mostly from my father, when he was alive, but …" I shrugged. My father had been a notoriously unreliable narrator.

"As you know, Cousin Jerry," she began, "many people in our family were Socialists or Anarchists. In 1965, I fled the United States, in particular the military-industrial complex." She sounded as if as if she were reading from a prepared text. I had served in the Vietnam War, myself, as a clerk at a naval base in California, but I did not think it would be wise to mention that now. After another sip of beer, she continued.

"So. I came to Pannonia with the notion that my skills as a translator could serve the Party." She shook her head in disgust. "Ha! Almost from the start, I was subjected to constant political harassment." She mimicked her harassers. "'Are you an American spy, Martha? Why did you really come here, Martha?' So. At regular intervals, I was thrown in jail. I was banned from all but the worst jobs, etc. etc." She shook her head again.

"Then, in 1993, Mr. Gorbachev 'tore down that wall.' "She mimicked Reagan poorly. "No more Russians! Wasn't that wonderful? Of course, ever since that 'seminal event,' after which our 'Communist oppressors' fled back to Russia with their tails between their legs, capitalism has been creeping and roaring across central Europe."

She paused to take a few bites from her sandwich and another sip of beer, which appeared to calm her down. "Now I work as a translator again, but I'm really just a poor old woman who has been left behind by history. So. Is Socialism even possible in the world, anymore? Where should I go now, Cousin Jerry?" She sighed deeply, looking so sad I felt like weeping, myself.

"Do you want to return to the States, Martha?" I asked. "I'm sure you've thought of it."

She produced a tired smile. "Of course I have. Hundreds of times. But no, I don't want to go back. Has anything really changed since Viet Nam? Only for the worse, I'm afraid." She shook her head in disgust. "Anyway, who would be glad to see me? Oh, I know everyone would be polite, and they would make sure I wasn't thrown out on the streets. But going back would be horrible. So. For better or worse, Pannonia is my home now. And the people you met the other night are my only 'family.'"

We lapsed into silence, and I thought of Henry James' dichotomy between American innocents and European sophisticates. Which was Martha?

Suddenly, my memory was flooded by horrible images of my family: all those sick people, the diabetics with amputated limbs, the sufferers from cardiac and other diseases, the schizophrenics and bi-polars. I forced myself to remember that there had also been people in the family who were relatively normal —like Martha's children, who, I had heard, were now an English professor, a psychoanalyst, and a successful something else. But this hopeful thought was driven off by a vivid memory of the day I had loaded my sister into an ambulance and shepherded her to a mental hospital, where, three years later, aged 29, she had died under "uncertain circumstances" — suicide, presumably. I also remembered the account my mother had given me, when I was "old enough," of the marriage of two first cousins from the Canadian branch, who had produced a handicapped child, after which the man had turned the gas on his little family.

For the minute or two during which I revisited these terrible memories, Martha and I sat in silence beneath our umbrella on the hot plaza. We picked at our food, twirled our beer glasses, and watched the trams and people come and go. Pannonians, I noticed, had a distinctive way of walking. They took stiff steps that caused a tremor in their whole bodies and held their arms stiffly against their sides. When the silence grew oppressive, I called for the bill and paid. Martha thanked me.

We got up and embraced (kisses on both cheeks, Pannonian style). Then, we stood on the pavement for another moment or two. She looked at me sympathetically.

"I'm sorry, Cousin Jerome. You should have stayed at home, or just skipped Pannonia." That was her valediction. We walked off in opposite directions, and I anticipated that I would never see her again. Would I even hear the news of her death --or vice-versa?

The Card Players

"Do you play Baseball, Elizabeth?" asked Judy, the dealer.

"Sure," said Elizabeth, throwing in a red chip, her ante. "Threes and nines wild, an extra card for each four, you can show a four-in-the-hole at any point in the hand." The stakes were penny (white), nickel (red), dime (blue), maximum of three raises ––the usual, for penny poker.

"Hey! There's a fox in the hen house!" cried Rose, the third player.

A friend from New York, Elizabeth was spending the week with Judy and her husband, Mel, at their summer place in Maine. The women were seated around an old oak table in the kitchen. Since Rose did not like games with multiple wild cards, which she called "*chazerei* poker," she looked a bit grim. ("*Chazerei*" is a Yiddish pejorative, derived from "*khazer,*" meaning "pig.")

Twenty years earlier, Judy and Mel had fixed up an old farmhouse on Bear Isle, a small island on the coast of Maine. This meant that they, like their good friends, Rose and her husband, James, who owned a similar house just up the road, occupied a middling position on the Bear Isle totem pole. At the apex were families whose progenitors had been resident "forever," followed, in descending order, by those who had bought, or built, houses within living memory, and so on, all the way down to summer renters, and, at the bottom, day-trippers. Even though she outranked only the day-trippers, had Elizabeth known about the totem pole, she would have been amused.

Judy dealt the first three cards, two down and one up. Elizabeth showed a nine, Rose, a jack, and Judy, a deuce. With a friendly smile, Elizabeth slid a red chip toward the center of the table.

"Oh, god!" cried Rose. "I knew we shouldn't have invited her!"

"I bet she's got an ace and a four in the hole," Judy guessed. Although her own hole cards were a six and a ten, she called Elizabeth's bet, and slapped a blue chip down on top of the reds. "Raise you a dime."

In fact, Elizabeth's hole cards were a four and a nine. Although Rose also had a four and a nine in the hole, as she added a blue chip and a red to the pot, she looked as if she were drawing her own blood. Elizabeth called Judy's raise.

Earlier in the game, Judy and Rose had been talking about their husbands. "Mel," Judy said, "thinks he can find places without looking at the map. The first time we drove up here —this was way before the GPS era-- we wound up in the village of Passamaquoddy —Ruth knows this story, Elizabeth-- because he didn't realize the sign wasn't for Passamaquoddy *Bay*--which is where this place, Bear Isle, is."

"Passamaquoddy is a lovely village," said Rose. "Maybe, we can drive over for a picnic this week. It's only about twenty minutes from here."

"Sounds like a great idea, Rose," said Elizabeth. "How do you spell 'Passamaquoddy'?"

"p-a-s-a" Judy began.

"No, two s's," Rose corrected her. "It's 'p-a-s-s-a-m-o' ... or is it an 'a'?

They all laughed, and, dropping the matter, resumed play.

As the last three "up" cards in the Baseball hand were dealt, the betting remained unchanged. Elizabeth, whose wild nine and king were still the high cards showing, kept betting a nickel. Judy would raise a dime, and Rose and Elizabeth would call, but not raise.

"This is getting too rich for my blood," complained Rose, who had been winning steadily since play began, about an hour before.

"Yeah, right, Rose!" scoffed Judy. "Too rich for your blood!"

Judy and Mel, and Rose and James, were all visual artists who earned the bulk of their middling incomes from teaching. Elizabeth, a widow, was the Director of a mid-sized social work agency.

By the time Judy had dealt the third "down" card, she was showing the deuce, a five, seven and jack. Since her hole cards were two sixes and a ten, all she had was a measly pair of sixes. Before the final round of betting could even begin, without deferring to Elizabeth's pair of kings, she tossed her cards onto the pile of chips, and declared, "Damn! I should have folded long ago."

Like James, her husband, Rose was a good player, which meant she kept track of the cards, and knew how to build a pot and, occasionally, to bluff, all without being obvious. But, also like James, Rose had a "tell." His was to push his glasses up on his nose when he was bluffing; hers, to complain when she had a strong hand. Judy had seen both of these "tells" many times, without recognizing them. Elizabeth, who was already wise to Rose's complaining, had sized her up as a greedy, but kind, person.

The physical and sartorial types of the three women, all in their sixties, matched their personalities. Impulsive and generous, Judy was wiry, gray-haired, tan and wrinkled — walnut-like. Her usual costume was a pair of old-paint-spattered jeans and a dark turtleneck shirt, also paint-spattered. Rose, slightly taller and much heavier, dyed her short hair black, and affected the garb of a latter-day hippie: non-leather sandals, Muu-Muu's in earth colors, and jewelry made from rawhide and Native American beads. Elizabeth, tall and hefty, wore elaborate make up, and dyed her hair a reddish-honey color. Deferring to the custom of the country, she was sporting blue jeans tonight —new ones --with a subdued green-and-brown plaid flannel shirt.

Judy's rashness was one reason for the single-sex game. Earlier in the summer, she had tried to fill an inside straight when all four sevens, the card she needed, were already showing. (There were no wild cards.) Pretending to tear his hair out, Mel made a joke about bankruptcy, and announced that he would never play poker with Judy again. After at least a decade of co-ed poker involving the two couples, plus Mary, the owner of a knitting shop in town, this was tantamount to more than a trial separation. The reason there were only three players this evening was that Mary had a prior engagement, a meeting of the Bear Isle Cemetery Committee.

Having drawn a three as her final hole card, Elizabeth turned over her four, and drew another king. Rose also turned over her four and drew the ten of spades. Elizabeth bet a dime, and, when Rose, whose third hole card was the Queen of Spades, pretended, once more, to hesitate, Judy piped up again. These interruptions were another reason Mel had banished her.

"I bet you didn't know," she said, "that two of the top three women players in the world last year were both named 'Vanessa'?"

When Elizabeth (willingly) and Rose (reluctantly) took the bait, the hand was temporarily suspended. After they had speculated briefly about names and personalities, the conversation turned to the more interesting subject of poker and gender.

"Why do you think?" asked Judy, "most of the top players are men?"

"Probably because," Elizabeth suggested, "most of the *players* are men." She pondered the question further. "Actually, all things being equal, I think women would be better. Aren't we more dispassionate? (Less testosterone.) And more sensitive to non-verbal cues?"

"On the other hand," Rose rejoined, "we may not be aggressive enough."

Elizabeth nodded in agreement.

"I sometimes think," Judy chimed in, with a wry smile, "that poker is an example of arrested development in men. Maybe, it's a socially acceptable form of the circle jerk."

Elizabeth and Rose laughed heartily, neither asking the obvious question of what Judy thought they, the women, were doing.

The moment of truth arrived. As Judy looked on gleefully, like a child at the circus, Rose raised Elizabeth's dime, a dime; Elizabeth raised her back a dime; and Rose raised a final dime. Rose seemed more nervous than ever, but Elizabeth was calm --as she should have been, with five kings, which beat the crestfallen Rose's straight flush. That it was a six-card straight flush made the defeat even more rankling. As she hauled in the largest pot of the evening, which amounted to about two dollars, Elizabeth felt sorry for Rose, whose pile of chips was now diminished to about the same size as her own, and for Judy, who was left with a forlorn little stack of eight or ten, most of them white.

"Wow!" said Judy. "That was exciting! Let's break for coffee and dessert now. Since I take regular, and Rose takes decaf, you can have either, Elizabeth."

"Regular, please."

The women stood up and stretched. Cream and sugar, and cups, plates, flatware and paper napkins had already been set out on the marble counter between sink and stove, and three high stools were also in place. Soon, the coffee was ready. Since Elizabeth was weight-conscious, when the blueberry pie, plus the vanilla *a la mode*, made its appearance, she demurred. Even so, she echoed Rose's "oohs" and "aahs." Judy was known, to locals and summer residents alike, as one of the best bakers on the island. Earlier in the summer, in fact, her upside-down pineapple cake, made from a modified old Fanny Farmer recipe, had won a blue ribbon at the Passamaquoddy Bay Agricultural Fair.

At that moment, coincidentally, the men were hoping the women would save them some pie. "Bad at cards, wonderful at baking," Mel quipped to James, who had known this for years.

They were in the red barn attached to James and Rose's house, inspecting James's new paintings. "I have a hunch our guest may be a sharper," Mel added. "Maybe, we should ask her to play with us."

"Sure," said James, "but, then, you'd have to let Judy back in."

"Good point."

James pushed his glasses up on his nose. "By the way, is Elizabeth married?" Mel raised an eyebrow. "Just curious," James added.

"She's a widow. At dinner last night, she told us all about her late husband, Bill. He was the Managing Agent for a string of apartment houses in Brooklyn. He sounds —sounded-- like an amusing guy. He barely came up to her shoulder, dressed like an old-fashioned *boulevardier*—bowtie, suspenders, silk vest—and smoked a pipe."

"Was he a poker player?"

"He didn't sound like one."

Mel was wrong. Again, by coincidence, still at the kitchen counter, Elizabeth was narrating Bill's exploits.

"He was really good," she said. "Because he was so short and tubby..." Judy and Rose laughed, Rose, at the matter-of-factness, Judy, at the image. "...the other players would assume he was a mark, a sucker.

"In one game, oh, ten, fifteen years ago, he was playing with this famous artist, who shall go unnamed, and a bunch of the artist's rich friends. The game was in the artist's loft. The stakes were high, the play, fierce. They..."

Rose interrupted. "Nickel, dime, quarter? Higher?"

"Much higher," Elizabeth replied. "I can't remember exactly."

"Wow!" said Judy, who was imagining Mel's reaction if she ever came home from such a game and told him how much she had lost.

"Anyway, there was a shark at the table, an investment broker, as I recall, and a collector-friend of the artist's. Talk about testosterone! This guy was later indicted for insider trading --it was in the paper. I can't remember if he was convicted. A real blowhard, the kind of guy Bill hated.

"Anyway, there was this hand where Bill saw a chance to pull one of his bluffs. The broker had been winning almost every hand and boasting non-stop. I'm sure you can imagine the kind of trash he was talking." She paused for a sip of coffee.

With a barking laugh, jumping to her feet, and clutching her crotch, Judy clumped menacingly around the kitchen. "Ha, ha, suckers!" she said, in a deep voice with an exaggerated New York accent. "Got you by the shorties now! Ha, ha!" Rose and Elizabeth laughed, Judy climbed back up onto her stool, and Elizabeth resumed the story.

"Anyway, it was a big pot, seven-card stud, nothing wild. Bill bet the hand as if he had a straight flush, but was betting modestly to keep the other players in. When the last card was dealt, he pretended to drop the pretense, and bet the max —oh, I remember now, it was twenty dollars." Judy and Rose whistled.

"By then, everyone else had folded, it was just Bill and the broker. When Bill made the big bet, the broker studied his own hand for a very long time and kept staring at Bill's down cards as if he were trying to see through them.

"The basis of Bill's bluff was that he was showing a kangaroo straight —six, eight, ten, Queen-- all hearts. The bluff, of course, was to act as if two of his hole cards were hearts that would have filled the straight flush." Elizabeth was discrete enough not to mention Ruth's losing Baseball hand.

"Eventually, the broker muttered a string of curses, slammed his cards down, and asked Bill whether he really had the straight flush. The host, who was pretty bold, himself, reminded the broker that, since no one had called Bill's last bet, he was not obliged to show his hole cards.

"'That's okay,' Bill said. 'I don't mind.' And, one by one, he turned the hole cards over, then scooped the money onto his pile. There must have been two hundred dollars in the pot. As I recall, what Bill really had was a pair of eights --or was it tens? The broker looked as if he were about to have a coronary.

"When he told me the story in bed that night, Bill ended by saying, with one of his little chuckles, 'Of course, I assumed the guy wasn't packing.' A gun, that is. Actually, Bill used to 'pack,' himself, sort of. When he went around collecting rents, he always carried an unloaded Derringer in his attache' case."

"Whew," whistled Judy.

"Wow!" said Rose. "He sounds like a pisser. What about the other game you mentioned?"

"Oh, that was years before the one I just told you about. We were visiting Bill's parents in Florida, and he got into a big game with some retired guys. I don't need to go into the details. The point is that, to these guys, Bill looked like a fish."

"Which he was anything but," said Judy.

Rose waxed thoughtful. "You know what the moral of that first story —both stories, really-- is, Elizabeth? I hope you won't think I'm being presumptuous, but it feels as if we're already friends." Elizabeth nodded encouragingly. "I think the reason Bill was such a good player was that he was a lot like a woman!"

Laughing heartily, the women returned to the table, and the game was resumed.

Ron Singer

A Nose for A Jacket

Sposibo, Nikolai

He looked like a man who might order tai chi in a Korean restaurant just for a joke. Fatuous smile, waiting for the "boom!" --you know the type. No doubt I only thought this because he was wearing my jacket and I wanted a pretext for aggression. Not that I'm into that tired stuff about nemeses or doppelgangers, but his age (early 60's), shape (pear top, stick legs) and stature (5'11", 175, 180), were so similar to mine that one glance told me the jacket was a 42 long. Of course, he did not otherwise look like me: red face, silver hair, button-nose. Never mind how I look; you don't need to know. Are you going to buy me? Turn me in? Too late.

His jacket was the prosperous twin of mine. The color was that mossy green, my second favorite. Mine, now milk chocolate, but still rich milk chocolate, thirty-some years old, was so torn and frayed it could no longer be mended, and it made people look at me as if I were homeless (which I am not). His jacket had so little wear on it that, for whatever reason, it must have spent most of its life in a closet --a second "reason" he did not deserve to keep it.

Without going overboard, let me say why I love these jackets. Made of durable, excellent material, they are beautifully tailored so that, although generously cut, they hang perfectly. And they have many capacious pockets. In fact, he had what looked like a trade paperback peeping from his left side pocket. Remember that.

I saw two options. I could cozy up to the guy. It was a nice Fall day, low humidity, crisp air, people in a good mood, corduroy jacket-wearing weather.

"Excuse me. Nice jacket! Isn't that an old Sweet-Orr Norfolk jacket?"

"Yes, it is." Smile of recognition. "Same as yours."

"Yup, but how come yours is still in such good condition?"

Then, I'd offer him a lot of money --say, $200, when the original had cost $30 around 1970, when I bought mine, and risen to $40 in the early 80's, which was when they stopped making them and were selling off the last few ...dozen? ... hundred? ... thousand? Of course, I should have bought five, but I had been brain-locked: the $10 add-on seemed outrageous. By now, both the $10 add-on and my reaction seemed quaint --stupid, that is.

The second option was to steal the jacket, try to arrange one of those eventualities for which restaurants "are not responsible." Of course, I had to decide in advance: if I approached the guy and he declined, there was no going on to Plan B. A court appearance with possible etcetera's was not an acceptable option.

I'm sure you already suspect I had come to this juncture by --as they say-- a tortuous route. Multiple mendings, obviously. There had been near misses in thrift shops --almost the right size, disgusting, irremediable stains or smells, ugly fading of one arm and shoulder. There had been attempts to cajole a jacket from my cousin (44 regular), who had met the $10 price rise more sensibly and bought an extra, so that both of his --one green, one navy-- were still in fair-to-good condition. And, recently, there had even been a forlorn googling venture -- "Sweet-Orr corduroy Norfolk jacket"-- which got me to

Sweet-Orr, which was (now?) a South African company that made many (other) fine products; and got me to many other, unwanted corduroy products; and to many jackets that were totally irrelevant; and to tourist web sites all over England--not just Norfolk, not even just coastal shires. E-Bay, too, in case you're wondering, was a bust: zero items. I hate going on-line, period, it's like jerking off with a parking meter ticking. Boom. Which brings us back to that fine Autumn day when I saw the guy in the green Norfolk jacket walking north on the west side of Broadway between 111th and 112th streets.

He was alone, not a window-shopper, but still with the look of an aimless stroller, or, more quaintly, someone out for an early evening pre-prandial. A self-satisfied type: look at me, I love nature, I have few pressing cares, my health is good for my age, enough money, big co-op on a fairly quiet street, wife loves me, retired early, nice profile, wise investments. Aside from the essential article, he wore khakis with cuffs and shiny brown loafers. In truth, he looked like a decent, unexceptionable, mind-his-own-business type of guy. Never mind, he'd pay for being alive (and having a nicer jacket).

I had trailed him for two blocks now, long enough to decide that theft was the better option. Why? He looked like a guy who wanted his old, good jacket more than money he didn't need.

How could I? Choose your own explanation: mid-life boredom (I was not currently "seeing" anyone), ennui from the recent retirement (ha!), or --let's get fancy-- the allure of a homeopathic remedy for danger in the post 9/11 world. That one could be a whole book --a whole bad book.

Are you bothered by my immorality --or is it amorality? I used to worry about things like that, but at some juncture impossible to identify I reached what might be called an ethical tipping point. Maybe it was Ruanda, a fight over a parking space, maybe Florida --who cares? All I cared about was getting the jacket and not getting caught. Which did I care about more? The next half hour or so would tell. Think of it as a trade-in: his jacket for mine plus seventy-three ethical gold stars.

I hoped he was planning to stop for an early meal at one of the rows of restaurants which dot both sides of Broadway between 110th and 116th streets. Pitter, patter went my heart. I hoped it would be a warm restaurant, a restaurant with a coat rack away from the booths, preferably up front. I hoped he would read his book (remember?) or be meeting a dinner partner he was interested in, so his attention would be elsewhere than the coat rack. I hoped there would be a bar or counter near the coat rack. Of course, all these hopes together were too much to hope for, but some of them might pan out. My plan, obviously, was to pull the old substitute-jacket caper.

You still don't believe I would steal the jacket, do you? You think I'm trying to con you. Oh, well, people crave explanations. It's the wiring.

One (repeat): temperamentally unsuitable for retirement.

Two (morally unhinged): eighteen months ago, and about three years after the "amicable divorce," my wife died, leaving a note for me --a cancer note, not a suicide—apologizing (sort of) for the fact that, for more than twenty years, she had been sleeping with a cousin of hers, female. As the boom-boom saying goes, she had been "seeing another woman."

Two-A (hidden anger): had I only known, I could have just cheated on her, kept it simple. I'm a "don't hit first but hit back hard" man. Witness my lame pretexts for stealing the jacket.

Three (same as Two): last Fall, a niece of mine, a nineteen-year-old college kid, asked me to sell her car for her. She chose me because I had the time (definitely) and because she was afraid to do it herself: the car could be relied upon to stall in wet weather. Does youth see into our souls? One sunny afternoon, I sold the car to an immigrant who paid cash, a shoemaker from Uzbekistan, an honest, hardworking man who kept saying, "I trust you, you look like honest man." The act caused me two sleepless nights and an attack of benign vertigo --dizziness, with the visual field broken into diamond-like patterns (very pretty) -- fender-benders on my ride down the interesting, exciting, wonderful slippery slope. I'm trying to remember the exact date of the car sale, sometime in late September. Maybe the jacket was an anniversary.

Four (disdain for law and order): for years, even before it became fashionable, I had been an inveterate jaywalker, on the theory that it is often safer to cross a street --cautiously-- wherever there is a break in traffic, than to risk getting salami-ed by a turning maniac at the corner.

My wife said, "There's something wrong with you, you love to take small risks and break small rules. A nine-year-old boy is trapped inside your brain, and, some day, if you don't watch out, he'll escape. Assuming you don't get puddled first."

Enough? Please say that's enough. Motives bad, story good.

My plan had a couple of things going for it. I would be seen coming in wearing a Norfolk jacket in a muted color and leaving in one. (If that advantage is not obvious, imagine me coming in wearing, say, a red baseball jacket and leaving in a green Norfolk jacket.) If I was stopped, there was even a chance I could pass off the failed theft as an "honest mistake." Finally, if he was as sensible as he looked, the victim would not even have to go home chilly: he could wear my jacket. Maybe, he'd leave a notice at the restaurant asking if "the person who innocently took my old green corduroy jacket instead of his own brown one at 6:15 on September 28th would kindly call [phone number]." Maybe, he'd even offer a modest reward. Sentimental value.

I was right about his intention to eat a 6:15 supper. Almost immediately, he turned into a small Korean place I had never been in before (Korean being about my eighth-favorite cuisine). One potential disadvantage was that there were sidewalk tables, but there was no one at any of them just now. It was lucky, too, that he turned into the restaurant only a few minutes after I had first started tailing him, and that the sidewalk was still crowded with people (unretired people) on their way home.

Through the door, I saw him (his shadow) make his way in, hang his jacket on the (yes!) coat rack across from the (yes!) front counter, then wait to be seated. He was led to a booth in the back, and I gave it twenty beats before I followed him in and hung my own jacket on the rack. His lovely jacket was right in front, unimpeded, like a ripe fruit on a low limb. I sat down at the counter and ordered a Korean beer and Korean pancake appetizer. Then, I noticed a negative: the whole place was mirrored. Without even turning my head at the counter, I could see him clearly all the way in back, studying the menu. The mirror mandated caution. But so what? Was I planning to be careless?

Given that most clocks are off by at least a few seconds, the caper worked like clockwork. Just as I finished my beer (lousy) and pancake (greasy, but not bad), he put down his (yes) book and headed back to, presumably, the rest room. The counter man brought my check --$8.35-- and I dropped a ten, pinning it with the beer bottle, the bottom of which I dried first with my still-clean paper napkin. Hurrying without hurrying, I put on his jacket, suffered an infarction which went into immediate remission, stretched, waited three beats for something to announce the collapse of my stupid plan, fought off the urge to put the jacket back and pantomime "What a dumb mistake," then walked out onto Broadway.

By the time I had sauntered across the Columbia campus to Amsterdam and turned back south, I had stopped sweating into my new jacket. I still had the urge to return the jacket, but I realized that, by now, "What a dumb mistake!" was, at best, problematic. Besides, the urge had grown weak, very.

The whole way across campus, past the big library, the steps in front, full of students reading and horsing around, and through the narrow file of buildings on the eastern end, I had been enjoying a blind inventory of the pockets. My best guess was that they contained a broken rubber band, a small plastic container of tic-tacs, some sort of business card, lint, a paper clip, and the stub from a theater, concert or movie ticket. In front of the big cathedral, St. John the Divine, I took the stuff out. The business card was from a midtown deli, the ticket stub from a Lincoln Center concert the week before (chamber music at the lovely Alice Tully Hall), and the tic-tacs, orange.

I waited until I got home, and, when I grew tired of checking myself out in the full-length mirror in the foyer -- great!-- I threw away everything except the paper clip, which I added to the half-full --not half-empty-- box on my desk. I then rinsed my sweaty hands and decided where to go in my new jacket. Amicably divorced (only her cousin knows), no children, recently retired with a well-planned 401k, I am, as they say, my own man. I would go for a long walk and a real dinner. Maybe a little shoplifting, for dessert.

A week later, I decided to try to snag a last-minute ticket for the Borodin Quartet playing Haydn, Dinklewasser and Beethoven at Alice Tully. Wearing the --my-- new jacket. Why?

I'll go with the homeopathic remedy for 9/11. Or maybe it was my wife's death/ death note. Or the used car deal. Or something. They say it's easier --to do wrong, to take ridiculous chances, whatever-- the second time.

This time, the clockwork malfunctioned. Not right away, though. I arrived with the clock (and my heart) beating right along and got a good seat. Why not? It was Tuesday, and chamber music is on demographic life support. I enjoyed the Haydn warm-up and even the Boro's strenuous attempts -- prodigious grunts, tinkles, shrieks and grinds-- to turn the modern pig into a silk purse.

Intermission. Heading out into the lobby for a pee and a look-see, I eagerly awaited the Beethoven, one of the Razumovsky quartets, which are among my absolute favorites. (I even love the name.) It was, as you must know, not to be. I barely made it out of the men's room.

"Well, well, well," said an unfamiliar baritone. A hand firmly gripped my left elbow, the clock stopped, and the urbane, the genteel, the civilized evening turned into a cartoon. The third thing I noticed, after his almost painfully strong grip and big, incredulous grin was that he was not wearing my jacket. Something tweed.

"Don't try to run, or I'll knock you down, dislocate your shoulder, and --see? over there? -- call for Security." He gestured with his head toward a large African-American about thirty feet away, wearing a green blazer, an ear piece and a bland half-smile, and leaning against a wall with his hands clasped behind his back as he scanned the crowd like a closed-circuit TV camera.

"But you can't ... "I started to bluff, gathering umbrage.

"Oh, no? Look-y here," and in his other hand was an open billfold with a big, real-looking gold shield. "This time, my friend, you picked the wrong guy."

"But how..."

"Are you kidding! All those mirrors? Jesus! Plus three solid wits. Stu-pid!"

"But who...?"

By now, he had put the billfold away, so he had a free hand with which to tick off the witnesses. "One. The counterman. Two: the Mexican busboy from the restaurant next door, who saw you go into the Korean restaurant wearing, quote, 'a brown jacket for a bum,' unquote. He wondered what happened in the half hour you were inside that 'change this shitty jacket to a green, nice one.'" The detective did a decent imitation. Three: the woman on the stool to your left. Did you think she was blind? 'When he put the wrong jacket on, his eyes were, like, pinball-ling. I really thought he was, like, going to faint.' "An undergrad at Barnard, very observant and also, by the way, attractive and funny. How could you not have noticed her?"

"I was busy," I muttered pathetically as he nattered on. But I saw a glimmer of hope: this was a vain man.

"Well, you'll get to be in the same room with her again, pal. Or the next one, anyhow. Of course, you won't get to see her, since she'll be behind a one-way mirror picking you out of a line-up." The glimmer faded.

By then, he had relaxed his grip, sensing correctly that I had no intention of trying to run. He went on talking, and, by the time the lights began to flicker us back to our seats, he had copied information from two pieces of photo I.D. and made a rude reference to the Mayor's crack-down on crimes just like the one I had botched. The only thing he omitted was the TV fright speech about what happened to guys like me in jail.

"Well," he said, when the flickering started, "you've finally found a little luck, my friend. I want to hear this. I love the Razumovsky. So suppose you call me at, say, 11:15 tomorrow morning, and we'll take it from there. Don't forget!" And, warning me what would happen if I did forget, he handed me his cop business card, the address on which, I noticed, was right near the deli with the business card that had been in his jacket pocket. Hindsight told me something I should have realized in the first place: who else carries business cards from delis?

"Are you, uh...?" He made a mock-courtly hand gesture to indicate that I could re-enter the auditorium in front of him. Inside, I could hear the quartet tuning up, but no Siren could now have coaxed me back in.

"No, thanks," I said, turning on my heel toward the glass doors, the entrance/exit of Alice Tully. "You've ruined my evening. But enjoy the music."

"Don't forget to call." And to come face the music.

As I hurried north on Broadway, I realized that the --shall we say? -- dick had not even made me give him back his jacket. Why should he have? And bother carrying it home? He knew I would deliver it to his office.

Out of his grip and presence, for the time being, at least, I semi-recovered and began to wonder what the other concertgoers had made of our chance encounter. Anyone listening might have assumed we were acquaintances who had run into each other and just agreed to meet again. What they would have made of the fact that one of the acquaintances looked as if he were tormenting the other --mortified-- acquaintance, you can decide. Most likely, nothing. This was

New York, where people are always fighting, always having these little vexed, overheated encounters.

I remembered a few years back to when I had my hernia operation. A week later, as the doctor was removing the stitches, I had been showing off what a brave, urbane fellow I was by regaling him with amusing patter. (Never mind that my dreams all week had been like Freudian mariachi events.) He had already asked me about the pain, etc., and I had John Wayned that part.

"Walking down the street, though," I admitted, "was something else. My, er, parts would get stuck to the bandage, and I'd have to reach in there to re-arrange things. I was afraid I'd be arrested for public obscenity."

"In New York?" Snip snip. He smiled. "No one even noticed." Snip.

"Afraid I'd be arrested." Very funny.

After a night you can imagine, and a morning spent walking around my neighborhood looking at clocks, I called him at the appointed nanosecond. He was there.

"Shepherd, here." Let that pass (the name).

"Hi, it's Wolf." That, too. The names are fictitious.

"Well, glad you called, Mr. Wolf."

"Did you expect me to flee to South America or something?" I was jumpy, of course.

"No, no, of course not," he chuckled. "Well. Are you ready to come turn yourself in? Bring the jacket, please. Be here at..." (pause to consult a palm pilot, no, desk calendar) "... at three-fifteen sharp. Tell the guard in the lobby you have an appointment with me, they'll let you through. See you, then." And, unceremoniously, he hung up.

I went, of course. To anticipate, with credit for time served, eighteen hours and twenty-five minutes, my remaining sentence was the equivalent of fifty lashes of mortification plus about fifteen minutes in the stocks.

When I arrived, wearing a nubby green sweater, his name, as promised/threatened, got me into the building. I rode the elevator to eleven, he was right there. Like a TV detective, his shirt sleeves were rolled up, tie loose. He took his feet off the desk, jumped up and, with a big grin, offered me his hand. Wondering which way the wind was blowing, I reached out to shake the proffered hand.

"Er, no," he said, still looking amused, and pointed toward the shopping bag in my other hand. I gave it to him, and he peeped inside. "Good. I assume it's in the same condition as when you stole it?" I nodded my assent, wondering what was next, and he put the bag under the desk. The stocks and lashing were next.

"Hey, everyone," he called in a voice which carried easily across the big room. Thirty or forty people looked up. "Check this out! Anyone who's free, come over here a minute. Come on, folks, up off your asses," he coaxed. "Believe me, this is worth getting up for."

And when the crowd had assembled --about half of those called-- he proceeded to a detailed account of the "crime." He was right: they loved it. Why should a group of hardened professionals have found a bungled theft so funny? They must have heard hundreds of these anecdotes, some of them hundreds of times funnier. How about the bank robber who signed the note with his real name? (And it wasn't "Smith" or "Jones.") How about the serial killer who had been illegally parked? That one wasn't so funny. Or did you hear the one about...

...the guy who tried to steal a detective's jacket from a small mirrored restaurant with his hands shaking like leaves, his shirt drenched in sweat, in full view of at least three wits before, during and/or after the entire felonious act? Well, don't ask me, they thought it was, duh, funny. I didn't, of course, but never mind. For me, there turned out to be a greater pleasure: relief.

Because, about five minutes into the uproarious anecdote, I realized this was to be my entire punishment. You will recall that I said we were about the same size? As we stood facing each other next to his cluttered desk, at first he swelled to about a foot taller than me, but, once I grasped the situation, for the remaining five minutes the size ratio altered at the rate of a few millimeters a second --you do the math.

It was simple. Common sense had kicked in. Would he really go through the whole hassle of arresting me, booking me, getting all the evidence together, coming to court, and so on, over a jacket which any decent defense lawyer could prove was virtually worthless, and which, who knows, given the vagaries of time and memory, a jury might even believe I had taken in error?

Yes, for the remaining five minutes, my confidence grew, and right near the end I was fortunate enough to be granted another key insight: all that remained was for me to be sure to let this guy have the last laugh. And he had to be sure he was having it.

Not to worry. When the last few drops of forced mirth had been wrung, and most of the Roman spectators in the arena looked ready to go home for a long drunken lunch or back to their forges and counting houses, he produced the punch line, all by himself. By now, it had even occurred to me that, even if he was, indeed, planning to hang a U-ey and charge me, after all, I was being police-harassed here, right in front of thirty or forty "wits." Which was twenty-seven or thirty-seven more than he (claimed he) had.

"Well, Mr. Wolf," he (shall we say) said. "Now comes the worst part." He made me wait a beat, or so he thought. "Sorry, my friend, but you're going to have to pay a huge fine for what you tried to do." What? After all this nonsense, was he really going to...?

He was not. Reaching behind him, he plucked my old jacket from the coat tree where, unnoticed by me, it had been hanging, in shabby absence of dignity, the whole time. With exaggerated care, he draped it over the back of his chair. In slow motion, with also exaggerated gestures, he closed his top shirt button, cinched up his tie, rolled down his sleeves, then slipped into my jacket, which, of course, fit him perfectly.

"Bye," he said. "Sorry! Evidence!" and waggled his fingers. Even though the remaining spectators all seemed to get the joke, it did not produce the huge response he had obviously anticipated: as I turned and made my way back across the room, I could not be said to have been followed by the old gales of derisive laughter.

There was a long wait for the elevator, and it stopped eight or nine times on the way down. I did not let my breath out until I was on the sidewalk. Then, for about a minute, I just stood there, breathing the heady air of freedom, but not too fast, because I was afraid of fainting. Then, I randomly turned left and headed south.

A few blocks on, as I waited for a light to change (even after all the cars and trucks had crossed the intersection), the office episode flashed through my mind. If anything, it seemed silly, pointless, just another in the endless parade of instances where, harrumph, the gap between the ideal and the actual in our so-called justice system assumes Grand-Canyon proportions.

Had I learned my lesson? Had I learned any lesson? If, by some freak, I ever wound up with a grandchild, would I take him/her on my knee and say that crime never paid? Nonsense. Or that you needed a combination of luck and skill to succeed in many of life's enterprises (crime included)? Obviously. I mean, a detective? a small restaurant with mirrors?

Well, forget the grandchild, I had learned my --or a—real lesson. I have concluded that I "suffer from" (actually, it's kind of fun) undiagnosed --self-diagnosed, now-- ADD. I hyper-concentrate, I obsess, I free-associate, I fly about. Another way to put this is, I'm constantly on the lam from depression and his/her hyperactive twin, anxiety. For instance, I don't allow myself to eat breakfast until I finish the *Times* crossword. (Some days, that means near-fasting, which is okay, too, since I'm vain about my small paunch-to-age ratio.) But I don't self-medicate I hardly drink, nor do I smoke or abuse other drugs.

So. (Or is it "But"?) Clinging to my old jacket to the point where I obsessively hunted for a replacement garment, then ran it to ground and seized it in my steely, pun-spewing jaws was a substitute pathology. I must have been "acting out."

And the lesson? *Must have been*, past conditional. By the time the light changed, I realized I no longer gave a rat's ass about old Norfolk jackets. It did occur to me to wonder what the detective would really do with mine --probably throw it in the garbage on his way out of the building. That would be just fine. I crossed the street and, starting to picture something along the lines of a blue-gray windbreaker, headed for Macy's.

Their Countries of Origin

An inveterate traveler and a retiree with disposable income, before Ngongo I had already visited Malta and Kosovo. These were the countries of origin of three of our building's many superintendents. But perhaps the most memorable was #4, Michael, a slacker who once had the temerity to announce, "Me Plumerian, you Chew. We same, no, Meester Bob?"

"Thanks a lot," I replied, but he was impervious to sarcasm. A super-duper.

Historically, it is true that Plumeria, a small island in the Black Sea, has been a football for the Germans, Russians, Turks, and Serbs. But the Plumerians can give as good as they get: their hands are stained with the blood of several other small nations and ethnicities in the neighborhood.

A far more sympathetic super hailed from Ngongo. His name was/is Tshombe --like the Congolese politician. Tall, thin, coal-black, agreeable and industrious, but with a modicum of skills, Pierre was only with us for six months, during 2010. He invariably addressed me as "*Monsieur* Sheh-*pard*." When he disappeared one day, we assumed he had been picked up by the Citizenship and Immigration Services. At the job interview, he had produced a green card, but our Board is careless about documentation.

"I wonder what happened to that African guy," I mused one evening, looking up from the paper. My wife turned toward me from her desk.

"Pierre?"

"That's right," I lied. "I forgot his name."

"I liked him, too. Everyone did."

"I was thinking of visiting his country."

She shrugged, raised her eyebrows, and turned back to the report she was writing. I took her non-response to mean she would not try to talk me out of my quixotic notion of a first trip to Africa. I appreciate the fact that she never tells me to "get a life."

While she was at work the next day, I googled *La Republique Federale d'Ngongo,* discovering a landlocked place the size of Luxembourg, tucked between the DRC (Congo) and Zambia. Their press releases emphasized economic development, many involving coltan, which is used in cell phones. The country's deposits are grossly disproportionate to its size and population (5.2 million, according to a 1992 census).

Ngongo also seemed exempt from the wholesale violence that dogs Central Africa, perhaps because it has been ruled for decades by an ancient dictator, who began life as a freedom fighter. Several times in recent years, this small nation has been flavor-of-the-month at Human Rights Watch. I speculated about the dictatorship's longevity. The capital, Fort Chaltin, is named for a major from the Belgian Congo. Why has the dictator not renamed his capital something more palatable, like *Lumumbaville?* Perhaps because the old name inspires fear, at least among his minions. More to the point, the city is perched on an escarpment, which must discourage coup-makers.

By early October, having obtained my shots, visa and plane tickets, I was ready to go. Despite the distance and airfare, $1400, I planned to be away for only a week. I would fly via Paris to Fort Chaltin, then either stay there the whole time, or make a side trip to Lake Tanganyika, which is just across the eastern border, 110 miles by road from the capital. I paid a night's deposit for a room at a *pension* I found on the Internet.

Having learned from previous red-eye experiences, I left N.Y. at 12:35 p.m., had a two-hour stopover in Paris, and arrived at 12:15 p.m. the next day. Even so, I was so tired I was glad I had not booked a rental car. I found a Citroen diesel cab to haul me up the narrow hairpin road from the airport and through the dusty town. It was the dry season.

Hidden by trees and flowering bushes, the *Pension Saint-Louis* seemed lovely. When I signed the guest book, the *patron* put my passport and most of my money in the safe, "for security reasons." I was given keys to my room and to the high iron gates in front, which would be locked between 7 p.m. and 7 a.m.

My second-floor room was kitschy, but spacious, clean and comfortable, with tile flooring, big windows, and a ceiling fan. To skim off the jet lag, I took a long nap, followed by a shower. After that, I wandered into Fort Chaltin.

My first impressions confirmed things I had read. The market kiosks were short of goods, prices were high --100 francs Gb., or about $3.50, for a small loaf of bread. The dirt streets were rutted and full of axle-shattering potholes. Clouds of dust and pollution from ancient vehicles made breathing difficult. It surprised me that I did not encounter any of the beggars I knew to be endemic, or the muggers and con men who brazenly accost tourists in places like Nairobi, a.k.a. "Nairobbery." But, as I roamed around, I began to understand this apparent absence of unfortunates and undesirables. Lurking in the shadows were men in dark, baggy suits, sunglasses and black Fedoras. These, I assumed, were members of the feared secret police, *La Force NKN,* said to number in the tens of thousands.

More blatant was the contrast between ubiquitous poverty and the few pockets of wealth, presumably created by the coltan economy, and presumably controlled by the octogenarian kleptocrat & Co. Clustered in a five square-block area of the *District Centrale* were skyscrapers, luxury hotels and upscale restaurants. *Pension Saint-Louis* was situated on a quiet street just south of this oasis. On my way back, I stopped at a kiosk for a meal of bread, goat meat and beer.

Behind the front desk of the *pension*, the *patron* stood reading a newspaper. "*Alors, Monsieur …*" he began, his eyes twinkling through his bifocals. "*Ca va?*"

"*Bien, merci.* So far, I like Fort Chaltin." My schoolboy French came back easily, so we continued in that language.

"Thank you. Are you here, *Monsieur*, on business or for tourism, if I may ask?"

"Neither. I'm here to re-connect with someone who used to work for me."

"How interesting!" He sounded wary. "And is this …reconnection your sole motive for visiting our poor, out-of-the-way land?"

"Well, mostly," I replied. We smiled and nodded at each other. "But tell me, *mon patron*, how might I go about locating this man?"

Again, he eyed me suspiciously. "What is the name, please?"

"Name? Robert Shepard. But… "

"No, no. *His* name, please?"

"Oh. Patrice —I mean, Pierre- Tshombe."

"Well, *Monsieur*," he said carefully, "'Tshombe' is a common name here. If I were you, I would check for an address at the Post Office." He pushed his glasses up on his nose. "This will be easier than trying to obtain a phone number, which would entail a big palaver at the *Ministrie Telephonique*." He stood up and stretched theatrically. "And now, *Monsieur* Shepard, if you will excuse me, I must see that the children are asleep, then go to my own bed. At what time would you like to take your breakfast, please?"

"Seven-thirty okay? I'll probably wake up early from..." (English) "jet lag."

"Of course, *Monsieur*, I am at your service. Good night, then. Please turn the lights off when you leave this room. There is a night light in the stairwell which you may leave on."

"Good night, *mon patron*."

We shook hands, and he went upstairs. I sat in the parlor a few minutes, my mind a welter of impressions. Then, I went up to my room. Probably because of my nap, I stayed awake reading for several hours.

My phone alarm woke me from a restless, dream-ridden sleep. I was the only guest in the small dining room. After a satisfactory continental breakfast, I wandered into the empty parlor, where I skimmed a week-old newspaper. Up in my room, I used the toilet and put the things I would need for the day (cap, cell phone, etc.) into a backpack with a small lock. Slathering myself with sunblock, I went back down, ready to walk to the Post Office.

In the vestibule, the *patron* lay in wait, polishing his glasses with a white handkerchief. After we had exchanged pleasantries about the forecast —hot and dry, chance of afternoon thundershowers-- he snapped his fingers, and a thin, light-skinned young man materialized from the parlor. Perhaps seventeen, he wore neat, but worn clothing.

"*Monsieur* Shepard, allow me to present my wife's nephew, Joseph."

I offered the young man, who bore little resemblance to the *patron,* my hand. With a small bow, he softly shook it, and we said how glad we were to meet each other.

"I have brought Joseph here," the *patron* explained, "because he can be of assistance in the search for your former employee." Before I could protest, he continued. "Please. Joseph will be most useful, *Monsieur.* The Post Office is difficult to find, and he will be of assistance in communicating with the employees, who speak only *Ngongienne,* with perhaps some Swahili, but little or no French. Assuming you succeed in acquiring an address, Joseph can help you to find the place. If your friend is absent, he will be able to communicate with the other residents. Fortunately, he is free to serve you all day. You see, *Monsieur,* the lack of school fees has forced him temporarily to abandon his studies. If you like, when you have completed the day's business, you will give him a small *pourboire,* to assist him in returning to the *lycee'* --just a few *francs,* you understand." The *patron* looked embarrassed, as did Joseph.

Before I could reply, the young man chimed in. "You see, *Monsieur,* as my uncle has explained, not only will the location of the Post Office be difficult of discovery, but the employees will speak mostly our own tongue, *Ngongienne.*" The *patron* solemnly nodded his agreement.

Fueled by two cups of espresso, my mind raced dizzily. In a dictatorship like Ngongo, citizens and visitors alike must live under a cloud of uncertainty. To evade my host's ministrations might stoke his paranoia, or that of the authorities. While I ran through these thoughts, Joseph and the *patron* gazed at the ceiling.

"Very well," I said. "I accept. *Monsieur.* Joseph." Another round of handshakes. "Shall we?" With a bit of "after you" farce, I preceded Joseph out the front door, which the *patron* closed behind us. We went through the gated entrance to find a big, old, black American car waiting at the curb. I was glad to get away from the officious *patron*.

"I have taken the liberty, *Monsieur*," Joseph said, gesturing to the car. "The Post Office is far." I got into the back, and without telling the driver our destination, Joseph took the passenger seat.

After all the preliminaries, the Post Office proved anticlimactic. Since there were few customers, there was almost no wait, but all that I —we-- learned from the polite clerk was that they had no current address for a Pierre Tshombe. As we exited the white stucco, colonial-era building, I began to wonder whether someone might not want me to find him. Our car was waiting. The driver had turned the motor off and sat dozing behind the wheel. By now, it was nine-thirty. Suddenly, I bridled at all the control.

"You know, Joseph," I said, "I think I'd rather walk back to the *pension*. I mean, all I've accomplished this morning is to eat breakfast, take a car ride, and spend ten fruitless minutes at the Post Office. Why don't I pay the driver and have him drop you somewhere? If I get tired, I'll find my own taxi."

Joseph became agitated. "But, *Monsieur*, this is impossible. It will be a too long walk, and my uncle will be very angry with me if I allow you, our guest, to lose yourself in this, our city."

"No problem." I opened my backpack and extracted the guidebook. "Look." I showed him a map that included the Post Office and the *pension*. "You see," I added cheerfully, "I'll be fine. Go on, please." Reaching for my wallet, I gestured to the car.

But he would not be shaken off so easily, and after some more back and forth, we reached an understanding: I would get my walk, but he would accompany me. After he had exchanged a hurried word with the driver in *Ngongienne*, I handed over what seemed a fair price, 150 francs GB, or about $5.25. The cab made a cautious U-turn and headed back toward the *District Centrale*.

"In this way, *Monsieur* Shepard," Joseph smiled, setting out along the edge of the road, "you will get to enjoy your constitutional, and I will preserve my uncle's good will. We can —how do you say it? —use one stone to kill two birds." I forced a smile and, careful not to fall into the drainage ditch, followed him in the direction my map said would lead us back to the *pension*.

The day had grown very hot. Glad that I had worn my lightest pants and shirt, I put on my cap and sunglasses. The blocks around the Post Office were a sort of suburb, quiet, with little traffic. Although the small one-story bungalows, made of stucco or whitewashed cement, were modest by American standards, they all had high iron fences with razor wire, and intimidating signs announcing that security companies patrolled the neighborhood.

Joseph saw me looking at the signs. "I think those are only for ... how do you say it... *dis...?*"

"*Dissuasion*," I said. ("Deterrence.")

"Ah, yes, of course."

"Are there burglaries?"

"Not many. But the property owners fear them."

"What of *La Force NKN?*"

He flinched. "Well, of course, there are those people." I did not pursue the point.

After several blocks, the street on which we had been walking, the *Rue de la Liberation*, brought us to a long row of small market kiosks like the one where I had eaten the previous day. Between them wound narrow paths leading back to mud huts roofed with thatch or rusty corrugated metal. Inside the open-fronted kiosks, men and women dozed on stools or chairs, or haggled over petty goods. Unconsciously, I moved my hands toward my pants pockets, and realizing I had neglected to do so, zipped them shut.

"Don't worry, *Monsieur*, there are no thieves —very few, anyway."

"Good."

But, as if to contradict Joseph's assurances, a few minutes later a tall, thin, ragged, dust-covered figure suddenly sprang out at us from a path between the kiosks. Before I could jump back, the man, who was somehow vaguely familiar, brushed against me, and I felt a hand at my right pants pocket.

"Shaa!" shouted Joseph, adding what sounded like a furious imprecation in *Ngongienne*. Several proprietors materialized, waving their arms and shouting similar imprecations.

"Sorry, sir!" the ragged man cried in French. "Please forgive me!" He spun around and sped back up the path, eluding the mob.

"I, too, am sorry," said Joseph. The merchants, some still muttering, wandered back to their kiosks. "I am afraid you have encountered one of our madmen. Very, very sorry."

"That's okay, Joseph." My heart was beating fast. "Not your fault." With trembling hands, I patted my pants pockets. In the left one, I could feel my wallet. But in the right one, which had held only a few coins and a roll of mints, the zipper was half open, and I felt something like a crumpled piece of paper.

In such situations, people tend not to notice much, but for some reason I had observed my accoster closely. His hair was filthy and matted. He wore ragged khaki shorts and a torn, once-white t-shirt. He was barefoot, and his face, arms and legs were covered with cuts and abrasions. I realized, then, why the madman had seemed familiar: it was Pierre. The image of our polite, meticulously clean super flashed across my mind. Instinctively, I patted the piece of paper in my pocket.

"Nothing missing," I said.

"Such people are not usually thieves. Would you like to sit down for a moment, *Monsieur*, perhaps to take a cold drink at a kiosk?"

"No, thanks," I said. "I have water." Unlocking the backpack, I took out the bottle. "Would you like some?" He shrugged and smiled. Taking a few long swallows, I put the bottle back and re-locked the backpack. "Shall we?"

We walked on until, forty-five minutes later, the tall buildings of the *District Centrale* loomed ahead. By then, I was exhausted. The intrepid traveler had never before attempted a long trek beneath the tropical sun.

"I give up, Joseph," I said, at last. "You were right." With a shy smile, he hailed one of the ubiquitous rattletraps, and in ten minutes we were back at the gates of the *pension*. I paid the driver and gave Joseph his *pourboire*, to which he responded with effusive thanks.

In my room, I locked the door and splashed tepid water on my face. Then, I unzipped my pocket and took out the piece of paper. It was a dirty, wrinkled, lined sheet torn from a notebook. In spidery handwriting, it read (in French):

Please, *Monsieur* Shepard, I am so sorry to impose on you, but this is a matter of life and death. Could you be so kind as to meet me tonight at the statue of Major Chaltin, which is on the road inside *Parc de L'Independence*, near the northeast border of the city? If you will call 23-004-91 at exactly 11 p.m., you will be picked up and driven there. The driver will be one of us.

"Your presence will indicate your willingness to help with an urgent matter. I will entrust you with a packet containing literature documenting the struggles and sufferings of our group. I will ask you to carry these documents home with you in your luggage, then take them to the address indicated. When we meet tonight, I will explain more completely. In case I am not there, you may assume I have been apprehended. The driver will drop you someplace where you can have a drink, and you will return by taxi to your *pension*. This should provide you with an adequate cover."

The letter was signed, "Your former employee and (still, I hope) friend, Pierre Auguste Modupe Tshombe, *Secretaire Generale, Cadre Pour La Liberation d'*Ngongo *(CPLN)*.

P.S. Please memorize the contents of this note and destroy it immediately.

Relying on memory for the other details, I wrote the phone number on a scrap of paper, then tore Pierre's note to bits, flushed it down the toilet, and flopped onto the bed. I imagined being stopped at the airport by *NKN* thugs, who would discover the packet. I would be thrown into a fetid cell, where demands to speak to my consul would be met with derisive laughter.

I spent the rest of the afternoon trying to nap and to read. For lunch and supper, I made do with some crackers and dried fruit I had brought along from New York in case the airline food was inedible. Towards evening, I e-mailed my wife. Trying to be circumstantial, I provided some local color and reassuring noises about my safety. Since I knew she would expect me to mention Pierre, I said I had unsuccessfully tried the Post Office. After that, I returned to my book, staring at the pages for a long time and remembering nothing.

At 10:30, I crept down the hall and determined that the *patron* and his family had turned out their lights. The *pension* still seemed to have no other guests, at least none that I had encountered. At exactly eleven, I called the number from Pierre's note, destroyed the slip of paper, tip toed downstairs and, as quietly as possible, un-locked the gates. Re-locking them behind me, I waited in the shadows. A quarter of an hour later, Pierre's man appeared, driving a battered old sedan. He carried me through the city to the statue in the park. No Pierre.

With growing anxiety, we waited forty minutes, until the driver suggested we leave. He dropped me at a bar in the *District Centrale*, where I had my drink, then took a cab back to the *pension*. As quietly as possible, I once again unlocked and re-locked the gates. Creeping up to my room, I re-read the Lake Tanganyika chapter in my guidebook.

After a restless night, at seven-thirty the next morning, I ate breakfast, paid the bill, and booked a room for the night before I was scheduled to fly home. When I asked whether I might leave some of my things at the *pension*, the *patron*, polite, but wary, agreed. He had already ordered the same car as the day before, which carried me to the bus station on the eastern edge of the city.

Purchasing a round-trip ticket, I squeezed onto a crowded bus that terminated at a resort town on Lake Tanganyika, just across the Zambian border. There, I spent four nights at an upscale lodge in Sumbu National Park. It was a lovely lodge in a lovely location, but I was so distracted I could hardly enjoy the spectacular shoreline scenery, or even the blue duiker, a small, rare antelope I was fortunate enough to glimpse from the lodge's Land Rover during a game-spotting ride.

On the fifth day, I returned to Fort Chaltin, arriving in the early afternoon.

Again, the car met me. Back at the *pension*, I still saw no other guests. When I asked conversationally after Joseph, the *patron's* reply was monosyllabic. When I said I wanted to stretch my legs after the bus ride, he shrugged.

Deciding to keep on playing the tourist, I spent an interesting couple of hours at the small *Musee' d'Ethnographie* at the south end of the *District*, six blocks from the *pension*. On my walk to and from the *Musee'*, I could tell I was being watched: the men in black were obvious. After returning to my room for a nap and a shower, I went down to the lobby, where I asked the *patron* to arrange for the car again, and to reserve a table at the *Grille Lapin*, an upscale place I had found in my guidebook. I waited while he impassively made the calls.

The car soon arrived, but with a new driver, short, silent, and scowling. Without a word, he drove me to the *Grille*, which was in the heart of the *District*. Not responding to my overgenerous tip, he said he would return in one hour and sped away. Not fifty feet from the restaurant, two *NKN* agents stood side by side on the pavement beneath a streetlight.

It was now seven-thirty, and the place was about a quarter full. As far as restaurants go, the *Lapin* looked like a good choice: immaculate and chic, with white tablecloths and black bentwood chairs. The server, a nervous, older man, seated me at a table for two in front of the window and immediately took my order. I hardly noticed what I chose. A glass of red wine appeared, along with a basket containing two huge rolls.

Five minutes later, as I was crumbling the second roll into pills, a black stretch SUV pulled up in front of the restaurant. Trotting around the rear of the car, the driver opened the back right door, and out came…Michael Milevski, my Plumerian super-- or someone very like him! Illuminated by the restaurant's red sign, this Michael wore a shiny, tailored safari suit with a dark fisherman's cap. Like his suit, Michael was shiny, smirking radiantly and glowing with health and confidence.

As he strode into the restaurant, his driver disappeared back into the SUV, which had tinted windows. I had never seen a bulletproof vehicle up close before, but there was something tank-like about the side panels of this one. Scanning the room, Michael spotted me. After a theatrical double take, he approached my table with a shark-like grin and outstretched hand.

"Well, well," he said, "of all people! Long time no see."

I stood up and returned his firm handshake. He exuded an expensive smell. The safari suit was light green and, I guessed, silk.

"Michael?"

With a perfunctory nod, he sat down. His backside had barely touched the chair when the server appeared, now wearing an anxious smile.

"The usual," Michael pronounced, in heavily accented French. "But no food tonight, Alain." The server ran back to the kitchen. "Well, Mr. Shep --Bob?" I nodded. "You look well. A little older, of course, but who isn't?"

I kept kneading the bread pills. A few seconds later, the server returned, holding aloft a silver tray with two glasses and an open bottle of what looked like champagne. Filling one of the glasses, he set it down in front of Michael and waited.

"Join me?" Michael asked.

"No, thanks." I lifted my own glass.

"Well, here's to ... success." I sipped my wine, and he drank some champagne. "Ah, delicious. You sure...?"

"No, thanks," I repeated. The server withdrew with the bottle. I hoped my coolness would prompt Michael to leave before the food arrived.

"Still traveling, I see," he remarked indifferently.

"Sort of."

"Someday, I hope you'll come to Plumeria, my country. Much nicer than this place, which, if I may say so, is the asshole of the world."

"Well, these days the world is full of assholes."

Rather than taking the sarcasm personally, he laughed so hard that several heads turned. "Very true. I've been to --and met-- many of them." He drank more champagne.

"Not to be rude, Michael, but what are *you* doing here?"

He laughed mirthlessly. "Certainly not mopping floors or delivering packages!"

"I can see that. But what *are* you doing?"

His expression became a caricature of thought. "How to put it... let's just say I've been spending a lot of time in Africa lately. I'm a ... businessman." He seemed pleasantly surprised by his cleverness in coming up with the word.

"And a very successful one, at least from the look of you. But what *kind* of business, Michael?"

"Well … *Bob*, let's just say I deal with African leaders whose names you would recognize from the newspaper."

That gave me a good enough idea: probably guns for diamonds, or here in Ngongo, guns for coltan. I dropped the subject, and for a few moments we sat in silence. The server reappeared, carrying a steaming plate of food and Michael's bottle. Consulting his smart phone, Michael waved him off.

"Sorry, Bob, I'm due at the Defense Ministry an hour ago, so I'll leave you to your dinner." He made no move to get up. "But before I go *—Bob--* I have a little message for you. Actually, it comes from the President of this country." He looked me in the eye, enjoying my alarm. "Unless you want to sample his special brand of hospitality, you should make no attempt to re-establish contact with that guy who accosted you the other day." He laughed harshly. "Who, even as we speak, is enjoying the President's hospitality!"

With a look of false concern, Michael switched from heavily accented French to heavily accented English (which I won't try to reproduce): "*Bob*, as someone who wishes you well, I really hope, *Bob*, you won't be *stupid* enough to meddle in things that are *none of your fucking business!*" To punctuate this rude peroration, he jabbed a finger in my face. This time, no heads turned. He stood up and, without shaking hands or even saying goodbye, strode through the door, slamming it behind him. A moment later, the SUV sped off.

Only then did I notice my food, a French stew served central-African style, and still hot enough to exude a delicious aroma. I ate what I could, washing it down with a second glass of wine, and paid the bill, which arrived just as my car pulled up to the curb. As I exited the restaurant, I looked to my left. One of the *NKN* men saluted.

Back in my room, it took me quite a while to calm down. I imagined a second conversation with Michael. "Hey, if I didn't do it, someone else would."

Had Pierre really been arrested, or had he failed to keep the *rendezvous* for a different reason? What would I do if he, or someone from his group, tried to contact me again before I left the next morning?

At about ten, to escape these unpleasant thoughts, I booted up and checked my e-mail. There were two messages. My wife's was short and sweet. She missed me, hoped I was still okay. She would see me soon. Love xxx. The second was a follow-up threat from Michael, this one texted from his phone. "BBQ at rsdnce of Jstce Mnstr Sndy pm. Wld lve hve yu for dnnr (ha ha). Pstpne flt, see the real Ngng!!! Wll snd car. Chrs, M."

I e-mailed my wife that I would take a taxi from the airport. I also promised to shop and cook dinner before she returned from work. To Michael, I wrote: "Sorry, urgent NY business, maybe next time." I signed it (ha ha) "B.S."

In the morning, I breakfasted, paid the new bill, and exchanged cool farewells with the *patron*, who was busy checking in some Chinese business types. I was driven to the airport in a random taxi. During the forty-minute ride down the escarpment, I worried obsessively that I would be detained.

Arriving just in time to check in, I entered the small terminal. Wearing the best smile I could muster, I wheeled my suitcase across the air-conditioned lobby to the check-in counter. The moment the perfumed, immaculately uniformed clerk, who was as beautiful as a model, began to process my ticket, her cell phone rang. For perhaps thirty seconds, she listened in silence, her perfect forehead beading with sweat.

"*Oui, Monsieur Le Capitaine., entendu*," she finally said, and closed her phone. Then, to me, also in French, "I am so sorry, Sir, but certain formalities require me to direct you kindly to proceed with your luggage to the gray door over there, the one marked 'SECURITY.'" She pointed a long manicured finger.

"But..."

"Please, *Monsieur*, it is necessary. I am sure you will not miss your flight."

With a sense of doom, I wheeled my suitcase to the door she had indicated and knocked.

"Come in, Bob, it's open," Michael called through the door, in English.

Dressed in another shiny safari suit, this one sky blue, he sat staring at a computer screen on a metal desk in a tiny, windowless office with fluorescent lighting. The only ornament was a huge, framed portrait on the wall behind the desk. It was the dictator as he might have looked fifty or sixty years before, wearing black framed glasses and a camouflage uniform. There was no chair for visitors, so I walked up to the desk and stood there. Without a word, Michael gestured for me to come around to his side. Complying, I saw on the screen several thumbnail photographs of a man under what I assumed was extreme torture. In one, he was dangling by his ankles from a meat hook with his hands tied behind him, his entire body covered with blood. In another, a close-up of a silently screaming face left no doubt who the victim was.

Barely able to keep myself from swooning, I leaned both hands on the edge of the desk. Michael's face displayed a look of false concern with an undercurrent of delight. He play-acted jumping from his seat and clasped me very hard by the shoulder.

"Please, Bob. Sit down! Sorry there's no audio. Can I get you a glass of water?" He gestured to the desk chair. I shrugged him off, and he smiled. "No? You're okay? If you don't mind, then, I'll just have a quick look through your bag."

Not trusting myself to speak, I gestured to the suitcase. He popped the snaps and cursorily riffled through the contents, then snapped the suitcase shut again.

"Good to go, *mon ami. Bon voyage.* Please give my very best to your lovely wife and to all the kind neighbors."

Hardly aware of what I was doing, I staggered from the office and wheeled back to the counter. With an apology, the clerk escorted me through a door that led out onto the broiling tarmac. In Paris, there was a three-hour layover, during which, still dazed, I sat by a window as the planes landed and took off.

During my first weeks back in New York, I told the story of Pierre and Michael to anyone who would listen: my wife (several times), friends, neighbors, total strangers. When I began to feel like the ancient mariner and she suggested I "give it a rest," I subsided.

Two months after my return, a torn, smudged Manila envelope arrived, covered with canceled stamps and containing incendiary materials. There was a slip of paper with the address of a Human Rights group, but no note. I brought the packet to the address, where an earnest young woman took it, earnestly shook my hand, and uttered an earnest speech of thanks. Since then, six or seven more months have floated past, as time does for the elderly. Hardly a day goes by, however, when my liberal heart does not bleed for Pierre Tshombe.

Ron Singer

When the Barber Died

Sposibo, Nicolai.

Last month, I needed a haircut and tried to call Angelo, but the number was not working. Later that day, out for a walk, I was accosted by his colleague, Giovanni, who was standing at the edge of a huge hole in the street, inside of which several workers were trying to lasso a damaged pipe. Shouting into his cell phone, Giovanni mimed for me to wait.

Finishing the call, he closed the phone and, with a solemn look, announced, "You must have heard the bad news. Angelo died."

"Oh, no!" I said. "When?"

"About a week ago."

"I knew he was sick, but..."

This was an understatement: Angelo had been afflicted with spinal cancer for three years, and had suffered through at least one operation, plus all sorts of other unpleasantness, which left him a pale bag of bones, permanently doubled over. Ever the stoic, he would deflect my health questions, and we would jump to our favorite subjects, used cars and fishing. Angelo was an aficionado of both. It amused me, a retired advertising executive with a Ph.D., to be schooled by a man who had dropped out of third grade in Sicily half a century before to become apprenticed to the local barber.

Each time I handed over the $60 (haircut, tax, tip), I would say, "You've done it again, Angelo. You've made a silk purse out of a sow's ear." The first time I used the expression, it sent Angelo, who had never heard it, into paroxysms of laughter.

This was several years before he was stricken, after which his laughter gradually grew softer and more contemplative. Recently, it had subsided into a sick man's smile. We went way back.

Angelo's haircuts were works of art. As I grew balder, and my face, more jowly, he would make subtle adjustments. Since I find it impossible to describe haircuts, let me paraphrase a conversation from the end of the most recent one.

I [looking at the back of my head in the big mirror, which reflected the small one held by the barber]: Perfect, as usual! I don't know how you do it, Angelo. You always manage to make a silk purse out of a sow's ear.

Angelo [with a wan smile]: Thanks, Mr. S. It's a matter of suiting the haircut to the head. If a man has a long head, you try to make it look shorter. If he is [laughs] --I mean, has-- a fat head, you make it look a bit narrower. If the hair is straight, you cut it one way; if it's curly, like yours [shrugs] ... If the hair is getting thin [smile], you have to...

You get the idea.

The conversation with Giovanni on the corner continued. "I tried to call for an appointment this morning, but..."

"The landline's down. I was just talking to the company." He gestured to his cell. "They're going to re-route the calls to our cells." "Our cells" presumably included Dave's, the other surviving barber.

"I'll call later, then." I stopped myself from adding, "to make an appointment." Instead, I substituted, "to get Angelo's address, so I can send the family a card."

"That would be nice."

Had Giovanni noticed the verbal hiccough? I did not want to make an appointment with either surviving barber. Giovanni was a blowhard; I just didn't like him. Dave was quiet and gentlemanly, but he always seemed depressed. Nor did what I had observed of their handiwork measure up to Angelo's standard.

When I phoned the next day, Giovanni picked up, presumably on his cell. After some small talk, I asked for, and was given, Angelo's address. Then, I said, "I think I'll wait a bit before I get a new haircut. I'm not quite ready to..."

"Of course, of course," said Giovanni solemnly. There was a silence.

"Are you and Dave going to look for someone else?"

"Well, we have to, but we'll wait a while. It won't be easy getting anyone suitable." I thanked him for the address.

As you must have realized, I'm a fussy person. Not just about haircuts, I'm a stickler about language and manners. Public farting and spitting provoke more than mild distaste, as does a *mot injuste*, or --even worse—a grammatical solecism such as, "Please send the check to Judy [my wife] or I." "Peevish" may be more accurate than "fussy."

The next day, I sent the card. Although I had never met Angelo's wife, I had heard enough about her over the years that I knew the tone to take. It was easy to find words to express my gratitude for the late barber's wonderful haircuts and conversation. There was no need to wax maudlin.

I recalled an incident from my working days that featured an observation a colleague had made at the airport. Having tendered awkward goodbyes to another, unpopular man, who was being transferred to our L.A. branch, we were walking back to the cabstand.

"You know," the colleague remarked, "it's easier to say goodbye to someone you'll actually miss. Someone you like."

"A paradox," I replied, "but true." I brushed some cement dust from a pants leg. Why are airports under perpetual construction? It makes them look like crash sites.

In the weeks after I sent the card, my increasingly shaggy head made me think of Angelo. Did I miss him more because of our quasi-friendship or because I anticipated how hard it would be to replace his haircuts? Like most people, my good feelings toward others include a healthy measure of self-interest.

I considered the options. When Angelo had been convalescing from surgery, I had tried Tanya, my wife's barber, who works at a Unisex salon in Brooklyn. (We live in lower Manhattan.) That haircut had been decent, but not up to Angelo's standard. Of course, grief over his death may have colored my memory of the other haircut. Cost was not an issue, since Tanya also charged sixty dollars, which seems like a lot, but may be the going rate these days.

"Maybe, I'll try Tanya again," I said to Judy over breakfast.

"Why not? You seemed satisfied last time."

I did not reply. Tanya was a single mom whose conversation consisted solely of chitchat --the weather, her children, etc. And even that was limited to small doses, since the haircut had been accompanied by non-stop radio music, bland "oldies." So I crossed her off my mental list. But I did not tell Judy, who thinks Tanya is "a nice person," and who does not mind "pop" music. Maybe, Tanya is also better with women or, at least, Judy, whose haircuts look stylish and age appropriate. She's sixty-four; I'm seventy.

Trying to picture the haircuts of past acquaintances, I remembered a good one, smart, but not trendy. Unfortunately, it belonged to a person of Chinese extraction. Since this man, Cheng Yi, a colleague in the Accounts department from my working days, had a full head of thick, straight, black hair, he might not be much help. But I called him, anyway, and he recommended a barber in East Harlem.

"Don't worry," he said, "His name is Mario, an Italian, but he cuts all kinds of hair. Try him, he's cheap, twenty dollars, tax and tip included. I don't think he even has a phone, you just go."

I proffered my thanks, and we made the usual noises about getting together. But Cheng was still working for the firm, and I didn't suggest lunch or an after-work drink. Seeing him would add to my frequent feeling, since retirement five years ago, of being ...well, useless.

When Judy got home from work (Office Manager, real estate), I described the phone conversation. She did not ask why I had decided against Tanya. Instead, she said, "That's nice, dear. Another Italian. Maybe, he'll be good, too."

The next day after breakfast, I googled "Mario's Barbershop." I found an address, but neither a phone number, nor information about credit cards or hours of operation. Since it was Wednesday, the middle of the week, the shop would presumably be open. In case the barber was busy or out to lunch when I arrived, I also googled the local library branch, where I could kill an hour reading. There were several "blogs" that review barbershops, but I did not bother reading them. Anyone can have friends who post complimentary lies, or rivals who seed the reviews with malice. The MTA told me I could reach the barbershop in thirty-seven minutes, via one train and a walk.

I brushed my teeth, used the toilet, and poking my head out the window to check the temperature, got dressed. Making sure I had enough cash, I set out for the station. I was excited. Angelo, I told myself, would certainly have approved. Like me, he is —was-- a man whose life was ruled by common sense — which is not really common, at all.

Catching the #6 to 110th and Lexington, I walked east. The streets were lively and old-fashioned, full of interesting little shops, in contrast with the banks, nail salons, chain stores and glass-fronted condo and co-op buildings of my own neighborhood. Even though it was one of those chilly, unpredictable days in early spring, men stood on the corners, some drinking, some just laughing and talking. There were even a few premature stoop-sitters in front of the run-down residential buildings, four- and five-story brownstones.

The website had said there was only one barber, Mario. Good, I didn't need to worry about having an assistant fobbed off on me. But there might be several waiting customers, and my library plan might make me lose my place in the queue. As I approached the address, I saw a striped pole and gold block letters on a very clean window. Even better, the place was open, the door being held ajar by a piece of string attached to the wall.

At the entrance, I had a stroke of serendipity: another customer rushed out through the doorway. Not only could I inspect Mario's handiwork, the other man appeared to be of either Mediterranean or Caribbean descent, which could mean he had the same tightly curled, springy hair as mine. On closer scrutiny, however, he did not have this kind of hair. In fact, he had hardly any hair, at all! Mario had shorn him like a sheep. A clipper job! No wonder he was so cheap! Thank goodness I had seen this man before going in! What could Cheng have been thinking?

I glanced through the open door. There were no waiting customers. Occupying the single barber chair was (presumably) Mario, a fat, exhausted-looking old man whose snoring could be heard from the sidewalk. Resisting the blandishments of tasty Latino snacks fried in unhealthy oils and sold from carts or store fronts --and still wearing my shaggy hair-- I took the subway home.

Enough was enough. I called Tanya, who happened to have an opening in two hours. Eating lunch and setting my watch alarm, I took a short nap. Then, I re-gathered myself and caught another subway, this time to Brooklyn. Twenty pop tunes, forty commercials, and an insipid running monologue later, sixty dollars changed hands, and I had a new haircut.

Back on the subway, I recalled my images in Tanya's mirror: before and after. From a shaggy, but beautifully sculpted head —almost Greek-- had emerged a neat, ordinary Middle American one. Oh, well!

Home again, I took a shower and read for a while. Then, I warmed up the leftovers from the dish Judy had prepared the previous evening —delicious vegetable chili. I boiled the rice, cut the bread, and set the table. My timing was perfect: just as the chili began to bubble, I heard her key in the door. Five minutes later, as we were sitting in our usual places, sipping water and waiting for the food to cool, she noticed my haircut.

"Well, dear," she said matter-of-factly, "not bad. It looks like your new barber gave you the same kind of haircut Tanya did. And you probably saved about forty dollars."

As I explained what had really happened, I could see her biting her tongue. Decades before, we had established a marital rule. Since we both hate to be told, "I told you so," the rule was for the person who was wrong to say, "You told me so." I chose to ignore the rule. Instead, I said, "Well, yes. But now that I've bought some time, I'm going to keep trying to find someone... good."

Looking thoughtful, she shrugged. Obviously, she was trying to compromise between what she wanted to say ("Get a life, you pathetic jerk!") and something a bit more sympathetic. After all, one of these days, she would be retiring, herself.

"You know, dear." Her smile danced on the border of empathy and condescension. "I'll say this for the thousandth time: you're a fussy man." I bowed my head, ready to be metaphorically shorn. "Some people think fussiness is a sign of anxiety, but I think it can come from loneliness." I opened my mouth to point out that, since I already had her, how could I be lonely? She made a stop sign gesture.

"Yes, I know, dear," she said. "You have me. And you're very sweet. But you don't have Angelo, anymore, do you? And you know what else? You and I aren't so different. I need women friends, and, thank goodness, between the office and the 'Y,' I manage to have a few." She reached across the table and touched my hand. "You need a new friend now, too, don't you?" She paused. "But why does it have to be a *barber*?"

She may have been right, but I was not ready to give in. Glancing up at her through my sheep's eyes, I could not imagine anything as satisfying as a perfect haircut accompanied by a wonderful conversation. By now, the chili had cooled, so we stopped talking and dug in.

Ron Singer

On Elizabeth Bishop's "One Art"

"The art of losing isn't hard to master."

Well, I don't know about that. I mean, I'm good at losing things, but I wouldn't call it an "art." To me, the trick ("art") is remembering *where* you lost them. And by "things," I mean both things and memories.

About a week ago, I thought I left my back support cushion on the subway. It wasn't on the chair where I always put it when I get back to the apartment (so I know where it is), and it wasn't in my backpack (where it always is when I forget to take it out and put it on the chair).

I prepared for remedial action. I would call the MTA, and since this wasn't the first time I'd left the cushion somewhere (at work, concerts, movies), I also decided to call the cushion company and order a backup. So I sat down at my desk and … kicked the cushion, which had rolled onto the floor: black cushion, dark brown floor. New rule: always use the strap to loop the cushion onto the back of the chair. But no need to order a backup.

That was just a trivial, preliminary example; now for the main event. This one is about memory, the forgetting kind of losing. And it's not just about where, but why.

The night before last, I was in a Turkish restaurant in New Haven. I don't live in New Haven, but I won't tell you what I was doing there yet, because I don't want to get sidetracked (or spoil the story). Although it was a very nice restaurant, I was the only diner, probably because it was so early, about 5:30. As soon as I was offered a table (in the front window), I looped the cushion onto the chair.

Of all things, the sound system was playing loud recordings of sentimental Italian songs. Although they were instrumental versions, I recognized two (out of two) of them: "Come Back to Sorrento" (or as my late wife used to say, "Snorento"), and that other one whose title sounds like "Non Dementica."

What could have been more incongruous? Here is this beautiful place --benches, cushions, carpets, lovely Turkish stuff-- and they're playing tacky Italian songs. So when the waitress, young, cute, and wearing a tasteful Turkish outfit, came over to take my order, I thought I'd say something. (I often say something. What do you have to lose? I've never found a pebble in my soup, or anything.)

"Hi, young lady," I said. "You know, before I order, I have a request. A couple of years ago, I was in Turkey (actually about ten, with my wife, but I decided to simplify). "Everywhere I went, I heard wonderful music --you know, in the restaurants and all the other places ..." She stood there smiling, looking patient. "...so I wondered, do you happen to have any ... Turkish music here?"

"Yes, of course," she said, with a warm smile. "I will change it."

She walked off into the back of the restaurant, and thirty seconds later I got a big surprise. Whereas I had been hoping for something traditional, some tasteful drumming, say, with a plucked string instrument or two, and maybe even some quiet, soulful singing, she replaced the sentimental Italian music with ...loud, horrible Turkish pop! Of course, I knew better than to ask her to change the music a second time. But that's not exactly the point, which, as I'm sure you remember, is about losing things.

After a minute or two, she padded back to my table. Was she wearing sandals? slippers? I didn't notice, but her approach was soundless. Maybe, there was a carpet --or maybe it was the loud music. She smiled again and handed me three or four menus —food, wine, specials, what-nots. Before I even opened the first one, I knew this was going to be expensive. And, to anticipate, it was, $43-and-change, tax included, plus tip.

"Which places did you go in Turkey?" she asked. I could tell she was being friendly, not trying to catch me (if I had lied to get the music changed), and not giving me a quiz (to see what a dumb tourist I had been).

This is where the forgetting part happened. "Well, we —my wife and I—stayed in Istanbul a few days, and then we flew down to … that big city on the coast, uh …" –I decided to skip the name-- "where we rented a car and drove further south."

"Oh. Along the Aegean?" suggested the polite young woman.

"Yes, the Mediterranean, too. It was all very beautiful, we had a wonderful time." Which was mostly true.

She was still standing next to my table, still smiling. It would have made sense to let it go at that and skip to the food ordering. But this is where I finally get back to the point: the art of losing isn't easy. Not even when it's not a matter of losing a loved one (which is the loss with which Bishop ends her poem).

See, the poet keeps listing all these things she lost, and saying how she managed to cope with each loss, building up to something that *wasn't* easy, which she loses in the last stanza — her lover. And, of course, she didn't have to tell *me* that losing things --all sorts of things-- really *can* be hard to master. This is sort of the deeper point of the poem, the way she gets the reader ready for the sort-of surprise at the end. I hope I've explained that clearly enough.

Lately, at least, for this reader, *any* losing, big or small, is hard to master --and I'm not just talking about my obvious loss, the death of my wife. You see, one of the things about losing your memory is that it doesn't happen in isolation. When the furniture starts to rattle around up there, it all rattles, and soon everything starts crashing into everything else.

Back to the restaurant. I don't know exactly why I said what I said next. It's possible you will attribute it to the stubbornness of age, which is, admittedly, one large piece of smashed furniture in my attic. But I think there was more to it than that.

"We flew to, "I tried again, "to … you know, that really big city, it's …"

"Antalya?" she suggested.

"No, no, not that one. It's …" And then I blurted out the part that surprised me, then, and still surprises me now. "You know, the one that used to be called 'Smyrna.'"

The waitress may have shrugged, still smiling --maybe. (I wasn't looking at her, anymore.) But she didn't provide the new name of the city. "I'll give you a few minutes to decide about the food," she said, instead. "I'll come back to take your order." And once again, she walked off soundlessly toward the kitchen area.

Why did I say "Smyrna"? Most Turks do not like to be reminded of the former name of this, the third largest city in their country. Since I can't assume you know these facts, Smyrna was the Greek name of the city when, in 1922, the nationalist Turkish army under Ataturk slaughtered Greeks, mostly, maybe as many as 150,000. After that, they —the

Turks-- changed the name to --yes, I remember it now-- Izmir. Most Turks are still into Smyrna denial.

"Izmir." If you happen to know Yiddish (a small number of Jews were also killed), there is a saying, "*Oy vay iz mir,*" which means, "Oh, woe is me."

Why did I say "Smyrna"? Why did I forget "Izmir"? Heaven only knows. Was I subconsciously trying to offend the nice young waitress? Was I making some stupid political point? All I can say is that it was nothing personal --it was me, not her. At any rate, the meal (though expensive) was excellent, no pebbles in the soup. And like most of the people we met in Turkey, the waitress remained polite and pleasant.

Was I angry about the music? Maybe so, plus stress from the long day —that's always a good excuse. At last, the "why."

I'll tell you how I had spent it now, the day, so you can decide for yourself: in a nursing home, with an old friend from college who has been paralyzed for five years, ever since a botched brain surgery. Here's one little exchange he and I had that may be related to what happened with the waitress.

"Remember that funny joke you told the time we were all walking back to the dorm during the big snowstorm —I think it was freshman year?"

"No, I have no memory of that," he replied matter-of-factly. "Or of anything else."

How sad! So I told him his own joke, which involved the expensive funeral of an aunt from Sicily, who had been a miser and had worked in a factory most of her adult life. After that, I told him several more of his own jokes, which he laughed at as if they hadn't been his, and as if he were hearing them for the first time.

Was that why I couldn't remember the Turkish name for the murdered city? Was that why I rubbed the waitress's face in her own history? Never mind. How can anyone really know about things like that? Maybe, I should take a short course in psychoanalysis for the senile.

Shall we return to the cushion? (I remembered to take it when I left the restaurant.) Or perhaps you'd like to hear another of my friend's jokes, the one about a rock collection and rows of cans in the supermarket. That one is really funny. No? Never mind.

Running the Diagonal

"Well," I whispered to Lou, "he did have a drop-dead drop shot."

"Very funny, Jake," he whispered back.

Lou is Louis M. Gordon, a Detective Sergeant-Supervisor in the New York City Police Department. Thirty years ago, he was a student in my senior English Honors class. "Mr. Jacobs," I was, in those days. My actual name is Jerome (no middle initial) Jacobs, nickname, Jake, not Jerry. Lou and I go way back.

The late James "Jumbo" Thurston had dropped dead of a heart attack while gardening. The Minister had run through his tropes: American dream (immigrant from South Africa), family man (married, one child), work (highly successful), fitness (committed squash player), irony of death (so young), blah blah blah.

Lou claims I taught him both to write and to stop horsing around. He once said that, if not for me, he might have wound up a dead junkie or an insurance salesman. From time to time, he still has me eyeball a few things he has to write, like evidence reports.

Even so, he was doing me a big favor by accompanying me to the funeral. Lou ranks high enough in the NYPD that he must have a perfect grasp of the calculus of the IOU or, as people in public life say, "I *owe* you."

Like most of the other men present, we were wearing dark lightweight suits and "tasteful" ties. We were marooned, for the moment, on a little island in the middle of the lavish country-club reception that followed the cremation. This was all taking place in Great Neck, a posh north-shore suburb just across the New York City line.

Or, as Jumbo would put it, "Location, location. Always go to the T, Jacobs! Prime real estate." And he would suit the action to the word, slamming his hip into me so hard that I would find myself two feet to the right of the T, whereupon he would feather a drop-dead drop shot into the front left corner, which, run as I might, I could not retrieve. Jumbo was, in short, a prick, which was related to my reason for having asked Lou Gordon to accompany me to today's obsequies for the deceased (or, as Mark Twain put it, "orgies for the diseased.")

After introducing ourselves to the Widow Thurston, who looked more worried than sorrowful (was she toting up putative bequests?), Lou and I were back on our island. I was uncomfortably aware that I was making him waste half a day during a week in which he was busy with, among other things, a horrific drive-by shooting in the Bronx, which was attracting all kinds of unwelcome attention, including mayoral.

Consummate gentleman that he is, Lou had already relieved me of this burden. "Not to worry, Jake, I don't mind getting out of the kitchen for a few hours. If God is watching, by the time I get back, my guys may have someone in custody." He had not even asked why I had invited him.

In forty years of teaching, maybe I had discussed too many books with too many students. When you're trying to fill up one of those long classes that can't seem to catch fire, you find yourself falling into what I call "the post-post school of lit crit" --i.e., anything goes. Let's say a student who seldom speaks, pipes up with an idea on the approximate level of fake news: "Wordsworth really loved nature, right, Mr. J.?" If truth were the game, I would have disabused him/her of the notion that fairness requires equal time for all views, a notion dear to many adolescent minds.

Ergo, this habit of multiple truths (let's be polite) may have been an indirect reason for Lou's presence. To get to the point, I could not entirely swallow the accepted truth about Jumbo's death. After reading the notice in the *Times* the other day ("massive cardiac infarction"), one of my first reactions was to suspect foul play. So I decided to seek a second opinion.

Speaking of multiple truths, there may also be a second opinion regarding my morbid hypothesis. Since, over the years in which we had played squash, I had resisted many urges to hurry this man toward his afterlife, could I have been projecting my own "deep and dark desires" *(Macbeth)*? For example, at the end of an especially contentious game a few months ago, I had stalked off the court muttering imprecations that may have included, "Fuck you! Drop dead, you fucking son-of-a-bitch!"

"Tsk, tsk, temper!" he taunted.

Jumbo's victory in that particular game had had the earmarks of a hostile takeover, which was among his off-court endeavors as an M & A specialist. The game still sticks in my craw. Even now, I can smell the cigarette smoke on the ginger-haired little bastard's breath.

To get back to the facts, as reported by our National Paper of Record, and fleshed out by gossip, on a hot and humid Saturday afternoon in July, after two hours of morning squash, followed by a heavy lunch, this fit man of fifty-six was felled by a massive heart attack. Like Marlon Brando in *The Godfather* (Part One), Jumbo Thurston dropped dead in his own garden.

On the drive back to the city, since Lou still hadn't asked, I decided to take the initiative. Because he was scrupulous about not using NYPD vehicles for personal travel, I was driving. Realizing how silly and trite my suspicions sounded (even to myself), I broached them indirectly, under the guise of revisiting the Minister's remarks. I also assumed the facetious tone left over from my teaching days, which ended in retirement six years ago.

"I wonder if you caught the undertone of the eulogy."

"'Undertone'? What?" Lou had been lost in his own thoughts. "Well, wasn't the 'undertone,' as you call it, what it always is, a bunch of cliché's papering over the dead guy's faults? You already told me you never liked him."

"Not to put too fine a point on it, he was a prick."

As we approached the merger with the Van Wyck, we got stuck in traffic, which always happens on the Long Island "Distressway." One minute you're sailing along, the next, it's stop and go —and stop. When I had asked Lou about this on the way out, he had made one of his dry ripostes.

"Why ask me? I never drew traffic duty."

"If you don't mind, Lou," I said now, "I'll explain why I called him that, by going back to the eulogy."

"Why not? I bet this will be like one of your crazy lit. crit. riffs. I always enjoyed those, Jake."

"Let's take it point by point."

"'Respect the text.'"

"Yup. Here we go." The traffic had eased, but that was not what I meant. "Number One: 'family first.' Yeah, right, husband, father, Indian chief! I don't think so. When we played squash all those times, he would brag about how many hours he also logged at 'the grind,' his job."

'You're talking to a cop, Jake. Do you know what our divorce rates are like? And do you know the principal cause?"

Lou said this knowing that I knew he was an exception. Jessica, his first, and only, wife, is a lawyer who works with the homeless, and they have two normal (whatever that means) daughters, both in their teens.

I kept hammering at Point Number One. "Plus, most Saturday mornings, he would take the train in for..."

"Okay, okay, I get the idea. You know, if you had one flaw as a teacher, Jake, it was that, when you were on a roll, you couldn't stop. Actually, I think you once acknowledged as much, when we were reading *Othello*. Remember? In the middle of one of your monologues, the passing bell rang. We had been discussing the drinking scene where Iago causes chaos. A bell rings, and he says something like, 'Time flies when you're having fun.' You ended class by repeating that line."

Instead of providing the exact quotation, I said, "You always had a good memory, Lou. Point Number Two: '... universally respected by colleagues...' Actually, over the years, Jumbo often bragged about that. Early on, he was a financial advisor to 'Preferred Clients,' which meant, as I recall, ten million and up."

Lou interrupted. "Jess and I keep our own fortune, which is closer to ten thou, in an Index fund. That's because we read that, in the long run..."

I finished his sentence. "...financial advisers seldom beat the market. But they always collect 'the vig.' "

"You said, 'Early on,' Jake. After that?" Lou was obviously interested in money. Who isn't?

"I think he became a take-over specialist. But he never went into the details. Since he was normally such a braggart, I always assumed he worked along the border of legality --or south of the border."

Lou nodded. "Jess talks a lot about that sort of thing. One reason she left a lucrative practice of corporate law was the stench of dirty money. But get to the point, Jake. We're close to the tunnel. So far, not many surprises. I'm afraid this may not be one of your better efforts."

"Lou, Lou! My feelings are hurt." He shrugged. Then, we hit another traffic jam, a big one this time. At least, the gods were not tired of listening.

"Point Number Three is where this gets really good. Remember when the Minister waxed elephant about the American dream, about how Jumbo, 'a native of South Africa, arrived on our shores two decades ago'? Well, never mind the inaccuracy of that statement: he was certainly never a 'native,' either before or after the advent of majority rule in 1994, the year before he cleared out. There's something else. Another guy I play with, at a different club, a grad student in Philosophy from Johannesburg... As I'm sure you know, they call the place "Jo'burg."

"Or 'Joeys,'" Lou added. "I was there for a conference in 2012. Good steak."

"Anyway, this guy told me a story that was all over their press in the 90's. Guess what?"

"I remember that ploy, Jake, a hoary, but goodie. In the middle of a lecture, you would direct a question to the student who was paying least attention. Remember the time you did it --I think we were studying *Huck Finn*—to Harvey Grunewald, when he was sleeping? We all howled."

"Did you ever hear what happened to Harvey?" I asked. "I haven't seen him at any of the reunions. Speak, Memory! Didn't he drop out in the middle of senior year?"

"Actually, he was caught shoplifting, for the third time, and it turned out he had a serious drug problem. His parents shipped him off to a private clinic in Texas. The Headmaster called a special meeting with our class and fed us a bullshit story about how the family had moved."

"Hmm. I wonder why he never told *us* that story." I welcomed this excursus into crimes and misdemeanors.

Lou must have read my mind. "Where is this going, Jake?" By now, we were inching through the tunnel.

"Bear with me a minute more. I promise, you'll know by the time we get to your office." Which was in the complex just north of City Hall, about ten minutes beyond the tunnel.

"Fine. South Africa?"

"In the early nineties, when petty crime in Jo'berg was spinning out of control, three or four young thugs tried to mug an upstanding citizen named J.J. Thurston. He pulled out a handgun and shot two of them. One died, the other was paralyzed from the waist down. The courts ruled 'Self-Defense.'"

At that point, Lou's light bulb flashed. (More literally, we had just emerged on the Manhattan side of the tunnel.) "Oh, no, don't tell me! Not that tired old crap about how 'he didn't die of natural causes.' Ah ha! So that's why you asked *me* to go to the funeral with you. Come on, Jake, why not get a..." And, instead of completing the insult, he blew out a long breath. Why had it taken him so long? Maybe because he had been resisting the idea that his dear old teacher was capable of such inanity.

"Okay, okay," I conceded. "I won't bore you with the rest."

We drove on in silence. When we arrived at Headquarters, I pulled over, turned on the blinkers, thanked him, and started to apologize. He cut me off.

"Never mind, Jake," he said, "what are friends for?" Halfway out the door, he paused, and added, "Besides, as usual with you, the *obiter dicta* of that ridiculous *schtick* were very entertaining. As we all knew back in the day, you might not have always been a reliable narrator, but you told a hell of a story. Just like Huck, as someone –Samantha Rodriguez, I believe it was—pointed out once, at the senior lunch table."

"Understood," I meekly replied.

Leaning down into the car for a fist bump, which revealed a small brown leather shoulder holster, Lou winked. "Suppose I call you as soon as I get the drive-by case under control. Lunch?"

"You're my hero, Detective." I turned left, headed south, and three minutes later, I was climbing the ramp to the Brooklyn Bridge.

When two months passed without a word, I began to wonder if I had put the kibosh on our friendship. Where, I wondered for the fiftieth time, was this foolishness coming from? Perhaps, like Don Quixote, the source was literary. Over the years, as a sort of brainwash for the heavier stuff I had taught, I had always been a big fan of mystery novels.

In at least a couple, corpses are dug up, and foul play is confirmed. Then, there's one in which the victim is injected with poison by means of an ingenious plastic syringe that leaves an imitation snakebite. In another, an old guy who has apparently been asleep behind a newspaper at his club turns out to be dead. (I think the solution depended on the time of death, but I can't remember what he died from.) And, in still another one, set either in a mansion or on an island, a hated figure is murdered, and the murderer turns out to be everybody. Murder by Committee.

Meanwhile, hours and even whole days passed, during which I pushed my suspicions to the back of my mind. No one can teach English for forty years without understanding how poisonous obsessions can be. So, possibly with more energy than usual, I kept up my routine as a retiree: I read, listened to records and CD's, watched nature programs on Public TV, and went, alone or with friends, to concerts, museums, art shows, and movies.

One of these friends was a retired colleague named Mary Robison who, like me, had been a teacher for several decades. ("*Not 'Robinson,'*" she would inform students at the beginning of the term, writing the correct spelling on the board.) A trim sixty-something (would that be a "sexagenarian"?), M.R.'s field was Biology. She is currently the driving force behind a consortium of Lower Manhattan community gardens.

Although Mary is a bit obsessive, for my taste, during the last couple of years, I have been, as they say, "seeing" her. (I realize the irony of calling someone else 'obsessive.') Ours is a relationship that chugs along at a low level. As far as I know, she has never been married. We both get what we need from the relationship, and I think she may be as glad as I am not to be asked for more.

I'll mention, in passing, that I don't believe in casual romances, especially for old widowers like me. According to one of my less prudent friends, most of the women you're likely to meet, at places like the Y, coffee shops, or even concerts, seem to be gold diggers, mentally ill, or both.

No more theatergoing for me, either. The few "classics" I attended before stopping, turned out to be anything but. Every single one was a mistake, transpositions of the originals that were designed to create "relevance," and that totally ignored the romantic side of the old plays in favor of the violent, cynical and disgusting. Why pay forty or fifty bucks to see the first half of another stinker?

And, of course, in the interests of fitness, sanity and fun, among my other activities, I kept on playing, yes, squash, two or three times a week. Here, of course, my "foul play" obsession leaked through my attempts to enjoy the game. For how could my partners have failed to mention the newly dead bully and cheat, James Jumbo Thurston?

"Anyone remember the match Jumbo and Jake played a couple of years ago?" The recollect-or was a motor-mouthed braggart and small-time movie producer named Marvin Bird, who must have bad-mouthed Jumbo to me behind his back twenty times when he was still among the living. No one bit, presumably because no one wanted to hear that story again. But Marvin is irrepressible.

"Jumbo was up, two games to nil, way ahead in the third. Then, suddenly, Jake was in the zone. Shot after shot, tremendous! Feathery drop shots, smashing rails, cross-courts, lobs that died in the back corner —plus, he was running the diagonal like a gazelle. Before you could blink, he had pulled even. And, once he won that game, in the next two, he blew Jumbo away. I think the final scores were 9-7, 9-1, 9-nil. Correct me if I'm wrong, but I think Jumbo smashed his racquet against the wall and stalked off the court without saying a word. Remember that one, Jake?"

"I do, I do." And leaving it at that, we resumed play.

Several weeks after the funeral, I read in the paper that two teenaged suspects had been arraigned in the Bronx drive-by shootings. There was a photo of police spokesman, Detective Sergeant-Supervisor Louis M. Gordon, smiling grimly into the camera.

Three months after the funeral, and about a week after I had given up, Lou finally called. After the usual prelims, he suggested lunch the next day, at a glorified coffee shop near Headquarters: big menus, big portions, big prices, and a rogue's gallery of former Miss Subway's. As usual, I was free.

"I would have called sooner, Jake," he explained, "but I've been checking out a few things for you. I assume you're still wondering who killed Roger Rabbit?"

"It's been on the back burner," I admitted.

"I dug up some stuff that might be of interest," he said. "I'll tell you over lunch." Oh, boy!

After we had ordered, and our beverages of choice had arrived, Lou jiggled the ice in his iced coffee, and, without preamble, began to talk. Every so often, he referred to what I assumed were notes, on his smartphone. When his club sandwich came, he pushed it aside, so I also waited before cracking open my chicken potpie, which usually burns my mouth, anyway. To cool my heated imagination, I clutched my diet ginger ale. This is the gist of what he said:

"Motive, opportunity, means. You've read the books and seen the TV shows and movies, right, Jake? Let's take them in reverse order." He ticked off the points on his fingers. "Means: no way to autopsy a cremated body, and, when the local police went in, at my request, they found no material evidence: no suspicious fingerprints on a coffee cup, no footprints in the garden. Of course, they weren't looking too hard, since the death cert already indicated a 'fatal cardiac infarction.'

"Opportunity? Lots of that! Jumbo was alone in the house. His wife was playing soccer mom to their son, an only child. Which brings us to the important element: motive. *Everyone* had a motive to kill this guy, Jake. Not to put too fine a point on it, but, as you indicated, he was an outstanding piece of shit.

"Luckily, you're not my only connection at the sports club. A couple of my colleagues play racquetball on a court adjoining the squash courts. These guys are loud --I mean, really loud. But they had all heard Jumbo repeatedly go off on people. Apparently, 'sportsmanship' was not in his vocabulary. I'm sure you had first-hand experience." I nodded.

"As for the domestic angle, Jumbo's narcissism —shall we call it that, instead of tiptoeing around it? -- probably did not include infidelity. In fact, he was loudly monogamous. If I may venture a comparison, he was something like all those swindlers who pride themselves on church or synagogue attendance.

"Let's follow the money. Naomi, his wife, *nee* 'Entitlebaum (just kidding), is a greedy woman given to large expenditures on bling, and such, and, yes, Jumbo carried a hefty life insurance policy. But she had no lovers, either (at least, none that I could find), and she already had a fat bank account of her own. Even so, when it comes to greed..." Lou shrugged, and consulted his phone.

"Work. As we've already said, Jumbo was a piece of shit: super-competitive, always looking for an edge, party to numerous dubious transactions. 'But,' you might object, 'isn't that the name of the game?' Still, we can't rule out an irate client who lost his shirt on one of Jumbo's bum stock tips, or an executive who worked all his life building up a business, only to be thrown out on his ass after a Jumbo takeover." Afraid to break the spell, I did not even sip my ginger ale. The potpie was no longer steaming.

"Okay. With all those possibilities, I could spend a year's budget, and tie up my whole staff, tracking them down. Could I justify that, Jake? Ha!" Lou finally came up for air, and took a few quick bites from his sandwich, before resuming the monologue. I doubt he had talked this much during the whole year he was my student.

"I've saved the most interesting part for last: the South African connection. Those three 'muggers' he shot? I exchanged a few e-mails with a 'tec' I met at the 2012 conference I mentioned after the funeral. Listen to this, Jake: Jumbo was working under cover for the South African Police, or SAP (unfortunate acronym). And the 'muggers' were actually militants who had sneaked back into the country from Zimbabwe.

"As you can imagine, the case was murky. The official line was 'shot while eluding detention for membership in the African National Congress,' which, at the time, was an outlawed, super-violent anti-apartheid group. Jumbo might have been stalking the three cadres, and they turned on him. Of course, none of that came out at the trial. Anyway..." Another deep breath, and a gulp of iced coffee.

"After the advent of majority rule, in 1994, when the ANC took power, he didn't stick around long enough to participate in what they called the 'Truth and Reconciliation' process, whereby many people buried the figurative hatchet, for acts they may have committed with real ones. The shooting gives us a bunch of new suspects to add to our already long list: fringe haters from the ANC, members of the victims' families. (As you may know, Jake, revenge is sanctioned in some of South Africa's indigenous cultures.)"

With that, Lou drew another breath, and turned his full attention to his sandwich. My chicken potpie was still untouched, and it crossed my mind to wonder whether the crust had kept it warm during the long monologue. Fork poised to find out, I could not resist one final question.

"So?"

"'So'?" Holding up his traffic-cop hand, Lou swallowed, gulped some more coffee, and wiped his mouth with the big pink linen napkin. "'So,' you ask, 'what does it all add up to?' I was just getting to that." He looked me in the eye.

"Although the number of suspects is legion, the fact is, Jake, I think *you* killed Jumbo Thurston." Was he joking? "You killed him right in here." Ignoring my look of astonishment, Lou leaned across the table, tapped my forehead twice with his index finger, and returned to his sandwich.

The Key

They were waiting for their flight to board when they discovered the key in Judy's handbag.

"But how did…" Dave started to say. Then he realized that, although the bag had been x-rayed on three separate conveyor belts, each time the key had presumably been identified and allowed to pass.

"Oh, God," she said. "I'm so stupid!"

He offered to retreat to the main terminal and look for a way to mail the key back to the hotel.

"No, it would be too complicated."

She was probably right. After all, even though there was plenty of time, they didn't speak Turkish, most Turks seemed to speak little or no English, stamps and an envelope or box would have to be bought, they had spent the last of their Turkish lira (on apple tea and a CD), and, since September 11th, airports did not even seem to have mailboxes.

"I'm so stupid!" she repeated.

Dave pointed out that they had woken up very early to get ready to leave, and he reminded her of his own, bigger mistake, discovered the previous evening when he was paying the bill. His failure to notice that the rate on the travel agency website was in euros, rather than in Turkish lira or even dollars, had meant that four nights in their lovely "bargain" boutique hotel had made a big crack in the piggy bank.

So they boarded the plane in possession of the key, along with the pebbles Dave had gleaned from ground on which Xenophon and Jesus' mother were said to have trodden—

different ground— and all their other carry-on items, old and new, and they flew back, non-stop, to New York.

At 7 pm (2 am, Turkish time), they were in their apartment. While Judy rummaged through the piles of junk mail, bills, and magazines, Dave emailed the hotel, typing carefully to offset jet lag:

From: "david schaf" djshaf@etherhead.net
To: contact@otelsiyahkalem.com
Sent: Sunday, April 23, 2006, 7:18 PM
Subject: key

I'm sorry we forgot to return your key. We found it when we got home just now. Shall I mail it to you? Again, we had a wonderful time in Turkey and at the Otel Siyah Kalem, in particular.

Regards,
Dave and Judy Schaf

"They'll just say keep it or throw it away," she guessed.

When they woke up the next morning—4am Eastern Daylight Saving Time—a reply was waiting:

Dear Mr. and Ms. Schaf,

We are really glad to hear you had a nice stay at our hotel. Many thanks to your kindness for informing us about the key. We are sorry we did not remind you about it. Please accept our apologies for this. We would be grateful if you could mail the key to us since the keys are produced by a company for us and even if one is missing, we have to order for the full pack including a key for each room. This makes us collect keys at numbers more than needed. You can use our address below on the pack. Many thanks in advance.

The address is:
Hotel Siyah Kalem
Sokak Sehit Mehmet Pasha No, 11, Sultanahmet
Istanbul, 34203 Turkey

Best regards,
Turhan Belevi, Manager

Judy and Dave smiled over the gracious Mr. Belevi's almost-English.

At 5:30 the same evening (Turkish time), seated at his cluttered office behind the desk in the small, but elegant, lobby of the Otel Siyah Kalem, Belevi Bay (Mr. Belevi) read the American's prompt reply to his own email:

Dear Mr. Belevi,
I just mailed the key, so it should arrive within 5-7 business days.
Dave Schaf

Mr. Belevi ran his hand over his right cheek and stretched. This reply was more than satisfactory. Not only had the gracious American been willing to take these pains, and so promptly that the manager knew it would be safe to rely temporarily on the hotel's single spare key to this particular room without incurring the cost of yet another replacement set, almost 100 YTL (New Turkish Lira), but the message was gratifying, in its own right. Though terse, by Turkish standards, it could be regarded as an example of the American style, so businesslike, that Mr. Belevi was coming to believe he should prefer it to the Turkish style, whereby so many un- and under-employed men spent so much time smoking cigarettes, sipping tea, making plans and gossiping, all to so little effect.

In fact, one morning only a few days before, in a conversation about politics and economics with Selim, the clever young university student who served as his night clerk, Belevi had upheld the American way.

"They are our lever," he concluded (they were speaking Turkish), "into Europe. Their own prejudices do not encompass the fact" (to transliterate) "Turks are Asians, used to put the boot for five-hundred years up in Europe's posteriors."

Selim, whose English was impeccable, had replied (still in Turkish), "Well, that is true, of course. But, excuse me, Belevi Bay, the conditions are different, and so is the culture. Americans do not have a general unemployment rate of 11.7%. And that is the official rate. Not to mention the millions who are underemployed."

"That is exactly the point!" replied the manager excitedly. "They are the ones can help us to at-long-last EU promise land of milk and honey. And one more thing about them, they like everyone to act the same as they do. It makes them feel comfortable, happy. This, as I am sure you realize, Selim, my son," (*oglum*) "is the nature of our own product," (he said the word in English) "our own business!"

When they had finished laughing, Selim told his employer an anecdote. The previous morning another American, this one a big fool, was parting from his wife in front of the hotel. (Selim had been able to see and hear them from his desk because it was warm, so the doors were open.) The man had said goodbye to the wife by pointing up at the hotel sign and calling out, "See ya! Get it?" The wife, presumably accustomed to these jokes, had neither laughed nor replied, at least not loud enough for Selim to hear.

Belevi Bay did not grasp the joke until Selim had explained it three times. Even then it was not funny, but he finally got the point, perhaps because it was his own point: fools or not, Americans did things their own way.

The manager tapped the space bar to wake up his computer. In the American spirit of promptitude, but also thinking that enough was enough, he replied to Mr. Schaf's email in a way that he anticipated would end this small matter.

Dear Mr. Schaf,
Thank you very much for your effort. We hope to hear from you again.

Sincerely yours,
Turhan Belevi

Mr. Schaf did not reply, but Mr. Belevi was wrong about the matter's having ended. On the sixth business day, the following Tuesday, the key did arrive, in a sturdy little white box, doubly packaged in a folded page from the estimable *New York Times*, inside a nest of wrapping material. Unfortunately, there was a problem. In addition to the two addresses, the box bore the frightening official stamp of the Milli Istihbarat Teskilati, or MIT, the Turkish National Intelligence Organization, which is the principal arm of the country's elaborate security apparatus, sometimes referred to as "the deep state". The box had been opened and re-taped shut. This stamped and re-sealed box spelled potential disaster. Having opened the box, if they had found anything at all that activated their preternatural antennae, the MIT could be counted upon to pay a prompt, unannounced visit to the hotel at any hour. And no one in his right mind would welcome such a visit, since MIT operatives were not known for tact or gentleness.

Luckily for him, however, Mr. Belevi held a potential trump card which he played immediately. Hastily locking the office, the Manager informed Deniz, his taciturn day clerk, that he was going out but would return shortly. Deniz replied in his usual way: a curt nod. Belevi hopped down the three front steps, turned left and, at the corner, turned right and ran uphill the five blocks to the National Court building, arriving at the entrance in a sweat. Passing through the metal detector without incident, he ran up the two steep flights to the private office of his first cousin (although on the mother's side). This man, Colonel Ahmet Fatiyeh, was Chief Army Liaison Officer with the MIT for the entire Sultanahmet district.

As he entered the large office of his cousin, who was about his own age, it occurred to Belevi Bay that it would have been more polite to telephone first. But no, he thought, this way he will sense my urgency. Colonel Fatiyeh rose, wearing an unsurprised and warm expression, as if the cousins saw each other every day. In fact, it had last been about a month, and that was at a circumcision ceremony, a mandatory event. They clasped hands, embraced, and exchanged the customary greetings:

"Hos geldiniz," said the Colonel. ("Welcome.")

"Hos bulduk." ("I'm glad to be here.")

"Nasilsiniz?" ("How are you?")

"Iyiyim, tesekkur ederim." ("I am very well, thank you.")

After three small glasses of black tea had been consumed by each man, and inquiries made and satisfactorily answered regarding the health of family members, Fatiyeh Bay lit up one of the foul local cigarettes he preferred. (Mr. Belevi was among the one-third of adult Turkish men who are non-smokers.) Then, allowing his anxiety to show, the visitor explained his plight. "Hmm," mused the Colonel, blowing smoke across the desk but to the left of his kinsman. "I wonder what their problem is with this small package. May I see it?"

The manager shrugged his shoulders and lifted his hands, as if imploring enlightenment from above. "I'm afraid I don't have it with me," he apologized.

Mr. Belevi had not thought to bring along the package, perhaps because the stamp had caused a certain superstitious dread of even walking through the streets with the package in his possession. He also noted with concern that Fatiyeh had used the present tense ("what their problem is...").

"But I have an idea," the Colonel continued. "Was there any message enclosed with your key inside the package? Words of any kind? A note? Anything like that?"

"Nothing, not a single word," Belevi nervously replied, trying to visualize the precise contents of the package.

"In what was the key wrapped?"

"[Bubble wrap]," Belevi replied. (He had to resort to a circumlocution, because the words do not exist in Turkish.)

"Nothing more?" the Colonel persisted.

"No…" Then he remembered. "Ah, but yes, inside the [bubble wrap] around the key was a page from an American newspaper. *The New York Times*," he added in English.

The Colonel looked pleased. "Ah well, there, quite possibly, lies your answer." He glanced toward the open door, then lowered his voice. "This is for you to know, Belevi Bay, but you alone. Of late, by means of intercepted emails, the MIT has become aware of yet another newly hatched conspiracy between separatist elements in our country and a few American sympathizers, these living in their district of New Jersey. And so…"

He shrugged. Mr. Belevi's face grew hot, and he opened his mouth to protest his innocence.

"No, no, of course not," the Colonel reassured him. "No one who knows you, Belevi Bay, could possibly doubt your loyalty to our nation, even for a single instant." He paused, and Mr. Belevi thought he might have caught a whiff of malicious pleasure. "But the MIT do not know you." The Colonel smiled, then added, "However, I shall have a word about your little box with my… counterpart at our meeting this afternoon, and, after that, the matter should hopefully be closed." He ended with what was presumably meant to be a reassuring proverb. "And, pardon me, Belevi Bay, but remember what our people in the hinterland say: 'If God wants to make a poor man happy, he first makes him lose his donkey, then allows him to find it again.'"

"Thank you very much, Fatiyeh Bay," said Belevi, getting up, "both for your kind offer of help and for your recitation of the comforting proverb."

Privately he was amused by the soldier's display of fidelity to his rural roots, when he had been living in Istanbul his entire adult life. In fact, like the lost-and-found animal in the proverb, the Colonel was a bit of an ass himself.

"I will take away no more of your time," Belevi added.

Colonel Fatiyeh also rose, tugged at the skirts of his khaki uniform jacket, then came around the desk to enfold his kinsman in a bony embrace.

"If you do not hear from me, Belevi Bay," he concluded, "assume all is well."

Mr. Belevi closed with the usual greeting, "Allahaismarladik." ("Goodbye.")

"Gule gule," replied the Colonel politely. ("Go your way with a smile.")

As he walked back down the hill to the hotel, the manager tried not to worry, but three small details from the conversation made complacency difficult. Colonel Fatiyeh had spoken of the problem in the present tense. Then, there were the words "hopefully" and "if you do not hear from me". Belevi had thought of asking "By when?" but doing so would have presumed too much upon his kinsman's limited obligation. So he would just have to wait. "Hopefully" he would never hear anything more about this matter, and the anxiety would gradually dissipate. One learned to live with uncertainty.

In their own way the Schafs were suffering, too. For one thing, although they had only been in Turkey sixteen days, the seven-hour time difference, the longest yet experienced on any of their trips, was proving very hard to overcome. Since they were both retired, they could take naps to compensate for waking up in the middle of the night (which had already begun to be a problem a decade before, when they had bumped into their sixties). But the naps caused the jet lag to linger, creating other difficulties. For instance, one morning about a week after they got home, in attempting to roll up a sleeve preparatory to washing his face, Dave landed a solid uppercut to his own jaw. And, as she worked on the daily crossword puzzles in the *Times*, Judy found herself experiencing uncharacteristic word retrieval problems.

In some surprising ways, the trip had also altered their perspective, especially hers. More visual than her husband, she thought New York looked different. The edges were squarer, and there seemed to be less squalor and teeming. In a wakeful dream, a haze, at about 5am on the tenth day back, she visualized the immense, perfect piles of perfect Turkish vegetables in the sprawling markets, and the vision gave her an unwonted disappointment that her own city was poor in consumer goods. The vegetable piles were succeeded by a vision of New York, but with a difference: it was somehow thinned out, culled of buildings, as if a sort of anti-neutron bomb had struck, not killing, or even injuring, anyone, but creating—or re-creating—big spaces between the buildings. Dave was amused by his wife's visions, which she shared with him. Having long given up trying to get back to sleep, they were sitting at the kitchen table drinking their morning coffee. By now it was after eight. A short silence followed Judy's confession (if that was what it was).

"I wonder if they got the key yet," she said.

"I know. But I didn't want to bother him again. Mr. Belevi."

"I'm sure he wouldn't mind an email."

Dave wiped his mouth on his napkin and, popping up like an unleashed greyhound, he rushed from the kitchen toward the study. Judy went on with the previous day's crossword. Although it was only Tuesday's, normally easy, the bottom-left corner remained a mass of blanks and erasures. Ten minutes later the corner had almost sorted itself out, and Dave was back.

"That's odd," he said, sitting down at the table again. "Belevi replied immediately. But all he said was that there'd been a problem with the package. He didn't thank me for returning it, didn't even say what the problem was."

Judy shrugged and returned to her own puzzle. Dave got dressed and left the apartment to do the day's food shopping.

Two days later, at just after seven in the evening when four big MIT men in dark suits showed up at the hotel, Selim, who had just come on duty, was coincidentally combing the page of the *Times* in which the key had been wrapped, searching for possible clues as to what had excited the interest of the authorities. Luckily, since it was the dinner hour, the lobby was empty when the men trundled in. He did not try to hide the page, which prominently featured a completed crossword puzzle. Seeing this page, the one who would do all the talking (obviously the leader, even though the four looked virtually identical) raised an eyebrow but made no comment.

Mr. Belevi was summoned, tea offered and refused. In the subsequent questioning—" interrogation" would be too strong a word—the MIT man never raised his voice, but he spoke in a sneering manner that seemed designed to intimidate. The implication was that Mr. Belevi would have had it much worse if not for his cousin, the colonel, who was not, however, directly mentioned.

There were no blows, no direct harassment, only the sneering tone and a great deal of aggressive questioning, starting with the details of the loss and return of the key. Since it was apparent that the MIT had already read all the emails concerning the key, including that day's exchange, Selim, a devotee of mystery and spy novels, surmised that they were trawling for lies or inconsistencies. Then came a demand for the names and addresses of all (fourteen) hotel employees, a puzzling question about the name of the hotel, and a few further, miscellaneous questions that seemed vague, even pointless. Selim wondered if any of their visitors raised an internal eyebrow when Mr. Belevi, in listing the employees, named Hezan, the old Kurdish man who, very early every morning, bought the food, then served the guest breakfasts.

Next, the leader and Mr. Belevi took the small lift to the fourth floor, while the other three MIT men sprinted up the stairs, Selim tagging along. Mr. Belevi was instructed to use the returned key to open the room. Although the possessions of the current guests— two unmarried German women—were scattered around, fortunately the women were out. After the three underlings had made a cursory search that left these possessions untouched and appeared to yield nothing in particular, everyone stood in the room while the leader asked a few more questions. Who were these Americans who had sent the key? Exactly when had it been carried off? And so on. It was a disappointment to Selim that the MIT did not dust for fingerprints.

After that, they all trundled down the stairs and piled into Mr. Belevi's small office, which could barely hold the six of them. Selim felt sorry for his heavily perspiring employer, who was forced to stand by while one of the underlings sat at his desk and copied the manager's email folder onto a blank CD (property of the hotel, not paid for). Selim, who discreetly read all of his boss's emails, blushed for the eight or ten of them in which, about a year before, Mr. B. had carried on a mild flirtation with a young typist, a distant relation of Belevi Bayan, Mrs. B. (on whom Selim himself had a mild crush).

Finally, donning hospital gloves, one of the MIT men dropped the key, all the packaging materials, and then the gloves into an evidence bag. Without providing a receipt, without explaining what might happen next, without so much as a parting greeting, they strode out of the office, across the lobby (blessedly, still empty), out the front door of the hotel, and down the street, presumably to the car park.

Neither Selim nor Belevi Bay cared to discuss what had just happened. With a shrug, the manager retreated to his office where, head in hands, he sat worrying his beads. Selim sought comfort surfing the web at the small computer behind the desk in the lobby.

A long time passed. At one point the two men's chains of thought converged, both wondering why the MIT had asked about the name of the hotel.

The exact question had been, "Who gave this place its name, and why?" Unbeknownst to the MIT (or to Mr. Belevi or Selim, for that matter), it had been the original owner who had named the smart new hotel in 1973, a decade before Mr. Belevi's tenure began, and seven years before Selim came into this world. 1973: a year in which, as it happened, in commemoration of the Republic's 50th anniversary, the city's Bosphorus Bridge had been built, linking Europe and Asia. In that year, too, several Turkish men and women had been born who would go on to achieve a small measure of international prominence in various fields.

"Who gave this place its name, and why?"

Mr. Belevi worried; Selim investigated. He vaguely remembered the name from his secondary school days, and, refreshing his memory via the Internet, soon re-learned the facts. Siyah Kalem was a 15th-century Ottoman miniaturist known for drawings of people, animals and mythological creatures— drawings of a striking, even violent realism. Selim accessed scores of images that reminded him of the main reason he and his classmates had been so excited to discover this artist from five centuries past: the man's work strikingly resembled the graffiti and "head" comics many of them adored. A second reason for the boys' fascination was that absolutely nothing was known about the life of this amazing genius. As he kept on trolling and scrolling, Selim was amused to discover that the name had also, in recent years, been "borrowed" by a horse, a valuable modern brood stallion. He wondered why, in the three years he had been working at the eponymous hotel, he had never once thought of the artist.

What Selim could not learn, even now, was the reason the name interested the MIT and their American counterparts in the constituent Agencies of Homeland Security—that post-9/11 alphabet soup of the CIA, NSA, and FBI. To these people the name of the hotel was a very red flag.

"Siyah Kalem," the artist's "pen" name (his real name was Mehmet), means "Black Pen," and the name had recently been borrowed for a third time, in this case for the Internet "handle" of a radical Islamist group, one of the numerous progeny of Black September. While the group had not yet taken credit for any specific acts of violence—they did not even have a website—" Black Pen" was under close watch for suspicious clandestine gatherings and bellicose email exchanges. Several of these emails, although none of the worst ones, had been traced to a town in New Jersey seventy miles from New York City, a town with a sizeable Muslim population that included eight or nine Turks and, as it happened, also the town where a first cousin of Judy Schaf's resided with her husband and their young son. The Muslims in question, especially a Turkish-American Middle-School Science teacher and his cousin, a gas station attendant, had been under surveillance for over a year. That the Turkish cousins often jogged together around the track at the high school in the early morning hours excited particular suspicion, for two reasons: an outdoor track is a good place to escape electronic surveillance, and one of the other runners, although he normally ran in the evening, was Judy's cousin's husband.

These "coincidences" were bruited by the polite pair of men in black who, after first telephoning, visited Dave and Judy in their apartment on the evening after their Turkish counterparts had called on Mr. Belevi. Initially, the two men spoke only of suspicious activity involving nationals of Middle-Eastern origin". They also mentioned the high-school track in New Jersey as a place where the Turkish cousins met almost daily. Then they zeroed in.

"If you don't mind my asking, are you close to your cousin and her family, Ms. Schaf?" asked Wattrous, the large African-American Agent.

"Not especially," answered Judy, who did indeed mind this whole vague, intrusive business.

Dave felt the same way. "What," he asked aggressively, "is this all about? We've been patient so far, but…"

The second man, Agent McCarthy, medium-sized, white and nondescript, interrupted. "Yes," he agreed, "you've been very cooperative, and we thank you for that, sir. Of course, I'm sure you also understand that the world has changed in the last five years, so…"

As Agent McCarthy nattered on in this vein, Judy noticed that even Agent Wattrous glazed over almost immediately. After about a minute McCarthy abruptly and bluntly got to the point.

"Okay," he said. "'What's this all about?' The name of the hotel, the 'Siyah Kalem', or 'Black Pen', is also the name of a suspected terrorist sleeper cell that these two men belong to." He seemed to sense their skepticism. "Not enough? Okay. When you mailed the hotel a key that you had apparently forgotten to return, do you remember how you wrapped it… the key?"

"Sure," Dave replied, "in bubble wrap, and in a small white box our new checks from the bank came in."

"And…?" Wattrous prompted.

"'And' what?" Dave asked.

"This."

Wattrous bent down and took a single sheet of paper from his old-fashioned brown leather briefcase. He held it out so both Schafs could read it. He and McCarthy appeared to be watching closely for a reaction. For a moment, Dave and Judy looked at each other, nonplussed. Then they both burst out laughing.

"Don't tell me…" Judy said, still laughing.

Dave began to shake his head. His face now wore a cynical expression that meant, "This is how they spend our tax dollars?"

"Look again," McCarthy suggested, pointing a thick forefinger at the page. "These lines and loops on the copy of your puzzle have been made by our cryptographers. The handwriting, the answers, as I'm sure you'll admit, is… are yours, Ms. Schaf."

For a moment, Dave and Judy, who were no longer laughing, peered at the sheet of paper.

"Oh, no!" said Judy. "I can't believe this."

"Is it time for me to say we refuse to continue this conversation without our lawyer?" asked Dave rhetorically, although he had a vague idea that the Patriot Act denied their right to a lawyer under the circumstances.

The cryptographers' markings consisted of two serpentine loops. One connected two answers by zigzagging from the top right corner of the puzzle to the bottom, left of center. The words that had been linked, unrelated in the puzzle, were "aye" and "wrack." The second, more elaborate, linking, this one connecting three answers in a pattern that crisscrossed the puzzle twice, involved the words "black", "pen", and "death".

"Thank you for your cooperation," said McCarthy, after a decent interval.

"We may need to speak to you again," said Wattrous, returning the copy to his briefcase. "Meanwhile, please do not share this conversation with anyone. Believe me, that way things will be better for all of us."

As they showed the men to the door of the apartment and locked it behind them, Dave and Judy held their tongues. A long discussion immediately ensued, a tissue of complaints and weak mockery that was really just weak bravado.

Thereafter the Schafs did their best to return to business (such as it was) as usual. However, despite Agent Wattrous's closing admonition, not many people—especially not underemployed people, which, after all, Dave and Judy were— can receive a visitation from "the deep state" without talking about it. Not that they needed to get a life or anything, but not even the busy round of shopping, cooking and dishwashing (cleaning and laundry were done for them), museums, books, concerts, Scrabble, Monopoly, and card games, occasional family "occasions", other family visits and telephone calls, restaurant meals and reciprocal dinner parties with friends, and (yes) crosswords (her) and gym workouts, emailing and Web surfing (him) could quite fill the long waking hours of the young retirees. As Selim had done, Dave immediately googled "Siyah Kalem," discovering the artist and stallion, but not the terrorist group.

Whatever the reasons, during the following week, waiting as it were for the other boot to fall, Dave and Judy were almost intentionally reckless in sharing the story of the key with family, friends, and even acquaintances. The only notable exceptions were Judy's cousin and her husband in New Jersey. To raise the matter with them would indeed have been imprudent. But the possibility that the story would get to the Jersey cousins via a third party seemed small enough to ignore.

Both by telephone and email, they went over the business with their daughter who lived in Chicago, whom they swore to secrecy, and who shared their indignation over the general erosion of civil liberties. Her husband, a corporate lawyer, had a very different opinion, which he expressed to his wife in his usual brusque manner.

"Look, those people have to do what they have to do. It's not your parents' world anymore."

His opinion was not shared with Dave and Judy. However, when most of the week had gone by without an aftermath, the Schafs finally did make a vow to try to stop talking about the key, both privately and with other people, not because they had been warned, but because talking did no good and, anyhow, they were sick of the subject. It took them about an hour to break the vow.

"I wonder what's happening to Mr. Belevi," said Dave.

"I know. I hate to imagine."

"Maybe I should send him another email—or call him."

"I don't like that idea, it could cause trouble. We don't have any idea what's happening over there, but it may not be so nice. EU application or not, their agents are probably a lot worse than that Wattrous and…what's his name, McCartney?"

"McCarthy," Dave corrected. Then they both realized the irony of the name and looked at each other with the "are you thinking what I'm thinking?" look. After forty-six years of marriage the answer was, as usual, affirmative.

At any rate, Mr. Belevi remained in their thoughts, but Dave, by now imagining tapped phones, intercepted emails, and further ingenious sleuthing (as with the crossword), did refrain from contacting him. They kept on complaining about the business to only thirty or forty of their closest friends.

"So. These facts I have been able to ascertain."

It was a week after the synchronized visits from the two security agencies. Mr. Belevi and his cousin, Colonel Fatiyeh, who had telephoned to invite him to lunch, were sitting at a small table in a far corner of a famous local kofteci (meatball restaurant). The L-shaped room was crowded, but the Colonel was in uniform and, anyway, he was well known to the proprietor, so the waiters did not pressure them to finish eating and leave. Belevi and Fatiyeh were being cautious. The restaurant had been chosen as a plausible meeting place and because, unless the proprietor were lying or unaware, it was free from electronic surveillance. As usual, the cousins spoke Turkish.

"They have now dropped the idea of a New Jersey terrorist connection," Fatiyeh divulged. As the conversation proceeded, both Fatiyeh and Mr. Belevi kept on eating and periodically checking their cell phones for messages. (Turkish culture permits multi-tasking.) "Mrs. Judy Schaf's cousin's husband, Mr. Irwin Nagel, is above suspicion. In fact, he has turned out to be a big judge, Judge Irwin Nagel, and a politically conservative Republican Party supporter as well."

"Why did it take them so long to discover this key fact?" Mr. Belevi wondered immediately if he should have bitten his tongue. Not that he regretted the half-intended near-pun. (In Turkish the word he had used, *ana*, although not identical with the noun, *anahtar*, is indeed related.) No, it was not the near pun he regretted, it was the too obviously implied criticism of authority.

Fatiyeh shrugged and did not answer. His expression was of studied neutrality. The same question had occurred to him but, of course, one did not share criticism of sister services with civilians, cousins or not. But Mr. Belevi was so annoyed that, even when he tried to move the discussion forward, his annoyance came through.

"Do I dare hope the business is accordingly resolved?"

The Colonel laughed. "Are we presently eating lunch in New Jersey, then? Am I dreaming, or is this not Turkey, [where] few things are ever 'resolved'?" (Turkish has no relative pronouns or relative adverbs.)

Mr. Belevi groaned. "Oh, well," he shrugged, taking another forkful of the now-cold pilaf and swallowing it without chewing. "So the poor man has once again lost his donkey. What is their problem now?"

Unlike the donkey, the reference was not lost, at least not on the Colonel, to whom his cousin's muted mockery came through loud and clear. And, although he would not admit it, Fatiyeh was amused and, in a way, even impressed, since after fifteen years' acquaintance he had covertly grown scornful of his wife's cousin for a certain timidity, a deficiency of spirit, having come to regard him as, yes, a steady and dependable man, but a drudge, employed in a generally demeaning business. In part, this was just the scorn of the soldier for the civilian. But now the hotelier's little joke improved the Colonel's opinion of his kinsman, and this, in turn, made him resolve the big question he had brought to the lunch— how much to reveal— in Mr. Belevi's favor.

"All right," he said, leaning forward, "I will tell you exactly [what] has happened."

"Efendi" [Sir], said Mr. Belevi, bowing his head.

"They have turned their attention to the [bubble wrap]. On both the key itself and on this material, they have discovered substantial residues of a powder they regard with suspicion."

Mr. Belevi almost lost it (his temper), right then. It was on the tip of his tongue to suggest to his cousin that he tell his MIT counterpart to search for powdery clues within his own anus. But then Mr. Belevi had a horrible thought: why was the Colonel suddenly being so accommodating? Could he be trusted? Trying to keep his tone from changing too obviously, and swallowing his rage, Mr. Belevi ventured a neutral question.

"'Suspicious' powder? In what way?"

The Colonel shrugged. "That information," he said slowly, "my counterpart did not volunteer. Your guess is as good as mine."

Mr. Belevi could indeed guess, but he thought it just as well to mimic his cousin's shrug and go on eating. Turning to family small talk, they soon completed the meal, after which they squabbled briefly over the check, the Colonel winning because he had issued the invitation, and was thus the host. With profuse thanks and polite disclaimers, and with the usual embraces and other formalities, they parted on the sidewalk.

Mr. Belevi's guess about the powder was based upon some articles, dating back about five years, in the Turkish edition of *Time* magazine, which he read about once a month on their website. (Occasionally, in fact, he would even do this with the English print edition alongside, in a half-hearted attempt to improve his rudimentary command of that impossible language.)

His guess was that the MIT, and perhaps their American counterparts as well, were testing the [bubble wrap] for anthrax or other poisons. How ridiculous! What likelihood was there that the genial, elderly American couple had been in possession of poisoned [bubble wrap]? Next to none, surely. Still, the guess was not comforting.

Mr. Belevi's guess was correct, but he was, as usual, behind the curve. The FBI Laboratory Division in Quantico, Virginia, had already tested the powder for anthrax, as well as for six or seven other poisons, passing their findings, all negative, along to the MIT. In fact, by the day of the lunch at the kofteci, the course of the forensic investigation had already tacked in a new direction.

By now, their son-in-law had communicated to the Schafs, via his wife—their daughter—that cooperation would be the best way to make the whole business with the key disappear in the shortest possible time.

"How long does he think that will take?" Dave asked. They were speaking on the phone.

She tried to be patient. "How could he possibly know, Dad?"

Despite the good advice, as they waited for the "Security Brothers," as they had dubbed them, to barge back into their lives, Dave and Judy were finding it hard to hide the fact that they were hopping mad. During the week that followed the first incursion not even all their loose-lipped complaints could inoculate them from the effects of the incursion.

They found themselves making an effort to hold their recent, marvelous vacation in a good light. More than once they looked over the 200 pictures they had taken with their new digital camera. One evening they edited these into a file of the "best" 65, marveling at how every ancient site had been a revelation, how they had never reached the expected state of "site fatigue". The same was true of all the mosques, museums and ancient churches. They remembered with special pleasure a Byzantine church-cum-mosque they had visited their last day in Turkey.

The aftermath of the visit, although nothing special, also remained a fond memory. That evening they had been back in the room, shoes off. Face to face on the big divan (a Turkish invention and word), they relaxed among the big pillows, enjoying the complimentary fruit and wine.

"Would you mind not pointing your feet at me?" Judy requested.

"What? Oh, sorry."

They had read in a guidebook that Turks considered foot pointing impolite. Although Dave knew the request was not serious, he shifted so that the offenders were aimed a bit to her left.

"That's much better, thanks."

After they had revisited all these wonderful places and recalled their last evening at the Siyah Kalem, as he was washing the dishes, Dave had a sad reaction: his pleasure dissipated almost immediately. But he decided to keep this to himself, not wanting to spoil Judy's pleasure. He also knew that she did not react kindly to strong doses of his pessimism.

By now it was mid-May and unseasonably warm. When the Security Brothers phoned one weekday morning around ten to announce a second incursion at one that afternoon, Dave and Judy had been about to turn on the air conditioner for the first time since the previous fall. But before doing so, they reacted to the call by hatching a plan. Like their inability to stop talking about the first incursion, this plan can possibly be blamed, at least in part, on their underemployment.

On the first visit they had observed that McCarthy was fair haired and red-faced, a physical type that does not usually come with an effective thermostat, and that Wattrous, although fit looking, was on the hefty side. Hence, the plan. After running the air for an hour and a half, they spitefully turned it and the circuit breaker off and left the windows closed, so that by the time the agents were due to arrive, the apartment should have heated up nicely. Since the windows faced west, and on hot muggy days like this any wind came from the south and east, they were betting that conditions would remain stifling even after the windows had once again been opened.

As zero hour approached, the conspirators synchronized their story: sorry, the air was not working. If it came to it, Dave would flip the air-conditioner switch on and off so the agents could see for themselves. If they mentioned the breaker, they would be told baldly that it was not accessible. The Schafs had both consumed plenty of liquids that morning, and no refreshments were to be on offer.

At first, this childish plan seemed to work. Within fifteen minutes, McCarthy had turned very red and Wattrous was sweating profusely. However, the Agents were trained to tough it out. After apologizing for having suspected the innocent cousin, McCarthy mopped his face and laid the ground for introducing new suspicions by offering up more generalities about the dangerous world. Wattrous wriggled in his too warm suit, well aware that regulations prohibited Agents in the field, who wore side arms, from removing their jackets. Maliciously, as McCarthy nattered on, Wattrous calculated that the Schafs would ultimately have to pay a percentage, though tiny, of the dry-cleaning bill for two soaked suits. He amused himself by trying to do an accurate mental calculation, but it was hard to get the decimals right.

As for McCarthy, since this was one of more than twenty pending cases with which he and his partner were doing their best to cope, and one of the least pressing, at that, he was forcing himself not to rush, not to reveal important facts prematurely. Both he and Wattrous had been well trained in this particular discipline, the "soft interrogation". The Schafs were obviously Category 3F's: mildly hostile, passive-aggressive respondents. (There are nine categories in all, with a total of 47 sub-categories.)

"We're not accusing you of anything," he said, in reply to Judy's nasty rhetorical question. ("So now that you've discovered your mistake about the Judge, why not just go away?") "But we do have to pursue the matter."

"Just a bit further, we hope," added Wattrous, playing good cop for the moment. "And please, you know how important something like this could be." A drop of sweat fell from the tip of his nose, and he deftly caught it on his tongue. He added another sentence or two about the threat of global terrorism, a threat he felt sure Judy and Dave were no more prepared to deny than most middle-class Americans, and he took their silence for confirmation.

"You see," McCarthy picked up, "our forensics people have been analyzing a substance found in the package in question. They have determined that this substance is a powder residue. INTERPOL…sorry, do you know what that is?"

Other than to glance at each other, the Schafs did not respond. Although he noticed the glances, McCarthy pushed on. "We learned from INTERPOL that…" Then he changed tack, abruptly and intentionally. "That bubble wrap had been used to transport tiles, right? Before you wrapped the, uh, key in it?"

"Yes, that's right," replied Dave, starting to overheat, himself, and finding it harder to stick to his son-in-law's advice. "But you're barking… "

"Right," McCarthy interrupted. "Indulge me here while I make a short detour. Actually, you may find it interesting. Are we okay with that? Ms. Scha…"

"Oh, just go ahead," said Judy crossly, unable by now to tell whether she was more overheated or angry. "Just stop stopping!"

Dave was also angry, and he piled on. "If you kept moving… Agent, maybe we could get to the end of this." He had barely refrained from saying "Senator".

"Sure." McCarthy smiled, his equanimity impressive. "Okay then, we're talking tiles, but not, I repeat, not, your common bathroom tile or the usual tourist—excuse me—crap."

Wattrous' function during this part of the interrogation was to observe the reactions of the subjects, trolling for specific visual clues. These "clues" were instantaneous, blatant and unexpected: at the mention of "tourist crap", both Schafs began shaking with suppressed laughter. He had to make a snap decision. He could either ask the Schafs what was so funny, thereby aborting the interrogation plan and ceding them the initiative, or he could wait a little longer, hoping an explanation would be forthcoming, assuming that they would want to explain. It was his call, and he knew McCarthy would not intrude. He decided to wait.

Without blinking, McCarthy launched into a disquisition on ceramic tiles. The purpose was to weaken resistance, to get the Schafs to lower their guard. But there was a flaw in this strategy: the disquisition was too interesting. Even though Dave and Judy had read all about Turkish ceramics in various guidebooks, some of the details the Agent now recited (from memory) were impressive. At least they have some skills, Judy thought. Even Wattrous enjoyed the erudite-sounding speech, which he thought would have gotten his partner an "A" if this had been a memorization exercise at the Academy.

"Okay, so…tiles. We're talking Byzantine here, late Byzantine to be more precise. Let me ask you a question. Have you heard of a church called St. Saviour's in Chora?"

"We visited that church," Judy admitted. "On April 22nd, our last day in Istanbul. It took a long, expensive taxi ride to get there, but it was worth it, a wonderful church. What about it?"

"Yes, we know," McCarthy said. "I'll come right back to that point. Bear with me for just another moment. Since you visited the church, I'm probably going to tell you some things you already know. It is an amazing place, isn't it?" Although he had never been to St. Saviour's, or even to Turkey himself, he had accessed world class images from the website of a German university. He slipped easily into guide-bookese.

"St. Saviour in Chora, or 'in the country'. It was originally called that because it was built outside Constantine's walls, sort of like 'St. Martin's in the Fields'. The church's splendid mosaics come from the period when it was rebuilt, 1315-21, during the final Byzantine flowering, a mere century before the Turkish conquest of 1453. The mosaics depict the lives of Mary and Jesus. There are also Italian Renaissance-influenced frescoes, magnificent too, exactly contemporary with Giotto. In the 16th century the church was converted to a mosque, the Kariye Camii, or 'church mosque', by one of those eunuch-grand viziers, I forget his name." (This last was true, an atypical lapse.) "After that the mosaics were obscured, buried by paint, dirt, earthquakes, whatever, until they were finally uncovered in the mid-20th-century. Sadly, the flight into Egypt had been destroyed, but the apocryphal fall of idols from the wall of an Egyptian town as the Holy Family passes through is still there." He paused for effect. "I say 'still there', but that's not quite true. Until last month, until sometime during the week of April 17th to 23rd, in fact, the 'fall of idols' was still there, reposing in a locked, but, alas, unalarmed, case in the hallway just to the right as you enter the church. Remember?"

Dave could take no more of this. "Okay, okay, that's enough," he said. "Stop, I confess. You've caught us: yes, some tiles from St. Saviour's cariye—that's how you pronounce 'church,' in Turkish, by the way, you should know that—were in our bubble wrap."

By now no one felt hot anymore. As if on cue, at some point during the half-hour conversation, if you could call it that, the weather had broken, and a fresh west wind made it feel as if the air conditioning had been on all along. No one had noticed.

Judy tag-teamed onto this delicious moment. "Except," she explained, "our tiles were, as you put it, 'tourist crap'. Eight kitchen magnet tiles, to be exact, costing a total of around four dollars, American. (Of course we were probably cheated.) We bought them from a transplanted German who runs a small shop right outside the front door of the church, just to the left as you leave. Do you know about him?"

"Why didn't you just test the powder before you got into all this…stuff?" Dave asked.

The reason, Agent Wattrous replied, they were not at liberty to divulge.

"But you must know about the shop," Judy said, to goad them further. "I mean, with all the other homework you two have obviously been doing."

In fact, Wattrous and McCarthy had viewed the shop, and about six others like it, on a hugely magnified NSA satellite map. The truth that could not be divulged was that all these coincidences, the theft and the visit to the church, together with the key, the name of the hotel, and the jogging cousin in New Jersey, could not, in the post-911 world of FBI bureaucratic shake-ups and security agency infighting, simply be glossed over. Were the Schafs likely to be tile thieves? Accomplices of terrorists? Of course not. But the security agencies of many nations had learned a painful lesson: ignore nothing, assume nothing. Of course, in practice, that was impossible…but they tried.

As things now stood, this particular case turned on perhaps eighty to one hundred thousand dollars U.S. from the black art market, passing sinuously through a network of terrorist money laundering channels. (In discussing how the St. Saviour's tile money might move through these channels, Wattrous, who had a tiresome propensity for puns, which McCarthy called "the slave's revenge", had actually used the word "Byzantine".) The key point was to pick up the trail before the scent faded. The object was to augment the agencies' knowledge of certain channels leading out of Turkey.

But now that the Schafs had said the magic words, in this case "tourist crap", now that they had filled in the final dots in their alibi, protocol dictated that it would be "wait for the tests", after all. In perfect synchrony each Agent unobtrusively scratched his chest, thereby turning off his wire, the micro-voice-activated tape recorder strapped with heat-resistant tape to his back. They stood up.

"Bill?" said Wattrous.

"Jerry?" McCarthy replied.

That was that. On to the next one! Politely they thanked the Schafs and promised they would receive a copy of the lab report within five to seven business days. The Agents reached the front door, the Schafs right behind them. Dexterously, making no false moves, McCarthy flipped both locks, and they were gone.

"Whew," said Judy, relocking the door. "That was…" But she did not know what to say it was. "Strange" seemed lame. And for some reason, perhaps the dramatic end of the early heat wave, she no longer even felt angry. If anything, she had ended by finding the Security Brothers amusing.

"Why did they use their first names like that at the end?" Dave wondered aloud. He, too, had put away anger.

"The personal touch, I suppose. 'We're only human, too'," she speculated. And she was right:

FBI 'Soft' Interrogation Manual #123B, Section 914, Para. 4:

When a soft interrogation is aborted because the innocence of the subjects has been rendered probable or certain, or an impasse has been reached, all efforts should be made to mollify said subjects. An excellent tactic is for each Agent to mention the Christian, or given, name of his or her partner. Data from our Psychological Personality Multiphasic Studies (PPMS) indicate that this tactic actualizes a significant (25-30%) reduction in subject hostility, as measured by blood pressure and adrenaline levels as well as by several other reliable indicators. (A caveat: these data have not yet been broken down by specific, possibly relevant, factors, such as age, gender, or ethnicity.)

Five business days later Dave and Judy received in the mail a #10 envelope, the return address of which was a box number in Quantico, Virginia. Inside was a personalized form letter, thanking them for their…and apologizing for…. It referred to them by their first names in three different places and opened with the phrase, "With regard to the matter of Turkish antiquities raised at your residence on the afternoon of May 15th by our Agents Jerome Wattrous and William McCarthy…" Enclosed was a second, more interesting, document, a copy of the lab report:

EVIDENTIARY EXHIBIT # 427568192

THE POWDERY SUBSTANCE HAS BEEN ANALYZED USING THE TECHNIQUES OF THERMOLUMINESCENCE (TL) SUPPLEMENTED BY OPTICALLY STIMULATED LUMINESCENCE (OSL) AND INFRARED STIMULATED LUMINESCENCE (IRSL), ALL THREE OF WHICH ANALYSES WERE CORRECTED FOR ANOMALOUS FADING (COMMONLY LEADING TO AGE UNDERESTIMATES). THESE TECHNIQUES WERE FURTHER SUPPLEMENTED BY USE OF THE NEWEST METHOD (2003), BY WHICH LIPIDS (ANIMAL FATS) PRESERVED INSIDE CERAMIC WALLS ARE SUBJECTED TO RADIOCARBON DATING TECHNIQUES. ANALYSIS BY ALL FOUR OF THESE METHODS YIELDS A SINGLE, CONSISTENT RESULT: TO WIT, THIS DUST REPRESENTS THE MOST COMMON SORT OF CHEAP ANATOLIAN CLAY, USED TO MAKE TILES SPECIFICALLY FOR THE DOWNMARKET TOURIST TRADE, DATING, IN THIS INSTANCE, FROM NO EARLIER THAN 2003.

Dave and Judy were interested to note that among the surprisingly long list of people to whom this report had been "cc'd" was one Mehmet Eymur, Director, Counterintelligence, Milli Istihbarat Teskilati. A fast Internet search told them that this "MIT" was the Turkish National Intelligence Organization, motto: "We are in the service of the great Turkish nation." The Schafs were also interested—and glad—to note that the first name on the alphabetical list was "Belevi, Turhan, Manager, Otel Siyah Kalem, Istanbul, Turkey".

If they were glad, imagine how Belevi Bay felt when he received his unopened, unstamped copy of the report (no letter) the following day! Accompanying it was the now soiled, re-re-sealed small box. And he felt even happier when Selim managed to translate the gist of the incomprehensible report to him and then at lunch, again at the kofteci, when Colonel Fatiyeh explained that, while his cousin would not likely receive official notification, he could expect no further attentions from the MIT.

"At least not," he added, since this was after all still Turkey, "with regard to this particular matter."

Ignoring the qualifying admonition, Mr. Belevi happily exclaimed, "My donkey, then, my dear little donkey! She has returned!"

The Colonel wondered, but did not ask about, the donkey's having acquired a gender. This time he allowed Mr. Belevi, who had requested the meeting, to pay the check. It was only proper, and he also knew that paying would add to his cousin's pleasure.

"Allahaismarladik."

"Gule."

After several hours during which he could hardly trust himself to attend to business, Mr. Belevi found himself in his office once again, where he decided to check his email messages for the first time since early that morning, before the report had arrived. There were two reservation requests to which he promptly and courteously replied. Then, his happiness leapt to new heights, for he saw that there was a new message from those excellent Americans, Mr. and Mrs. Dave, and Judy, Schaf.

Opening this message, the manager sat back and slowly did his best to decipher the gratifyingly long text, written, he suspected, by Dave Schaf, who seemed to be the family amanuensis. Later, of course, Selim would be consulted, but Belevi wanted to enjoy the first fruits. As he read, he mentally reacted, and composed answers to, those points he was at least fairly sure he grasped. Below the usual heading, the email, which was really more like a letter, began like this:

My Dear Belevi Bay (Oh, ho! I will respond in kind, with 'Schaf Bay'):

I cannot tell you how happy I was to see your name on the list of those to whom copies of the FBI report… (Of course, I, too, am very, very happy to be on this list!) With this report, and its conclusion that the box and its contents were completely innocent, (totally) I feel certain that the matter of the key, so mystifyingly persistent, (?) has at last been resolved. ('Insh'allah' to that 'resolved'!) I can also imagine that you may have suffered worse effects than we have from this unpleasant process, which Ms. Schaf and I set in motion, however inadvertently. (internet definition: 'accidentally.' Of course, my friend, of course you are forgiven.) For any such effects, my dear Mr. Belevi, please accept our heartfelt apologies…

At this point, tears required Mr. Belevi to suspend reading for a few moments. Before he could resume, there was a knock at the door. It was Selim, and Mr. Belevi invited him to enter.

"Excuse, Efendi," said the clerk. (As usual, they spoke Turkish.) "I saw on my monitor that an email has arrived from the kind American gentleman, Mr. Schaf, and I wondered if I might assist with its decipherment."

Mr. Belevi understood immediately that, while the offer was sincere, the motive was double: to say that the always-helpful Selim was curious about this email would be as superfluous as saying that he who does not heed proverbs does not avoid mistakes. Since Mr. Belevi also suspected that his clerk possessed the technical skills necessary to have read the email undetected, he mentally credited this apparent restraint to the young man's already impressive ledger sheet.

So they went over the message together, starting from the top again, with Selim translating the hard bits and Mr. Belevi reciprocating by filling him in on those developments in the investigation which had been disclosed by Colonel Fatiyeh, but which solicitousness for the boy's peace of mind had hitherto prevented the manager from sharing.

When they were finished, Selim offered to help with the reply as well. But, since they were now in the busy season, and guests could be expected to begin returning from dinner and other evening activities at any moment, Mr. Belevi told Selim to get back to his post in the lobby. He promised to send the reply, ASAP. (Insh'allah, of course) to Selim's computer so that the clerk could translate it in the quiet hours of the early morning. Pleased, Selim bowed his way out of the office.

Alone again in his quiet sanctuary, from the bottom right desk drawer, Mr. Belevi drew the key that had caused so much trouble, now relegated to service as a spare. It was still resting in the [bubble wrap] in the small white box, residue from the white powder still faintly visible. Gazing at the key for a moment, he had a brilliant thought: why not send this key to the Schafs as a memento, but this time wrapped in a bit of precious old silk, the purchase of which would augment his own pleasure?

But it had grown late, and Mr. Belevi was tired. So, deciding to sleep on the new idea, he finished up the last details of the day's business. Then, nodding politely to a young couple from England who were enjoying a late-night glass of wine in an alcove across from Selim's desk, and quietly explaining to the mildly disappointed Selim that the reply would not be drafted until the following day, after all, he walked down the hill to the car park and drove home to his sleeping wife and children. As his wife understood, Istanbul traffic made these midnight returns more of a luxury than a trial.

It was perhaps fortunate, Mr. Belevi would later tell himself, that he had prudently decided to sleep on the idea of sending the unlucky key to America. Whether rational or not, in the next morning's light superstition prevailed.

Accordingly, at his employer's request, late one overcast night the following week, with the taciturn day clerk Deniz staying on for an extra shift, Selim took the ferry across to Uskadar, in Asia. To be certain he was not being followed, he made use of spy craft he had learned from novels. When the ferry reached the middle of the watery expanse, he slipped out onto the deserted deck and opened his backpack. Then he dropped the key, in a zip-lock bag weighted with a piece of lead, over the side. The roar of the ferry's engines made the splash soundless. A gull dove, and so did Selim's heart. But the bird came up empty, the key went down—and stayed down. There it rests, presumably, in the depths of the Bosphorus, among the detritus of at least three millennia.

Ron Singer

Part Three: And After--

"Is this the promised end?" –*King Lear*, 5.3.279

Ron Singer

Total Body Crumble

-1-

(2017)

"Has anyone else heard what Dinesh is thinking of doing?" No one had. "Well, there's this new German procedure where they inject synthetic stuff into your knees to replace the cartilage."

"When it comes to ingenuity, leave it to the Germans!" said Rob, who works as an actuary for a re-insurance conglomerate.

That was too good an opening for Steve to resist. "Right!" he said, "and when it comes to weird experiments..." Having lived in Berlin for a couple of years, Steve considers himself an authority on German culture.

We were sitting on folding chairs behind the squash court, resting between games.

"How's Dinesh doing these days, Jerr?" asked Ari. "Other than his knees."

"Same old, same old."

I was Dinesh's official e-mail conduit to the group. A few years before, after an interim in the U.S., he retired from his lifelong career as an investment banker and moved back to Sweden. Although his principal motive was to be closer to his son and ex-wife, the decision also entailed his becoming primary caregiver for an older sister, an invalid. Another, perhaps decisive, factor was that he had never taken American citizenship, and returning to Sweden meant generous health benefits for his declining years.

Dinesh comes from an exotic background. He was born and raised in India, and judging from his aristocratic bearing, and from the fact that he wears an amulet on a thread around his neck, I've always assumed he was a Brahmin. His relatives, many of them doctors, are heavily involved in philanthropy, such as sponsorship of village clinics, which he periodically visits.

"You think they cover knee jobs in Sweden?" asked James. "If it were here, they'd say it was elective, and wouldn't pay a dime." James is a globetrotting hustler who produces Broadway musicals.

"What a joke!" said Steve. "Don't those fools in Washington know that squash is life?" And that bad knees are squash-death.

"Some of the politicians play," I pointed out. "So, maybe, it *is* covered."

"'I got the total body crumble blues,'" sang James. Although we had heard that one before, we dutifully laughed.

"Okay," said Rob, springing to his feet, "let's play some squash!" After a bit of shuffling, we realized it was Ari's and my turn, so Rob sat back down.

Since squash is a young person's game, and since most of us are in our sixties or seventies (all but Ari, who, I think, is about fifty), physical problems are a serious concern. These are the ones I know about (in order of age, from youngest to oldest):

Ari: none (other than recent back spasms).

Steve: a heavy knee brace, complaints about a stiff back.

Rob: either none or isn't saying.

James (if he can be believed): a broken leg, cartilage replacement in his right (squash-playing) wrist, laser surgery for an enlarged prostate, broken clavicle (in youth), and replacement of about a foot of his small intestine, because of Crohn's disease, a chronic inflammatory condition. Plus minor stuff, --allergies, dietary restrictions, etc. James describes himself as "a one-man med-school curriculum."

Jerry: With me, everything is incipient: pulmonary weakness, knee twinges, rotting teeth, etc. According to Joanne, my wife, "if you ever went to a doctor, dear, you'd discover that you're a very sick man." To which I riposted, "And you're a very sick woman to point that out. Just kidding, dear!'

(And returning to) Dinesh: a bypass (double, I think) in his fifties, and now the knees.

But, for someone approaching eighty, when Joanne and I saw him in Stockholm last summer, Dinesh seemed very spry. Or, as he put it during dinner at an Indian restaurant, "Except for all the things that are wrong with me, I'm a healthy man." When I complained that the curry was too hot, Dinesh laughed himself silly. All three of us shed tears over that dish, I, from the spices, and Dinesh and Joanne, from laughing at me.

A few years back, I had a philosophical discussion about body crumble with another old (in both senses), but non-squash playing, friend. Marty is a retired accountant, stereotypically methodical. Our specific topic was body-part replacement, and we began by listing the current options.

Marty: Let's see (ticking them off on his fingers): One: hip. Two: knee.

I: Heart, kidney.

Marty: That's four. Oh, the liver. They've recently started making tiny livers from stem cells. And that's significant, because livers have been called our second brain, the brain of digestion.

I: We are what we eat —and digest.

After that, we got into other anticipated replacements involving stem cells: bladder, trachea (windpipe), eyes (retina only, so far, the eye being the most complex body part), pituitary gland, and bones. Of course, as we listed these synthetic —or should I say organic-- organs, we cracked lame jokes, such as using Carrie Nation's stem cells to make new kidneys and bladders for drunks. And, finally, we noted, a tiny brain had just been created.

Marty: If, god forbid, you were to contract brain cancer, Jerr,' would you go for a new brain?

I: Nope, I think I'd draw the line at that. Not to sound religious, or anything, but, if the brain isn't the real you, what is?

Marty: Agreed.

-2-

(2027)

Over the next decade, of course, the expected —and unexpected-- happened. Once again, in order of age:

Ari moved to Israel. The last I heard (a postcard, a few years ago), he was living on a kibbutz near the Syrian border. Since he had always been a daring shot-maker in squash, I suppose he's still a risk-taker.

Steve has retired, not to Germany, but to Majorca, or someplace like that. According to James, he is living with a "babe," a twenty-something. "Expect a cardiac infarction," James prophesies.

I heard (again, from James), that Rob, who is also retired, is considering hip replacement.

As for James, he now sells high-end co-ops and condos here in the city. I'm not sure whether he's also still producing musicals. Once or twice a month, we meet for a game, and he boasts about all the money he's making. He wears so many bandages —knee, calf, ankle, forearm and elbow—that he looks like a mummy.

I'm the second oldest, you'll recall. About a year ago, when I went to Sweden for Dinesh's memorial (he was almost ninety), I detoured to Berlin and had my knees rubberized. I don't know how long they will last, but so far, so good. Besides routinely trouncing James, not to brag, or anything, but last week I won the consolation round in the 80-and-over flight of a local tournament. Of course, I was the only participant who could run. The seven others all wore Darth Vader braces on one or both knees.

Marty is also extant. In order "to keep my hand in," he still does a few friends' taxes, mine included. Three months ago, when we met for lunch, I noticed a few signs of Alzheimer's, like restlessness, asking the same question more than once, and confessing that he often misplaced his keys and glasses.

Marty: By the way, Jerr', have you changed your mind about brain replacement?

I: Haven't given it much thought lately. I guess I'm still riding the high from my German knee job. What about you?

Marty (after putting ketchup on a French fry, and nibbling it): Not so sure, anymore.

I changed the subject.

-3-

(2030)

Although he died two days ago, that was not the end for Marty. Without straying into a full-blown Science lesson, let me explain. Starting a few years back, patients with blood diseases, such as leukemia, began to be given lab-generated versions of their own healthy cells. These acted like stem cells —i.e. they could replicate. This was an advance over the old method, bone marrow transplants, which required compatible donors.

Inevitably, the new method has been expanded to include cells from organs, such as the brain. The extension involves getting non-blood stem cells to act like blood stem cells, which was made possible by the creation of things called "induced pluripotent stem cells," or "iPS cells." The science is complicated, but the key point is that further issues of compatibility have been resolved, so that we can now regenerate diseased cells, including brain cells, from healthy cells in living donors. The result is a new generation (no pun intended) of cell donors, something like organ donors, in the old days, or blood donors, in the old-old days.

About a year ago, when Marty's Alzheimer's was approaching full-blown, the five survivors in our squash gang, plus him, formed our own small private brain-cell donor bank. (By then, Steve had broken up with the "babe," and was back in the city.) Cell banks are something like autologous donations, in which friends and relatives band together to bank their blood for specific recipients. I should say that this technology is still, if not in its infancy, in the toddler stage. Generous, as always, even Ari joined our brain-cell bank, sending his contribution from a lab in Tel Aviv, via El Al Airlines, which transported the cells *pro-bono*.

Two days ago, when Marty died, his children directed their lawyer to have us sign release forms for the banked brain cells. Yesterday, with the temporarily deceased in an induced coma, the transfer was affected, and, in a few hours, we hope, Marty will be awakened. Since computers have also made remarkable strides, in recording and transcribing brain waves, Rob, Steve, James and I crowded into Marty's room where, huddled in front of a monitor at the foot of his bed, we all -even James- read in complete silence.

-III-

MARTY'S BRAIN, VERSION #1

Hello again, dear friends. How can I begin to thank you for this? Although, as you know, I spent my entire working life as an accountant, I cannot possibly calculate, in monetary terms, the extent of my indebtedness to you. The bottom line, however, is simple: I owe you. Big time! On second thought, however, it might be possible to calculate the debt, and rather precisely, at that. It would involve a simple set of extrapolations, using stochastic calculus formulae from my own field. Hey, hey, let's not go there! We're doing this as a *mitzvah*, right? Why has this begun to sound more like a diplomatic conference than a message from Marty's brain? Children, children, let's not squabble! Agreed! Before we nickel and dime the deceased, let's remember that it may soon be someone else's turn! Speaking of which, when are we going to start talking about knee-cell banks, elbow banks, dick banks, etc. etc.? Hey! What's going on here? My new brain seems to lack executive function. What the heck has happened to my prefrontal regions?

Oh, no! We stopped reading, aghast at what seemed to have happened. Soon, we agreed that what we had heard must have been a composite. To put it mildly, the procedure for brain-cell transfer had not yet been perfected. Running the tape again, and stopping this time to identify the source for each bit, we sorted it out, as follows:

MARTY'S BRAIN, VERSION #2

Hello again, dear friends. How can I begin to thank you for this? Although I spent my entire working life as an accountant, I cannot possibly calculate the extent of my indebtedness to you in monetary terms. The bottom line, however, is simple: I owe you. Big time!

[What a pleasure to hear Marty's old methodical, generous voice! This must be how monotheists feel about the afterlife.]

On second thought, however, it might be possible to calculate the debt, and rather precisely, at that. It would involve a simple set of extrapolations, using stochastic calculus formulae from my own field.

[A different kind of methodicalness: Rob.]

Hey, hey, let's not go there! We're doing this as a *mitzvah*, right?

[Generous, as usual: Ari.]

Why has this begun to sound more like a diplomatic conference than a message from Marty's brain?

[Me?]

Children, children, let's not squabble!

[Steve?]

Agreed! Before we nickel and dime the deceased, let's remember that it may soon be someone else's turn! Speaking of which, when are we going to start talking about knee-cell banks, elbow banks, dick banks, etc. etc.?

[James, obviously.]

Hey! What's going on here? My new brain seems to lack executive function. What the heck has happened to my prefrontal regions?

[Marty, again.]

By then, we were so dispirited that we turned the monitor off. Two hours later, when Marty was brought up from his coma, he seemed at least as confused as the rest of us. Promising to try to get to the bottom of this mess, we mumbled our goodbyes, and fled the room.

-IV-

Last night, I dreamt of Dinesh —his ghost, that is. (Don't Hindus have a notion about astral bodies, reincarnation, and dreams?) He addressed me as if he were looking into a camera:

"Hello, Jerry. I hope you're glad to see me again. By the time I got the tape you sent, I'd already heard about Marty's new brain, through the astral grapevine. I'm so sorry I wasn't around to help sort things out. Although I never had the pleasure of meeting Marty, you made him sound like such a kind, straightforward gentleman. But now..."

This evening, the survivors (minus Ari, but including Rob, whose new hip is pretty good) will be playing squash again. Although we still play every other month, our game has deteriorated --seriously. One of us serves a soft lob. If it lands in the back corner, unhittable, the opponent picks it up, using his racquet and the side of his sneaker, like a lazy tennis player. We then switch sides, and the server serves again. When a serve is a bit less accurate, and hence returnable, the opponent hits a drop shot that the server does not bother to run for, and we switch roles. For old times' sake, we keep score. Like our game, my rubberized knees seem to have deteriorated, to the point where they are as useless as the old ones. The warranty has expired.

This time, of course, the squash will only be a sidebar to the serious part of the gathering, which will be to discuss what, if anything, can be done about poor Marty's brain. For now, the doctors are keeping him in the hospital, because his behavior is so unpredictable. Since we all have an obvious stake in the outcome, they have asked us to try to reach some sort of consensus before we consult with them next week. Or, as my wife puts it, "A brain re-set, by committee!" Marty's relatives, I imagine, are frantic, probably screaming about lawsuits.

To lighten the tone of tonight's anticipated conclave (or, perhaps, to rub in its hopelessness), James has e-mailed us a new verse for The Song:

Got a new brain, nothin' to lose,
'ceptin' my mind. But never mind,
I got the total body crumble blues.

Sources:

- "I got the total body crumble blues." --from a (?) Bristol University Medical School skit, seen by the author at the Edinburgh Festival, 1979.
- https://theawarestudy.com/?utm_source=google&utm_medium=cpc&utm_term=alzheimer%27s+symptoms&utm_campaign=Alzheimers+Symptoms+&+Treatment&utm_content=Alzheimers+Symptoms&gclid=CLKYhdndmtUCFYSFswodYIoJDw
- https://www.himalayanacademy.com/readlearn/basics/karma-reincarnation
- https://qz.com/342830/you-have-a-second-brain-in-your-gut-and-it-wants-cake/
- http://www.telegraph.co.uk/news/science/science-news/10275996/The-body-parts-which-can-be-regrown-in-a-laboratory.html
- https://www.scientificamerican.com/article/lab-grown-blood-stem-cells-produced-at-last/

The Old Avatar

Shopping (cheap) was his hobby. He spent summers at the flea markets along Route 1 in Searsport, Maine (salt air, old glass bottles and dishes, especially blue, rose, and green), and the rest of the year at the Odd Lots bargain emporium on Church and Chambers streets in lower Manhattan (thumb tacks, masking tape, traffic fumes).

Around the time he retired (from work, not shopping), e-bay put a serious dent in the non-virtual bargain business. Owing also to the events of September 11th, 2001, Odd Lots closed its doors, as did (also owing to e-bay) most of the Searsport fleas (their booths).

But e-bay did not do it for him (call him set in his ways), so he soldiered on at the few fleas left standing (or hopping) and at the extant New York schlock emporia. The latter, although they could never match the selection or deep discounts of Odd Lots, were harder to kill than Dracula. No sooner had market forces driven a stake through the heart of one of them than ten more popped up (like umbrellas when the rain starts to fall, or bats flitting into the evening sky).

"*J'achete, donc je suis,*" he waggishly quipped (to himself), paraphrasing Rene' Des(shopping)cartes, although he did not subscribe to that philosopher's pernicious mind-body dualism. Shopping, for example, was something you did from the heart, but the brain never said, "Stop!" at least not to the selective, joyous shopper like him.

It was a life (so to speak). He shopped in New York, drove up to Maine, shopped in Maine, drove back to New York, shopped in New York, drove up to ....

Eventually, he waxed (waned) old and (nothing special) died. Acceding to his wishes, his relations (family) had him (his corpse) cremated. But when the ashes were scattered, in a wooded area on the larboard side of Route I North, something inexplicable happened.

The dead shopper coalesced into a giant papier mache' sea captain (old avatar), wearing a yellow rain slicker, boots, and hat, smoking a corn cob pipe, and sitting in a giant wicker armchair in front of a diner on the starboard side of the highway just south of Searsport.

"Well, I'll be darned," said the owner of the diner when he arrived for work that morning. But he left him there. (Why not?)

The Captain's advent took place (so to speak) several years ago. He still sits in his chair, holding his smokeless pipe, with the rain or snow dripping or melting down him (when it rains or snows), none the worse for wear, except for a few places where the paint has chipped off, creating white spots (like snowflakes) amidst the predominant yellow (rain gear), white (hair), and rose (hands and face).

"Welcome," calls the shopper-cum-salt to passing motorists (many from New York) as they whiz, hum, or creep past at the start of their summer vacations. "Up here to enjoy the sea air, are you, my friend? Why not stop for an hour? Grab a bite and a cuppa, browse a bit, maybe even buy a little something, then go on your way. Believe me, you'll be the better for it (stopping). And later when you're back in town, please remember to spare a thought for your old pal, Captain Nelson Billings.

Acknowledgments

— *Garbage: Starry Night Review*, 2007
— *The Silent Treatment: Pilgrimage*, 2008
— *A Dream of Trains: Word Riot*, 2008
— *Glen's Vintage Tin: Sage of Consciousness*, 2006
— *The Technicolor Meal: big bridge*, 2007; *Exterminating Angel (the Magazine)*, 2018 *(Pushcart nomination)*
— *W4 ™: Mad Hatters' Review (print & Mp3)*, 2011
— *In Ethiopia, Once: Transnational Literature*, 2015
— *A Reading at the Library: Starry Night Review*, 2014
— *Spots: big bridge*, 2007
— *A Game of Lies: Phenomenal Literature*, 2015
— *A Nose for a Jacket: Willow Review*, 2005;
— *Imitation Fruit*, 2017
— *Their Countries of Origin: New Maps*, 2013; *Transnational Literature*, 2014
— *When the Barber Died: Exterminating Angel (the Magazine)*, 2019
— *On Elizabeth Bishop's "One Art": Third Wednesday*, 2010 *(Pushcart nomination)*
— *Running the Diagonal: Boned: A Collection of Skeletal Writings*, 2018 *(Pushcart Nomination)*
— *The Key: Sage of Consciousness Online Magazine*, 2006; *The Second Kingdom, Three Novellas, Cantarabooks*, 2009
— *Total Body Crumble: Jelly Bucket*, 2018
— *The Old Avatar: Avatar Review*, 2009

About the Author

Ron Singer, b.1941, has been both a lifelong resident of New York City, and one who has traveled to, lived in, and written about the wider world. For forty-four years, Singer was a teacher and writer. Singer's life and writing have both featured political activism. For instance, while he was in South Africa working on a book, he was invited to read poetry at a memorial for activist/poet Dennis Brutus. The book is *Uhuru Revisited: Interviews with Pro-Democracy Leaders* (Africa World Press, Red Sea Press, 2015). It can be found in libraries around the world.

About the Press

Unsolicited Press is based in Portland, Oregon. The small publisher produces fiction, poetry, and nonfiction from award-winning authors. Learn more at www.unsolicitedpress.com.